BEYOND
SEPTEMBER

SEPTEMBER

BEYOND

SEPTEMBER

BECK STANLEY

Softcover ISBN: 978-1-950880-11-9
Hardcover ISBN: 978-1-950880-90-4
eBook ISBN: 978-1-950880-13-3

Typeset by Medlar Publishing Solutions Pvt Ltd, India.

Printed in the United States of America.

Published by Author Source
Kansas City, MO
www.AuthorSource.com

MY GRATITUDE

First and always, I am thankful and grateful to my Heavenly Father for creative gifts and hanging on when I let go.

Thank you to my husband, Chuck Stanley, who believes in me, encourages me, and often kindly tolerates me when I'm writing.

Thank you to my son, Dr. Robert Pippin, who taught me far more than being a mom. To my sister, Pam Ryan, for being my first best friend and always the leader of the cheering section. To LeeAnn Hunter, who joined me for an adventure that inspired a novel. To Dr. Kate Determan for nudging open that first door.

Thanks to Early Ford V8 Club members Dave Sanderson, who provided technical guidance on vehicles, and Dean Neubauer, whose beautifully restored '48 Ford Pickup inspired me to put it in the story. Thanks to Adair County Sheriff Jeff Vandewater, for tireless research and input on weapons, coordinating with timelines and professions. He quickly learned that I seldom had just one more question. Thanks to Char Loudy, whose nursing experience in trauma and orthopedics helped with medical terms and clarifications in the story. Each gave credibility to this work.

Thank you to my early readers, who gave input and spotted errors: Brenda Stanley, Lynn Heinbuch, Julie Woollums, and Dave Sanderson.

Thank you, Julie Sorensen, for giving me (and the world) your marvelous word, *pondercate*.

A special thanks to my friend, mentor, and man of many titles, Dr. Simon Presland. His ability to peel me off the ceiling with a kind word or prayer is a blessing. Thank you to Mike Owens and the AuthorSource Media team for producing a quality book. Working with you is a pleasure. Your patience is immeasurable.

Thank you always to my loyal readers, for asking for and waiting for this sequel to be completed.

Beck Stanley

PROLOGUE

The handsome couple walked toward the train station where passengers would soon emerge from the mass of steel heading to Glenwood Springs. The vibrant town of over 6600, was a hub for tourists heading for skiing adventures at Snowmass and Aspen or planning nothing further than the Hot Springs and a few days of relaxation. Many of the town's residents were anxiously awaiting the arrival of family and friends coming to enjoy the Thanksgiving holiday, a familiar scenario played out in towns across the nation. This would be a true holiday of Thanksgiving for the two people who watched and listened for the approaching train.

Gregor and Lenore Parishnikov had met in this friendly town the last weekend of September, 1990. Their separate lives had been full of complications, and neither of them were prepared for the ramifications of falling in love. When they both realized it was as inevitable and natural as sunrise following a dark and lonely night, they embraced the fullness of their relationship.

Gregor Parishnikov had been comfortable in his new country, after having chosen to defect from the Soviet Union where he had been a valuable KGB operative. He had also left a brother behind; a situation he planned to remedy.

Lenore Appleby had chosen that weekend in Glenwood Springs as a vacation destination with her best friend, Leah Chase. Away from stress and routines, she could gather strength to proceed with plans to divorce her cruel, abusive husband and continue raising her teenage son alone.

Gregor knew Lenore was the woman he wanted to spend the rest of his life with the moment he saw her, but he also knew that a woman's heart is a difficult thing to capture when it is held so protectively behind a wall of hurt and betrayal. Over time, Gregor had convinced Lenore of his love for her, then disappeared from her life for nearly a year. Sitting isolated in a Soviet prison had been endurable only because he held on to the hope of someday returning to the United States to be with the love of his life again, and to have his brother beside him. It was unrealistic to believe. His chances of release were minimal and his hope of Lenore waiting for him seemed even less likely.

Yet, somehow God had a hand in it all. There were torturous events to overcome. Gregor's were physical. Lenore's were locked deep within in a broken heart. When John Dixon III, a CIA agent who befriended Gregor, began monitoring Lenore in hopes of finding the missing Russian, he soon became torn between duty and hidden love. He pushed hard for answers and the return of Gregor. He knew Lenore could never be his until she faced the Russian to make her choice.

Leah Chase, Lenore's best friend, provided the thread that unraveled the mystery of Gregor's disappearance. Her gift of communication and recalling details from her own conversations with the Russian man, gave Dixon a variety of leads. Lenore had always joked that the ever-cheerful Leah would be a valuable government agent in the task of interrogations. It proved far truer than she could have imagined.

In a time of tumultuous political and social change in The Soviet Union and in large part due to the information from Leah, Gregor Parishnikov and his brother Alexander were located by CIA operatives. With help from the Swiss Consulate and the US Embassy, they were allowed to leave The Soviet Union and come to the United States.

When Gregor had at last been able to see Lenore, the painful questions were answered and the love he had once captured was once again, his. It had never been given to anyone else.

Now, over a year later, Gregor and Lenore stood at the train station, holding hands, both knowing that they would never take their love for granted.

* * * * *

The late November air was seasonally cool, but Lenore wished she had worn a lighter sweater instead of the jade-colored turtleneck under a denim jacket. The unbuttoned jacket flapped with her constant movement, and long dark hair moved in sync with her motions; its shiny fullness catching the sunlight in an unfettered display.

"What if they missed the train?" Lenore let go of Gregor's hand and paced.

Gregor smiled as he reached out and pulled her to him. "They would have called. We left the house only an hour ago."

"Are you certain you don't mind everyone being here? It'll be quite a crowd." She nestled into his arms

"My beautiful wife, this is something I've waited a lifetime to enjoy."

Lenore looked up into his handsome face. How she adored this man.

A year apart had not changed what he held inside. Gregor's well-trimmed beard and thick, black hair on his head, now bore strands of silver. The light that shone in his eyes when he looked at Lenore had only become brighter and his generous smile came easily.

Gregor's five-foot nine stature had remained, but months of grueling torture in a Soviet prison had lessened his former athletic physique. He took every opportunity to be outdoors, to climb and hike, further strengthening his agility in the mountains he loved. Lenore's healthy cooking aided his efforts.

Sounds of the train emerging from Glenwood Canyon brought their attention back to the platform where dear friends and family would soon be wrapped in the love and hospitality of the newly married couple.

* * * * *

The man who watched the couple from a comfortable distance tried to blend in with the growing crowd. At six feet, one inch, dressed in jeans and a blue plaid flannel shirt, his stature looked out of place in this very casual town. He stood far too straight, seemingly at attention. His sandy-colored hair was cropped close, military style; unusual for the times. Dark glasses protected eyes that moved constantly to scrutinize the crowd, always to return to the woman. A professional, he also had a visual on the CIA agent surveilling the Parishnikovs. That agent, assigned for their protection—and also in the event the former Soviet KGB operative not being as pure as he wanted everyone to believe—had no clue he was being surveilled as well. This was easy for the tall man, who had been trained well for this task. No one would question his presence. Until very recently, *he* was the assigned CIA agent to surveil Lenore and her husband. Abruptly removed from surveillance duty under the pretext of being sent back to Langley to train for a covert overseas operation, he knew they only wanted him out of the way.

Now, it had become a matter of survival.

Lenore's.

CHAPTER 1

"There's Leah!" Lenore waved to her best friend, the fashionably dressed blonde lady standing on the platform of the train station, dressed in a dark brown mid-length skirt, a soft beige cashmere sweater and tall, tan suede boots. A long necklace caught the sunlight and sparkled, as if announcing her presence. When Lenore finally caught her attention, Leah disappeared in the crowd, emerging close to Gregor and Lenore. Hugs and giggles, along with a few tears, reunited best friends.

Gregor watched for and managed to direct Leah's husband, JD and Lenore's sons Joel, and Grant over to the group. Warm embraces and assurances of a pleasant journey precluded the gathering of luggage. Urging and ushering the group to the waiting vehicles, Gregor never lost sight of his wife. She smiled and laughed through tear-glazed eyes.

JD helped Gregor fasten the overflow of luggage to the top of the Nissan Pathfinder. Lenore talked with her sons and her best friend, while sorting luggage for the Saab.

"Are you sure you're doing okay living in the dorm, Joel?" Lenore asked her youngest son. "Are you eating enough? Can you get your studying done?"

Joel rolled his brown eyes and smiled at his mom. "I promise everything is fine! I'm comfortable, my roommate is tolerable, I go to the library or the student union when I need peace and quiet. And with Leah insisting that I eat at their house at least two nights a week, I'm well fed." He patted Leah on the shoulder, producing a smile from his mom's best friend. "She also sends enough juice and cookies and fruit back with me, that I think I'm gaining weight." He rubbed his trim tummy.

Lenore knew Joel's naturally slim physique had not changed. He loved to hike and ride his mountain bike in the foothills around Fort Collins, and with the necessary activity of being in the Ram's marching band at Colorado State University, his athletic physique could easily be maintained. His straight light brown hair could use a little trim, she thought. His eyes were bright and observant, exuding enthusiasm for life and natural curiosity. Lenore knew Joel was becoming a confident young man, but she could still see the little boy she knew so well.

"I know, you're probably fine, but you know me," she said, hugging her son. "I'll always worry about both you boys."

She turned to Grant as they stood beside the Pathfinder. "What about you? Is your job still good? Are you making enough to live comfortably? You don't have Leah to feed you twice a week, so are you eating properly?"

Grant Appleby, Lenore's firstborn, and a gentle giant of a man, stood six foot three. His full, dark-brown hair, blue eyes, and clean-shaven good looks made women turn their heads. His broad shoulders and well-defined muscles were partly the result of genetics and partly due to his disciplined exercise regime. His sometimes-sedentary profession as graphic designer could quickly result in becoming overweight, if he wasn't dedicated to healthy eating and an active gym membership. His quiet demeanor was never taken as an indication of weakness by those who worked with him or any who were close to him.

Grant hugged his mom. "I'm doing better than I ever imagined I could. The job is terrific. It's challenging and I'm making enough to live comfortably, and saving some, too." He tossed his jacket onto the back seat. "Joel and I talk every couple of days and he knows I can be there in an hour if he needs me." He laughed. "Half-hour if it's an emergency!" He nudged his brother, who looked back with a grin. "Our concern is you, and from the looks of it, none of us have anything to worry about. I've never seen you so happy." He gestured toward Gregor. "He's a great guy, Mom."

Leah had been keeping an eye on the two men arranging the load on top of the vehicle. "Hold it! Hand me the small case." She pointed with a well-manicured finger. "There's no way my make-up is riding outside of that vehicle if I'm on the inside of this one."

"I'm sure the boys could give you a lift." JD laughed as he pulled the case from the load and gave it to Leah. "It might get too quiet in there if you're up here, though."

"I may just have to choke you for that remark." Leah threatened, accepting the case and the gentle teasing from her loving husband as she walked to the Saab and secured the case in the back. Her retort made them all laugh, having witnessed the infamous throttling. She would throw herself onto his lap, place dainty hands around the base of his neck and pretend to choke him, making JD laugh, then tickle her until they both collapsed in breathless giggles.

The handsome man beside JD winked at Lenore and she smiled back at her husband, both silently communicating the same deep devotion and love that flowed between Leah and JD.

With all luggage accounted for and loaded into two vehicles, the guys climbed into the Nissan Pathfinder. Lenore and Leah would travel together in the silver-brown Saab to the Parishnikov home. It provided a little time to catch up on a couple of months of separation. Not nearly long enough, but they would have ample opportunity with the guys heading for the ski slopes in the morning.

* * * * *

Lenore reached behind the seat, opened a small cooler, and took out an icy can of Diet Coke for her friend before pulling into traffic behind the Pathfinder.

"I thought you might be needing one of these."

Leah took the can, carefully opened it, and took a sip. "Oh, absolutely! No Diet Coke on the train!"

"Really?"

"Yes, really. Isn't that just unbelievable?" She took another sip. "Absolute and total deprivation of one of the necessities of life."

"You poor thing!" Lenore sympathized and shook her head. She checked her rearview mirrors before passing the vehicle between them and the Pathfinder. "I'll send a little cooler home with you with a stash to tide you over until you get back to civilized territory," she added, using her most proper imitation of a British accent.

"Oh, God bless you, Lenore; it will be my own private little treat." She sipped again and noted Lenore not having a Diet Coke of her own. "Speaking of treats, where's yours?"

Lenore dropped the accent. "Well Leah, when you live with the healthiest man in the world, you start listening to his logic, and his logic is that water, tea and some juice is far healthier than Diet Coke."

"Oh, my goodness. I can't believe it. Don't you miss it?" Leah turned in her seat to face Lenore, awaiting tales of total withdrawal symptoms and misery.

Lenore glanced at Leah, and reading her thoughts had to laugh. "Well, I can't say it was easy at first, but once I sort of went cold turkey, I've not missed it. Think of how healthy Gregor is and how that lifestyle of good food and such, basically kept him alive during his time in the Soviet prison. Ya gotta figure he knows what he's talking about."

"Oh, I'm so proud of you, Lenore. I really wish I had your tenacity. I will honestly consider following suit. Maybe not just yet, but soon."

Keeping her eyes on the road, Lenore reached over and patted Leah's hand. "You do what is best for you. I am certainly not going to tell you what to do. That stuff has been a great part of both our lives for a very long time! I will always keep a generous supply at the house for you or anyone else."

"You're so thoughtful." Leah looked at her nearly empty can and sat it in the aftermarket cup holder just behind the center console.

The friends were quiet for only a moment, letting the soft music from the radio fill the void. Leah broke the silence, as usual.

"The sky is such a beautiful blue today." Leah noted as she admired the landscape. "It just makes everything look so fresh, even in the throes of autumn."

"Yes, I absolutely love Colorado blue skies. Heck, I don't even mind clouds anymore." Lenore laughed. "I don't have any idea what winter is going to be like, but I know I'm safe and warm and comfortable, so whatever it is, I'm ready." She pointed at the horizon. "We've already had some snow in the higher elevations."

The duo had fallen a couple of vehicles behind the Pathfinder and Lenore checked mirrors, waiting for an old VW microbus to pass before she entered the passing lane to go around a horse trailer being pulled by an old white pick-up truck. The ancient driver looked familiar.

"Leah, check out the driver. Do you suppose that's Gus from the dance we were at when we met Gregor?"

The passenger, intent on watching the bus, shifted her focus to the truck and its driver. He waved and she waved back.

"Oh, it must be. He said he lived around here. Hope he knows you're married."

Lenore laughed and passed another truck. They were still behind the VW bus.

"That's what had my attention," Leah pointed. "That's an old hippie bus."

"I guess I've gotten used to seeing it on this road a few times. The old hippies are alive and well and living in Colorado. No big surprise."

The VW microbus passed the Pathfinder which allowed the Saab to fall in behind the vehicle carrying the guys and far too much luggage.

"Lenore, you look so happy. It makes me happy, but I sure miss us living closer."

"Me, too. A phone call helps, but not nearly as much fun as our marathon movie nights and just driving around together." Lenore sighed. "Maybe we can make up for some of it with this holiday together."

"Isn't it just going to be the greatest holiday ever? I'll bet Alex is excited."

"Oh, excited it hardly the word. He loves this new family thing." Lenore glanced in the rearview mirror. "Looks like Gus turned off back there."

Leah looked in the side mirror. "Well, home must be that way." She turned back to Lenore. "Is it awkward having Alex living with you?"

"Never, Leah. He's quiet and polite and cleans up after himself. He loves being outdoors and watching television game shows and, of course, he's hooked on the Weather Channel. Since he studied meteorology in the Soviet Union, it helps with learning English. He understands what they talk about, and the terminology." She laughed, then added, "I've also detected expressions from Sesame Street."

"Oh, how smart! Might as well learn like the little ones."

"Exactly! Alex struggles, but he's getting better all the time. We're proud of his efforts."

"Do the two brothers get along?"

"Oh, absolutely. You know, until we got here and settled, I'd never really heard those two interact as brothers do. They get just silly sometimes. And then there's the laugh." Lenore giggled at the thought. "I call it their Parishnikov laugh. It's huge and deep and it's simply infectious and impossible to not laugh along with them."

"I can't wait to hear it."

"Oh, you will love it. I crack up at some of Alex's attempts at American slang. That's a subject they didn't have in Soviet schools."

Lenore pointed to a small herd of deer in a meadow as they passed, and commented, "The herds are usually not active during these hours. Hmm, something must have stirred them." She shook her head then glanced back at Leah. "I know I should probably correct Alex when he makes errors, but it's like … when your child says something cute. You just hate to correct it."

"No doubt Joel and Grant can teach him a little English slang. Maybe he could teach them Russian!" Leah turned to Lenore. "You're learning Russian, aren't you?"

Lenore shook her head. "Some, I guess. I'm not as motivated as Alex to learn a different language, but I'm picking up phrases and things. I have the rest of my life to learn."

"Of course." Leah tilted her head, and raised her brows. "What about privacy? Is that a problem?"

"No. When Gregor had the house built, after he first arrived in the United States, he purposefully made an area that Alex would be able to claim as his own. He knew he would never stop trying to get his brother out of the Soviet Union."

"How thoughtful and positive thinking," Leah said.

"Yes." Lenore laughed, "I told Alex he had a *bachelor pad*, which proved to be a challenge to interpret." He's so proud of it and his status as a *bachelor*. He's got a nice bed, desk and chair, a comfy sofa, and tables; even his own TV!

"He has his own bathroom, of which I assured him *he* is responsible for keeping clean and I will always check to make sure it is!" Glancing at Leah, she raised her eyebrows for emphasis. "We all share the whole house. It's not like he is required to just stay in that part. We cook and eat together. We share household duties. It works out great!"

"What fun you must be having, seeing him settle into living in America."

"Gregor and I both do." Lenore smiled. "Leah, he's such a sweet guy. I hope someday he finds someone special to share a life with."

"With the family good looks, he shouldn't have any trouble." Both women agreed.

* * * * *

A thirty-minute drive, and with Leah's concerns for Lenore's happiness calmed, they followed the Pathfinder into the driveway and parked in front of the garages. The two-story home seemed nestled into a picturesque valley, with rises of heavily wooded hills on the north, east and west. The home faced southeast rather than a true north and south. The southern area from the valley opened to capture views of snowcapped peaks in the distance. The white clapboard home featured dark green trim around windows and doors. Native stone accented the front of the home and a sturdy rail surrounded the wide front porch. The deep double garage had dark green doors with small windows high enough to prevent someone from seeing inside, while providing daylight to fill the interior. As the doors raised, they could see the rare 1969 Boss 429 Ford Mustang sitting in the garage; it's red paint glistening.

Two large white dogs ambled down from the front porch, greeting the familiar vehicles with curiosity and wagging tails as passengers in the Pathfinder got out.

"Those are some big dogs, Gregor." JD said as he stood outside the van. "Do they bite?"

"Only on command." Gregor assured him, with a friendly chuckle.

Lenore started to exit the Saab, but knowing Leah's apprehension regarding dogs she turned to her friend. "They're very gentle creatures. The worst they would do is drench you in slobber." She hesitated, then added. "If we weren't here with you or they didn't know you, it could easily be a different matter."

Leah slowly got out of the passenger side of the Saab and wasted no time coming around the vehicle to stand next to Lenore.

The dogs' excitement grew with all the company, and they began circling and barking their greetings. A voice sounded from the front porch, "Nyet! Sidet! Nicolai, Marushka, nyet!"

"There's Alex! He's been waiting patiently for everyone to get here." Lenore said, as Alex, Gregor's younger brother, tried to corral the excited dogs. "Either that, or he's anxious to eat the food I've talked about for two weeks."

Alex greeted the family and friends he knew and assisted with carrying luggage into the house. After being evaluated at Langley, confirming that he and Gregor were not a perceived threat, Alex had been introduced to everyone upon their arrival in Colorado. He had stood proudly beside his brother when Gregor married Lenore in late September, and delighted in having two nephews and the extended family of Leah and JD. Familiarity of love and family fueled the grin on his face.

Alex was a handsome man in his late thirties, with strong European features. Six feet tall, trim, and muscular, he stood three inches taller than his brother, with light brown hair streaked with even lighter highlights. Lenore knew some of those highlights were white hair, due to his experience in the Soviet prison. He and Gregor had aged beyond their years in some ways. The white strands had appeared in the hair of both men. Their happy demeanors had erased any traces of other ill effects.

Alex was calm and quiet and ready to assist with any task. He always wore blue jeans, saying they were what Americans wore. His eyes were dark, but unlike Gregor's, they had not witnessed the onerous challenges of a KGB operative, nor the extended torturing his older sibling had endured. He smiled easily and Lenore had never seen him frustrated or angry, as if that gene simply had not been included in his genetic make-up.

Alex, Joel, and Grant found common ground and managed well with language limitations, when it came to the ski equipment. The trio put their ski equipment in the garage alongside equipment belonging to Gregor, Alex, and Lenore. The five men would spend the day before Thanksgiving skiing at Snowmass while Lenore and Leah shopped and baked for the Thanksgiving Day feast. Lenore approved of the arrangement, though she loved skiing. She and Leah were due a marathon talk session.

After they settled luggage into the guest rooms, the group migrated into the living room, where Alex had built a cozy, crackling fire in the stone fireplace. Hot cocoa with peppermint schnapps was offered to those who wanted it. Evening settled in outside of the house aglow with lights and filled with laughter and love. Trays of food were nibbled from amid healthy doses of conversation.

Lenore and Leah opted out of the hot cocoa fare and went to the large eat-in kitchen. Lenore opened the refrigerator and handed a can Diet Coke to her best friend.

"Oh Lenore, I wish I didn't want it, but thanks. I promise I'll cut back and even stop one of these days."

"Your choice, always. I don't expect you to do what I do just because I did it."

Leah laughed. "Well, a good example is a good example. I absolutely do want to try. I could set a good example for my grandsons as well."

"True, but do it in your own time."

Lenore had prepared a large pot of chili earlier in the day, and delighted in revealing the primary ingredient to be ground elk meat along with the ground beef.

"Wow, you guys do eat healthy, don't you?"

"Yep. Elk meat is lean and healthy and Gregor has a lot of locals around here who offer him elk and deer. He offers to pay them and they just won't hear of it."

"Sounds like he's well thought of."

"Um, yes, he is. Can you grab those napkins?" Lenore pointed with a finger as she held a stack of seven bowls in her hands. "When we returned, the paper interviewed us. Gregor tends to be a little private, so he only gave the barest of information. It sure didn't stop the rumors." She raised her eyebrows as she arranged the bowls near the steaming pot of chili.

"Utensils?" Leah asked as she fanned out the napkins on the end of the island separating the working kitchen from the dining area. "Rumors in a good way or bad way?"

Lenore pointed to the center drawer of the island. "Oh, a little of both. Doesn't matter. Those who know the truth can correct those who don't know. We have a life to get on with and correcting rumors is not on the agenda."

"I agree with you. If they matter, they know."

Lenore stirred the large pot of chili. "There's some shredded cheese, sliced pickles, and jalapeños in the fridge, middle shelf, right side."

Leah retrieved the offerings and put them on the island.

With steaming hot chili and a large assortment of accompaniments, the women urged the guys to help themselves. An hour later, bellies were full, the kitchen clean, and the lights turned off. Everyone settled in for the evening in the cozy living room.

CHAPTER 2

Lenore's sons and their Uncle Alex sorted through maps of the ski slopes they hoped to visit Wednesday. The two couples sat comfortably admiring the fire's glow.

"You sure have a beautiful home, Lenore." JD noted, glancing around the room. "There's plenty of room for company and it feels very comfortable."

"I can't take credit for the house, JD. Gregor had it before we ever met. All I've done is a little decorating and furnishing and filled in some of the blank spaces." She squeezed her husband's hand and added, "He was very fortunate to have been able to hold onto it while he, well …" she paused, choosing her words … "had been a *guest* of the Soviet Union."

"Remind me to never accept one of their invitations." JD replied, laughing.

"It wasn't so bad." Gregor said, which produced raised eyebrows from JD and Leah, and a look of astonishment from his wife. Even the three young men standing near the table full of ski maps turned. A big, hearty laugh erupted. "Unless you prefer freedom, cleanliness, warmth and the loving arms of the woman you plan to make your wife." His demeanor faded just a bit. "If I had not believed daily, that I would have Lenore to come home to, I would not have survived." He caressed Lenore with loving eyes and touched her beautiful face. "Nor, would I have wanted to."

"That's the most beautiful thing I've ever heard a man say to his wife." Leah said, her voice wavering with tears.

JD offered levity. "Leah, I say beautiful things to you all the time." His wife cocked an eyebrow as he continued. "Don't I tell you all the time that you have the cutest little hangy-down parts I've ever seen?"

Gregor and Lenore laughed as Leah stared at her husband, who was obviously proud of himself.

"Yes, Dear. I forgot what a romantic devil you can be." She rolled her eyes and shook her head.

Alex, Joel, and Grant had stopped their mapping to join the others. Lenore's sons understood the silly terminology, but Alex seemed perplexed.

"What is hangy-down parts?"

As Gregor proceeded to explain in Russian, what the conversation had been about, Lenore's sons settled near her. With the explanation complete, first Alex blushed, then laughed.

"I see this joke, I think. My brother is also very happy with Lenore's hangy-down parts."

Lenore decided a change of subject was in order.

"I've been working on my play room. Anyone want to see it? I hesitate to call it my art room since for the time being, all I do is play with paint."

"I want to see it!" Joel said, getting up from the floor.

"Me too!" Grant stood, offering a hand to his mom.

Lenore glanced at Leah and JD.

"We'll check it out later." Leah affirmed with a smile. Lenore and her sons needed *Mommy* time.

Lenore led her sons out of the room, down a short hall to a room she called her own. As they surveyed ample supplies and the half-finished works in the room, Lenore hugged her two sons and listened with pride as they told of their latest adventures and accomplishments. She missed having them nearby.

"Do you guys feel deserted by my moving here with Gregor? Are you okay with this? I just miss having you guys closer."

Joel slung an arm over his mom's shoulders. "I can't speak for Grant, but I'm okay with it. I know what it took for you to get here. I miss you, but practically every freshman at CSU is in the same boat." He tickled his mom's nose with an unused paintbrush and she pushed it away, laughing. "I always have JD and Leah close, and they're family. I know Gregor loves you." He hugged his mom and rested his chin atop her head. "Are you shrinking, Mom?"

"I agree with Joel," Grant interjected.

"You think she's shrinking, too?" Joel laughed.

"No, I agree Mom's happy and deserves it. I like Gregor. He's interesting." Grant flipped through the mostly blank pages of a sketch pad. "I like Alex, too. He sure seems a lot younger than he is."

"Oh, I think part of that is his youthful exuberance of discovery. He lived a sheltered life in the Soviet Union, and this is all new to him." She took *weapons* away from the boys who had begun playing dueling paintbrushes. "We take all this for granted. He finds wonderment in things like seeing people wearing blue jeans everywhere and the quantity of goods in a grocery store. He still needs to master the language and the cultural changes before he can find a job and settle in. We all need to help."

"Joel and I can teach him how to meet women!" Grant said, wagging his eyebrows.

"That doesn't seem to be a problem." Lenore placed the paint brushes back into the quart canning jar holding a variety of brushes. "He's handsome and has the same disarming smile as his brother. The ladies are always anxious to meet Alex."

Joel and Grant looked at one another for a moment, then smiled, sharing a mischievous thought, which Lenore noticed.

"What does that mean?"

Grant replied, "Maybe we can catch some of his cast offs tomorrow. I'm really looking forward to skiing, how about you, Joel?"

"I've got Kim, but I can't say I wouldn't mind the view from the sidelines. I'll let you two work the harvest."

Spot, a very spoiled calico cat, meandered into the room, drawn by familiar voices. Joel scooped her up and settled into a comfy chair. He scratched and massaged an area just behind Spot's ears and she rewarded him with very loud purring.

"Look Mom, she remembers me."

"Of course, Joel. I'd say there's no doubt." She smiled at the two reunited buddies.

"Maybe next year, when I move out of the dorms and into my own place, I can take her back to live with me."

"She's a lot of responsibility, Joel. You'd need to be able to provide care for her if you traveled, even for a weekend." Lenore didn't want to sound too negative about the idea. She knew her absence in Joel's life had to be painful at times. It wasn't just the cat he missed. "I know you miss her and it would be very nice for both of you if you find a place that'll accept pets. I'll help all I can."

Grant had been listening as he went back to admiring his mom's artwork. "I could always watch her in a pinch," he assured his brother. He looked up from the sketch pad. "How does Spot do with the dogs? They had to look huge to her, and never having to share life with a dog before must have been traumatic."

Both boys watched their mom as she smiled and walked to where Spot nestled comfortably in Joel's arms. "Let's just say I'm very glad the dogs mind as well as they do. With some discipline, they curbed their instincts. They frightened her initially, then she decided aloofness would be the best defense."

"So then, they get along?" Joel asked.

"I'd call it a respectful tolerance." Lenore stroked the top of Spot's drowsy head. "The only issue came when Marushka gave her a lick on top of her head. *That* crossed the line." She tickled under Spot's chin. "A hiss and a bop on Marushka's nose with Spot's paw confirmed it."

Spot flipped her tail, as if agreeing.

"The dogs don't come into the house very often. Mostly when the weather is going to be particularly bad. Gregor says they prefer the cold to the warm house most of the time, because that's what their thick fur is designed for." Grant showed a sketch to Joel as she spoke. They both gave an approving *wow*.

"They have a very comfortable shelter outside. It's big enough and cozy for two big dogs if they choose to get in it. When they do come inside, they like to hang out with Alex in his part of the house."

"I sure think they're beautiful. No offense Spot!" The comfortable feline didn't appear insulted and stretched in her familiar human's arms, yawning, as if bored with the subject.

"Let's go back and join the others. You guys are feeling okay with where I am?"

"I can't speak for Joel, but I'm sure alright with it."

"Hey, you're happy, that's great. We get the bonus of a cool stepdad, an uncle, two dogs and a great place to visit." Joel put Spot down on the floor, stroking her back from neck to tail, where her rear end naturally lifted. As Joel abandoned the chair, Spot reclaimed it, nestling into the warmth her favorite human had provided.

Lenore ushered her sons back into the warm living room. She sat near the fireplace and watched the people she loved talk and laugh. As the group changed and rearranged, Gregor held a hand out to her. She walked to where he sat on the sofa, and grabbed a floor pillow to sit on the floor at his feet. Gentle, strong hands massaged her shoulders as they talked with JD and Leah. This was the way life should be; soft, warm, and comfortable.

The warmth of the room and the hum of conversation soon worked its lulling effect on Lenore and she had a hard time keeping her eyes open. Gregor kissed the top of her head as she yawned.

* * * * *

The warm autumn day had given way to a cold night. The man continued to stand next to his truck, watching the house through high-powered binoculars from a road in the hills east of the valley. The extra guests would sideline his plans for a few days, but they would in no way stop him. He thought how easily he could have picked them all off, one by one with his Walther .380, as they stood outside the house earlier. He really didn't want to kill anyone. Yes, he was almost certain that he didn't. If anyone tried to stop him, well, that would be a different matter. Then he would have no choice. He lifted the binoculars once again and adjusted the focus until he could see her face through the un-curtained window. Soon her smile would be for him alone.

With a groan, he lowered the binoculars and got into his truck. He became uncomfortably aware of the swollen manhood inside his pants, and muttered to himself, "Got to save it for her."

Later, in the dark confines of his remote cabin, it would relieve itself of the pressure. He knew it would happen. His nocturnal encounters with Lenore always produced the same effect. They would not be dreams much longer.

CHAPTER 3

Gregor stood in the doorway of the kitchen sipping hot tea as he watched his wife put the finishing touches out for the breakfast buffet. He loved watching her. She radiated happiness. Even doing the most ordinary household chores, she smiled, occasionally whistling, or singing. It wasn't altogether uncommon for her to break into a dance if a lively tune inspired her. Gregor, Alex or even a handy broom would suffice as a partner.

Lenore adjusted and checked temperatures on the warming trays, poured herself a cup of coffee and walked to Gregor's side, slipping her arm around his waist.

"Are you hungry? Do you think there's enough?"

He kissed her lightly on the temple. "There is plenty. You have done a beautiful job. My hunger is not for this fare, however."

Lenore sat her cup down, took Gregor's cup of tea from him and sat it beside hers on the table. She put her arms around her husband. "It's only been an hour."

Gregor slid his hands under her loose sweater and gently cupped her breasts. "My mind knows this, but my heart hungers for you again. It is not aware of the time."

Lenore moaned and pressed herself into his strong hands, then leaned back and unbuttoned his shirt. She found a turtleneck sweater covering the strong, hairy chest she loved to caress. He laughed at her pouty lips and touched them with his smiling lips. Releasing her breasts to take her hand, Gregor led her out of the kitchen and upstairs to the sanctuary of their bedroom. He closed the door and removed his shirt and the offending turtleneck sweater. Lenore removed her sweater and they embraced, bodies fitting together in a familiar pattern.

Lenore let herself be distracted for only a moment when she thought of her guests. "What will everyone think when they come to breakfast and we aren't there?"

Gregor led her to the bed, gently easing her onto the satiny comforter. "They will know, or will think they know. It is something married people do when they are so much in love, is this not true?"

Lenore answered by pulling her lover down onto the bed and they entwined in a kiss, struggling out of their remaining clothes. Gregor's boots proved to be an easily ignored hindrance, with one removed and the other securing his pants to one leg.

With hands curled into the thick black hair covering the strong, firm chest, Lenore met her husband's rhythm until they were both satisfied. They kissed and held each other until breathing and heartbeats returned to normal. When they sat up and saw the mass of clothing tangled around Gregor's left leg, laughter erupted.

"I hope that wasn't too uncomfortable for you. I just couldn't wait any longer."

Gregor shook the bundle dangling at the top of his boot, turned and kissed Lenore softly. "I promise, my Lenore, it could not distract from you in any way. We should join our guests. I am certainly hungry for your cooking now."

Lenore ran her fingers through his hair, smoothing soft curls back into place. "I need to remake the bed and clean up a little. There's one thing in favor of using protection; it's not quite as messy."

"This is true, but then we could not be making a baby."

"True! Race you to the bathroom."

Lenore won easily with Gregor having a slight disadvantage with the bundle of clothes attached to his leg by a hiking boot. He finished his routine before Lenore and walked back into the kitchen, reclaiming his cup of cold tea.

"Good morning! Is the breakfast satisfactory? I apologize for our absence."

JD answered. "No apology needed. Great breakfast!"

Leah looked at the faces of Alex, Joel, and Grant for their reaction to the situation. Alex continued to eat without interruption, apparently used to their absences. Joel and Grant looked at Gregor, then to one another, raised their eyebrows. They understood, and seemed perfectly comfortable.

Lenore blushed a little as she walked into the kitchen. "Good morning. I hope you like the breakfast." She picked up her cup of coffee, walked to the sink and emptied her cold brew before pouring another cup. Affirmations from everyone eased her embarrassment.

She started another pot of coffee and turned the fire on under the tea kettle. She took a piece of bacon and sat down next to Leah.

"While you guys go skiing, Leah and I will go into Glenwood Springs and finish shopping for tomorrow's dinner. Then we'll come home and start baking pies. How late do you think you'll be?"

"It will probably be after dark. We will go to Snowmass today for skiing. It will take a little time to drive home if we stay until the last run, but the roads are clear. You will be careful in your trip to Glenwood."

"We'll be fine." Leah answered. "Lenore's the best driver I know."

Lenore patted her best friend on the back as she got up to pour Gregor's tea. "Thanks Leah, but that's not what he worries about. He worries about someone interfering or bothering me when I'm without him."

The silence in the room made Lenore look up. Her guests had stopped mid-chew and were staring at her.

"Oh, for goodness' sake! Nothing's going to happen. He worries too much. I can out-drive practically anyone on the road and once we get back here, there's Marushka and Nicolai, and a Taurus revolver I've been practicing with." She announced proudly. "It uses .38 specials so the kick isn't as bad." The stares and silence continued, until Grant spoke up.

"Mom, if that's supposed to make us feel better, it didn't work. If you've been taught how to use a gun, then it's because Gregor has a valid reason to teach you." He turned to his new step-father. "Gregor, do you think there's a threat of someone trying to hurt Mom?"

Gregor shook his head. "The CIA assures us there is no problem, but they continue to monitor our lives. Perhaps they are not so sure as they say." He added, "I also believe every person should know how to use a weapon. This is the reason your mother knows how to use a variety of them. We do have bears in the area." The answer seemed to satisfy the young men.

"Is John Dixon still assigned to you, Gregor?" Leah cringed after she asked the question, not knowing if the prior relationship with Lenore created a problem between them.

"Not in the same capacity as before," he explained, sensing Leah's concern. "The agents here report to him. It is a promotion for him, and he is the head of the mountain west area. He will be joining us for this holiday and is to be arriving sometime today. He is a very good friend to this whole family." After a final sip of his hot tea, he stood. "We should be leaving. The lifts will be operating soon."

Gregor walked to where Lenore sat and gave her a kiss that lasted a bit longer than the day's absence would normally dictate. Grant, Joel, JD, and Alex stood, waiting near the door. Alex sighed and opened the door.

"If we do not leave now, they will disappear again. We will never find any snow rabbits that are worth our trouble."

"Bunnies!" Joel and Grant corrected as they followed Alex out the door. JD blew a kiss to Leah, who giggled and blew one back to him.

Gregor gently caressed Lenore's face. "Have a good time today." Then he kissed Leah on the cheek, "I am glad you are here Leah."

As the door closed, Leah turned to Lenore. "Are good-byes always such a production?"

"Always! Maybe someday they won't be, but it's still too fresh a memory of how long a good-bye had to last one time."

Leah nodded. "That must haunt you both. In many ways, I hope you never take good-byes for granted. You're truly happy, aren't you, Lenore?"

"Truly happy!" She sighed, a smile settling gently in place. "I'm so very in love with my husband. It's sometimes a little frightening to have so much love for another person."

Breakfast dishes were cleared and put into the dishwasher as the ladies talked and laughed.

"How are Shelly, Dustin and Danny?" Lenore asked as she made one final swipe across the counter with the towel.

"Oh, my gosh! I forgot to tell you! Shelly moved to an apartment of her own, has the boys with her now and has kicked that guy she thought was so great, *and wasn't*, to the curb!" Leah beamed as she closed a cabinet door and straightened the knife holder. "I'm so proud of her."

"Wow! What got her motivated?"

"Honestly? You!" She caught the towel Lenore tossed and hung it on the rack near the sink.

"Me?"

"Yep, she said if you can start again and have such a great life, she knows she can do it, too. The boys are just so excited. They have a big room to share and they live just a block from their favorite park."

"Please tell her I'm proud of her. I can't wait to see them when we come to the front range. She's going to make it just fine with you guys providing a great support system for her." They headed upstairs to the bedrooms. "Want to take a dip in the springs while we're in town?"

"Sure, but isn't Gregor going to mind?"

"I don't think so. Why?"

"Well, it wasn't on your itinerary when they left. He sure seems to worry about you."

"Leah, it's his nature to worry. With an agent following me and watching me, there's nothing to worry about." The friends reached the top of the stairs and stopped. "The only reason there are agents here at all is because of John."

"Is he a problem between you and Gregor?"

"I've never detected it if he is. As a matter of fact, Gregor invited him to join us for the holiday."

"Must be some pretty good friends." Leah followed Lenore to the master bedroom.

"The best!" Lenore went to the walk-in closet, opened a drawer, and began sorting through bathing suits. "I have several suits if you want to try them."

"Oh, I brought two of my own, just in case." Leah watched Lenore making her choice. "I've always wanted to go there in cold weather, just to see the steam, rising from those heated pools."

"Two suits? My goodness, you did come prepared!"

Leah nodded her approval of the suit Lenore held up. "You're the one who said it's always better to have it and not need it, than to need it and not have it."

"I taught you well! Go get them and we'll dress in here."

The two friends laughed and talked as they dressed for their excursion. With bathing suits on under sensible clothing for the autumn day, they started for the door. Lenore handed Leah the shopping list, then went to a panel on the wall.

"Check the list and see if I've forgotten anything while I set the alarms. Gregor pulled the Saab out of the garage for us, so I'll meet you at the car."

With alarms set, Lenore closed the door behind her and turned to see Leah backed against the Saab with two Great White Pyrenees dogs very intent on keeping her there.

"Marushka! Nicolai! Nyet! Nyet!" She stormed toward the car. "Sidet! Dammit, get back!"

The dogs obediently backed away from Leah and ambled toward Lenore, who strode past them and put her arms around the visibly shaken Leah.

"I'm so sorry Leah. I just didn't think when I sent you out here alone. I just figured they would remember welcoming you yesterday and know you are a friend. Did they hurt you?"

Leah lowered herself back down to her original five-foot frame, after having stretched as far above the dogs as gravity would allow. She started laughing and Lenore didn't know if she had missed a joke, or if her best friend had gone into hysterics.

"I'm fine! They just startled me. They never growled or acted like they wanted to bite, they just kept pressing up against me." She continued laughing.

"You sure you're alright? What's so funny?"

"It's no wonder they wouldn't mind me and back off. They only understand Russian, right?"

"Believe me, they're learning plenty of English!" As if to prove a point, Lenore turned to face the two creatures, shook her finger at them and scolded. "Bad dogs! This is a friend!" She hugged Leah. "Go to the porch now!"

Marushka and Nicolai lowered their wagging tails and obeyed. Sitting side-by-side on the porch, they watched Lenore and Leah get in the car and pull away, then laid down in resignation.

Leah watched the dogs as the Saab pulled away from the house. "I can't believe you can control those huge animals. Aren't you afraid of them?"

"Nope! Never, Leah. I just decided if they were going to accept me, they would have to obey me as well. I give them a lot of affection and attention. They trust me and they know I love them." She smiled. "I suppose they would tear someone apart if I gave the order, but they usually just like to make their presence known."

"Boy do they ever!" Leah agreed.

Lenore glanced at Leah. "Did they slobber on you?"

"I don't think so." Leah checked her jacket front and sleeves.

"Nothing quite so disgusting as dog slobber." Lenore noted, wrinkling her nose. "Those two seem to have an abundance of it."

They drove several miles with silence; an oddity for them. Lenore glanced at Leah

"What are you thinking about so seriously?"

"Oh, just pondercating." Leah had created the special new word, *pondercate*. She said it meant something between pondering and contemplating. Lenore loved it and giggled.

"About what?"

"What did you say to make them stop? It sounded like the same thing Alex said when we arrived. I figure *nyet*, of course, means no or stop, What's the "*sid-yet*" mean?"

Lenore smiled at Leah's pronunciation. "You're correct about the first. The second, *sidet*, means to sit, sort of. I intersperse Russian with a heavy dose of English. They get the drift."

"Okay. What's the order?"

"Of what?"

"The order you give to make them attack?"

"I won't tell you." Lenore shook her head and glanced at Leah. "If you would happen to say it, they would go nuts."

"How do you know I won't say it by accident?"

"It's Russian."

"Figures." Leah looked back at Lenore. "But what if I *need* them to attack?"

"No!"

"End of discussion?"

"Yep!"

The silver-brown Saab 900 Turbo cruised into town with the passengers admiring familiar territory and reminiscing about their adventures in Glenwood Springs.

* * * * *

A light gray 1948 Ford pickup truck followed at a safe distance behind the assigned agent's car, allowing several vehicles between them. The agent was intent on keeping Lenore's vehicle in sight. The driver of the pickup did, too. He just wanted to make sure the agent didn't pay attention to vehicles behind him.

When the cars turned toward the Hot Springs after crossing the bridge, the truck continued straight. He turned into a parking lot and waited ten minutes before getting out. He walked toward the springs, making sure he saw the assigned agent before that agent spotted him. He knew Lenore would be in a bathing suit, exposing most of her beautiful body. She shouldn't be quite so comfortable in the bathing suits. Men watched, wanting her. None of them wanted her as badly as he did. He would have her. Soon.

CHAPTER 4

With belongings secured in lockers, and a final check to make sure nothing showed that shouldn't be showing, the best friends walked to the pool.

"This is fantastic!" Leah said. "Tell me madam, do you come here often?"

Lenore replied in her own British accent "But of course. It is, after all, what one does when one is a local." Their towels were placed upon a lounge chair on the north side of the pool and robes dropped alongside. It took little time for them to get into the soothing, warm water.

"How foolish of me. Of course, that would explain your tanned body in the throes of autumn."

"Well, yes," Lenore agreed. "But it is also a result of nude sunbathing on the balcony at home. Gregor joins me. He missed the sunshine so much while he was in prison."

Leah raised her eyebrows as she looked at Lenore, her British accent gone. "Don't you worry about the surveillance team getting to know you a little too well?"

"No, it's enclosed. The only way they could see us is from a helicopter or hot air balloon." She leaned back and dipped her long hair into the warm water. "So far, they've not used those."

Leah had no intentions of getting her hair wet. "Does it bother you, being watched and followed all the time?" Shoulder deep would be her limit.

Lenore closed her eyes as she hooked her elbows on the edge of the pool and let her legs float in the warm water. "Not really. There are times I wish I could just go for a drive all alone and not have someone behind me. Someone following sort of ruins the effect. I know it makes Gregor feel better about letting me go places alone."

"Remember when you outdrove Frank?"

Lenore nodded. "After Kansas City I felt like an ass for what I'd said to him that day. He was only doing his job. If it hadn't been for him, they wouldn't have found Sergei and the other one." She shook her head. "The USSR assured our government the third one is back there, being *dealt* with. I just need to trust it's true."

"Boy, I'd demand proof."

"The Soviet Union has made some significant strides, but they're not there yet. We can't *demand* anything."

"Does it keep you awake at night worrying?"

"Nope, I sleep like a baby. Well, unless Gregor wakes me." She winked. "I don't mind being awakened by him, ever!"

Leah laughed. "Did you finally go on the pill, or are you still using rubbers?"

"Nope."

"Nope to which?"

"Neither. We aren't using anything." Lenore stood up and pointed. "Is that who I think it is?"

Leah stared at Lenore, not wanting any interruption at that moment, but turned to see where Lenore pointed. She recognized the agent with whom she had spent so many hours on the phone when Gregor had been in prison in the Soviet Union. John Dixon emerged from the sturdy old red sandstone building, standing beyond its shadow, appreciating the sun's warmth. His blue eyes were hidden behind dark glasses and his normally well-behaved soft, brown hair reacted to the gentle breeze. John combed through it with the fingers of his free hand as he scanned the area, deciding where best to enter the inviting thermal waters.

"It's John!" Leah confirmed as the two women began waving.

"I don't think he sees us. I'll go get him." Lenore turned and got out of the pool, the brisk air chilling her. She walked near the edge as she called out to him.

John held a towel in one hand as he walked around the pool to the sunnier side. His robe hung open, revealing a well-chiseled physique. When he heard his name called, he saw Lenore wave and began walking toward her. As he neared, he could see her nipples hard and erect, pushing against the soft white material, reacting to the cold air.

"Lenore, I didn't expect to see you here. Better get back in the water. It's cold out here."

He welcomed the quick hug she gave before she sat down, easing back into the water.

"Put your stuff over beside the teal-colored towels." She pointed, then said, "Look who else is here! Hurry and get into the water with us"

John hoped the baggy swim trunks he wore would hide the reaction his *little agent* had upon seeing Lenore so close to naked. It brought back familiar feelings. He still loved her. He would always love her, but she belonged to Gregor now. Lucky bastard! He dropped his towel and robe near Lenore's and got into the water. He laughed as both women hugged him and talked at the same time.

"When did you get here?" Leah asked.

Lenore added, "and why didn't you call and let us know you were here?"

"Why didn't you come on the train with the rest of us yesterday?" Leah continued.

"We're so glad you decided to come. Gregor is just so excited to have everyone here." Lenore giggled as she hugged him.

"Hey, slow down!" John laughed. "Two against one isn't fair, especially when it's *you* two!"

The two women relented, the trio still embracing in the warm water. One of Lenore's legs innocently entwined around John's, which did nothing to suppress what he tried to ignore.

"I flew into Aspen yesterday and rented a car. Well, a truck." He struggled to concentrate. "I decided it'd be better to have a four-wheel drive, just in case the weather turns bad. I wouldn't dream of missing your first holiday together. I appreciate the invitation."

"I have to whizz!" Leah announced.

Lenore looked at her friend and titled her head. "You just went before we got in the water!"

"That's been nearly an hour ago and all the excitement and warm water isn't helping. I'll be right back!" Leah maneuvered to the ladder and got out, grabbed her robe, and sprinted to the bath house. John and Lenore watched her go, then focused their attention back on one another.

"I swear, she has the tiniest bladder of any human being I've ever met." Lenore laughed.

"Lenore, you look beautiful." John looked into her eyes. "I've missed you."

The smile remained on Lenore's lips, but moving a leg to adjust her balance, she became aware of just how much he missed her. She was suddenly embarrassed to be standing in the water, still embracing John, and tried to move away without looking too obvious.

"I've missed you too, John." She moved to the edge of the pool and held on, letting her legs move freely in the water.

John moved to her side and floated on his stomach as he held onto the side. "Sorry Lenore, I hoped you wouldn't notice. I know you're a happily married woman, but I'm afraid parts of me just don't have good manners."

They looked at each other for a minute, then smiled. John knew it would be alright.

"You look very happy. I guess that means Gregor is being good to you."

"Yes, he is, John. I'll never be able to thank you enough for bringing him back to me."

"I didn't do it alone. I just gave the information to the right people and they took it from there." He smiled. "Our friend with the tiny bladder and good memory did the most." He wished he could kiss the smile that played across Lenore's lips. Instead, he sighed and tried to converse. "How's Alex adjusting?"

"Quite well. He's like a kid in an amusement park. I should quit taking him to the grocery store with me though. He just stands there in awe of all the choices and quantity." She imitated Alex's gaping expression, then shook her head. "It can get downright embarrassing!"

They both laughed at the vision. John started to reach out and smooth a strand of hair from Lenore's cheek, stopping before he completed the gesture, and returned his hand to the edge of the pool. "Do you think he could handle a job yet?"

"Doing what?" Lenore absently stroked the hair away from her face, unaware of John's intended desire to do it for her.

"A television station in Denver is looking for a meteorologist and I put his name in the hat."

Lenore arched her eyebrows. "You mean he would be on TV?"

"No, at least not for a while." He turned, hooking his elbows on the edge of the pool and allowed his legs to float in the mineral enriched water. "At first, he would be behind the scenes, tracking storms, working on forecasts and such. Eventually, they'd give him air time." John was aware the little agent in his swim trunks had stopped saluting Lenore's presence. "They're very interested in having a former Soviet citizen on staff. It would be good publicity, of course."

"Oh, Alex would be ecstatic, but you'll have to talk to him *and* Gregor about it. He'd have to move to Denver, and I don't know if he's ready for that."

"He could stay with me. Not a problem," John said.

"I'm sure that would make Gregor feel better about it."

John nodded. "Yes, it cost him nearly a year of his life to get his brother here. I doubt he'll be very anxious to let Alex out of sight. I'll discuss it with Greg before we approach Alex."

"My thoughts exactly," Lenore replied.

Leah returned and joined her friends in the warm water. "I don't know why bathing suits are so hard to get off and back on when they're wet! Sorry it took so long." She nestled neck deep into the water. "How's life in the world of good guys and bad guys, John?"

John laughed. "Leah, my world now consists of too much paperwork and too many phone calls. I haven't had time to do much else. How about you and JD?"

"Same old routine, except mine isn't nearly as much fun as when Lenore lived there. Sounds like we all needed this trip."

"Will you stay through Sunday?" Lenore asked.

"Depends on my beeper. If duty calls, I'll need to go. I'd like to get some skiing in." He would enjoy getting to see Lenore without the crowd today and be assured, or maybe a little disappointed, in her happiness. "I got here yesterday and settled at the lodge. I told Greg I'd be coming today, so I used the time to relax and get some extra sleep." John hoped that sounded reasonable. "Why didn't you go skiing?"

"We're supposed to be grocery shopping and baking pies today." Lenore continued before the ensuing lecture about changing plans could start. "We just couldn't resist coming here for a little while. We need to leave in about a half hour if we're going to accomplish our goals though." She patted John's arm. "You need to check out of wherever you're staying and meet us at the house in about an hour and a half."

"Check out?" John asked.

"Of course! You're staying at the house. You should have come to the house yesterday. We have your room ready."

He shook his head. "I'm fine where I'm at. You don't need the extra company. I'll just come out and wait until the guys return."

"Nonsense!" Lenore scolded. "Gregor won't understand your refusal. It would be an insult. You aren't company anyway. You're family!"

"She's right," Leah added. "Besides, it's going to be like a huge slumber party. You wouldn't want to miss it!"

The two beautiful ladies stood on either side of John. He looked from one to the other and shook his head. "You're ganging up on me again, aren't you?"

"Yes!" They answered in unison. John nodded in submissive acknowledgment. They hugged him, though Lenore was a bit more reserved than before. John didn't appear to notice.

CHAPTER 5

Leaving the historic Hot Springs Pool complex, Lenore and Leah headed for the grocery store. John returned to his room at the lodge to gather his belongings. He closed the door where he had only spent one night and walked to the office after loading his truck.

The affable innkeeper waved as John entered the office, but had a phone to his ear. The smell of fresh coffee greeted his senses, and a stuffed black bear near the door seemed to salute. John waited near the desk until the call ended.

Bart sported a generous belly covered by a crisp white shirt buttoned to the top, and he wore a seasonal cardigan. John wondered if the bowtie he normally sported, had been forgotten or lost. His well-trimmed gray hair was combed straight back and showed no signs of thinning. His cheeks were plump and became even more round when he smiled. His efficiency and cordial manner, honed by years in the hospitality industry, came naturally. His wire framed glasses caught a glint of light as he ended the call and looked up to address John.

"Hello Mr. Dixon. What can I do for you?"

John reached into his jacket and retrieved his billfold, "Bart, I'm going to be checking out. I hope that's no problem. I'll go ahead and pay for my entire intended stay since this is short notice."

"Oh, no need to do that. It's not going to be a problem renting it. I'm always full up this time of year. People wait in line for a room." He chuckled, his belly punctuating the effort. "I sure had one that got upset when I had to tell him we were full a couple days ago."

"How upset?" John asked, signing the credit card receipt and only half-listening for details.

Bart shook his head. "Oh, he made a threat that he could come and make me do it. I told him I could sure handle people like him if he did." He reached under the counter and produced a sawed-off Remington 870 12 gauge. "This usually calms folks right down."

John whistled appreciatively. "Yes, I think that would settle most issues."

Bart put the weapon back under the counter; no doubt handy, but safely stored. "I've had a couple of revolvers through the years; a Taurus M66 being my favorite, but the older I get, I've decided I don't want to have to worry about aiming." He chuckled.

"You'd have a pretty wide pattern when that shotgun fires," noted John.

"Yep, it's my persuader. I'm sure I'll win most arguments."

"No doubt, Bart. Now, about the guy who threatened you. Pretty insistent, huh?" John put his pen back into his inside pocket.

"Oh yes. I even told that fella I'd be happy to check around for a room available somewhere else. He got damned angry and said it had to be this lodge and a particular room." He shook his head. "Something about that room, Mr. Dixon." He frowned and scratched his head, then smoothed and patted his hair back into place. "I recall two ladies from Fort Collins had that particular room two years in a row for their weekend getaway." He handed John a copy of his credit receipt.

"Oh?" John was suddenly very attentive.

"Such nice people, those two. Always smiling and friendly. I can even recall their names; Appleby and Chase." He chuckled. "You know, that Appleby woman married a fella from around here. He's from Russia. Good folks. He brought a brother with him back from Russia. Nice story they had in the paper." He chuckled again. "Too bad for me she won't be needing that room again."

The hair stood up on the back of John's neck. The old guy had a good memory. Of course, Lenore and Leah were easy to remember.

"Can you tell me anything else about the guy who called?"

The clerk looked out the window and pulled a neatly folded handkerchief from a back pocket. He removed his glasses and gently rubbed at the lenses, giving serious thought to the question before replacing the glasses, refolding the handkerchief, and swiping his nose back and forth with it. He answered as he tucked the cloth back into his pocket. "Fella said he would be staying maybe a week for both business and pleasure. Then, when he found out he couldn't get that specific room he insisted upon, he got kind of ugly."

John reached into a coat pocket, pulled out his billfold once again and retrieved two one-hundred-dollar bills and laid them on the counter, along with his business card. "This should help in case that room isn't rented today. If you happen to hear from that guy, give me a call. If he shows up, call the police if you can. Show him that persuader of yours if you can't." He patted the hand reaching out scoop up the cash and business card. "Oh, and I'd appreciate it greatly if you didn't mention this little arrangement to him or anyone else."

The clerk looked over the business card. His eyebrows raised. "CIA huh? I understand why you ask so many questions. Nature of the job, huh?" He chuckled. "Well, I'll keep my mouth shut about it. Haven't been in this business forty-eight years by tellin' everything I know."

John walked out of the office and got into his truck. He wasn't convinced the clerk knew how to keep things to himself, but he hoped it didn't matter. It might just be some business man who always stayed in the same room, or it had been his honeymoon suite at one time. He just couldn't ignore the uneasy feeling building. John needed to get to the Parish's home.

* * * * *

Lenore and Leah put groceries in the car, apparently too involved in the task and their conversation to be aware of anyone other than the usual surveillance. The man in the gray pickup truck waited and watched. Agent Barnes, assigned to watch the ladies, got out of his car to assist. What a perfect target. A calculated shot would put him out of the picture in an instant. The young agent appeared too relaxed in his task, and ignorant as well. He should have been at least aware of the truck and its occupant. Instead, Barnes had been reading a paper while the women shopped. This could be a much easier task than he had ever dreamed.

He had become irritated with Lenore and her behavior at the pool. Hanging on Dixon the way she did; well, it was just wrong. Yes, he would teach her to always behave as a lady. She would learn. She would never parade around in skimpy clothes. No one would stare at her again once he freed her from the fools who held her now. He would go shopping to get her some decent clothes to cover her beautiful body. Soon, she would show it only to him.

He watched the Saab pull out into the southbound lane of traffic, the agent following. He knew the destination. He could follow at a reasonable distance, then watch the house from the hilltop through binoculars. It was a poor substitute for being the agent surveilling her, but that would all change; soon.

He had been infuriated when Dixon reassigned him, and even more pissed at agent Pete Kelly, for telling Dixon about his friendship with Lenore. They didn't understand.

Dennis Halvorson decided it had to all be part of their plan to keep Lenore with the Commie. She wasn't even given the freedom to have friends of her own choosing.

He had been told to report back to Langley for training on a covert duty overseas but he knew they weren't needing him to be trained for anything. They were just trying to get him out of the picture. That Commie had them all fooled. No, he was determined to rescue Lenore and have her for himself. She needed to be with a good upstanding American. She deserved nothing less, and he would provide it.

* * * * *

"Lenore, before we get to the house, you have to tell me what you meant when you said you weren't using anything for protection," Leah said.

A normal occurrence for them, Lenore picked up the threads of an old conversation.

"That's it. We aren't using anything."

"Well, I know you're not afraid of disease, but what about pregnancy?"

"We aren't afraid of that either." Lenore passed a Chevy suburban, who's occupants were busy admiring the scenery, weaving in their lane of traffic. "Those folks need to pull over and take pictures."

"Is Gregor sterile, or are you?"

Lenore glanced at Leah. "I sincerely hope neither."

"You *want* to become pregnant?" Leah's eyes grew wide.

"Yes!"

"Lenore, you're not twenty years old anymore. Are you sure this is a good idea?"

"I've never been so sure of anything in my life. I've had a good physical exam. Doctor said I'm healthy, and all my parts are in excellent condition, so I can handle a pregnancy."

"But your babies are all grown. You want to start over again?" Leah was certain Lenore had lost her mind.

"Leah, there's such a difference now. I had Grant at a very young age. Their dad and I married because you were supposed to do that back then. You grow up and get married." She sighed. "I had Joel three years later. Don't get me wrong, I loved being their mom; still do, but their dad and I were going in different directions. We both knew we wanted out of the marriage. It remained amicable and I really don't think the boys ever gave it much concern."

Lenore checked her mirrors before pulling back into the right lane, aware of the ever-present agent's car following, though several vehicles separated them. "Still, I had a hard time, trying to raise the boys perpetually on my own. An every-other-weekend stay with their dad and a pittance of child support meant I needed to work every hour I could; six and seven days a week. When their dad moved away, they had two-month summer vacations with him, and holiday visitation schedules."

An older beat-up Jeep pulled out in front of them from a side road. Lenore slammed on the brakes, producing a shriek from Leah and a resounding "Dammit!" from herself.

"Where in the blazes are their heads today? They're not even tourists. Local plates!" She pointed, then glanced a Leah. "Sorry. Are you ok?"

Leah popped the top on her can of Diet Coke purchased in the grocery store. She sipped long, then put the can into the caddy. "I'm fine. If we can catch up, I'll stick my tongue out at 'em." She shook her head. "Brats!"

Lenore accelerated a little to make Leah laugh and lighten the mood again.

As they settled back into the ride, Leah turned back to Lenore. "Please continue."

"Well, you know, after the fiasco with Nick," She made a face at the recollection. "I had become convinced that true and devoted love just did not exist for me."

A smiled bloomed on Lenore's face. "And then I met this guy who decided to turn my world upside-down and shake out all the bad, leaving room only for love." She glanced at Leah. "This child will have parents who not only love him or her, they will always know how very much we love one another."

Leah sat quietly absorbing what Lenore said. "But Lenore, you remember the diapers and two in the morning feedings? It's still a life-long job and you're just now starting to enjoy your life like you always should have."

"Leah, *this is* the life I always should have had. The diapers are such a short time of it. This isn't going to be one-sided parenting. I want to give Gregor a child to raise and bestow all the love and knowledge he has. He will be such a good father, and I *know* the love he has for me won't diminish." She glanced at Leah. "He deserves to know those feelings of watching a child grow and learn. Before we know it, we'll see this child graduate from high school. The only thing I think about is whether the boys will understand."

Leah sipped more of her beverage. "Lenore, they love you so much and you have such a great communication with them. They know your life with Gregor is what you want. I'm certain that if you don't make them feel they're taking a back-seat to the new little one, I think they'll be fine."

"Gregor would never allow that. He sees them as an extension of *me*. He's so enjoying getting to know them better and would do anything for them. He offered to have them live here with us." She signaled the turn, to proceed down the road to her home. "He's paying Joel's college expenses above his scholarship. I guess because he had been denied a normal childhood, he cherishes the family unit."

"Lenore, your family is going to have one very special baby."

"At the very least."

"I hope you mean quality and not quantity there."

Before she could address the statement, they pulled into the drive and saw John sitting on the steps with Marushka and Nicolai laying quietly on either side of him. The man and the ever-watchful dogs stood and descended the steps to greet the Saab and its occupants.

Leah watched the two dogs amble towards the car. "Would the dogs ever attack John?"

"Oh, no, they're old friends." She laughed and waved at John. "Remember, he was assigned to watch Gregor for two years. He also speaks enough Russian to control them."

"Does he know the word?" Leah asked.

Lenore knew exactly what Leah asked about. "Yes. Gregor thought it necessary."

"Oh sure, he knows but I can't be trusted to know." Leah feigned a pout.

Lenore looked at her friend and raised her eyebrows, "I know you realize that pouting will not change my mind."

They got out of the car and the three of them began unloading groceries while Marushka and Nicolai supervised. Leah even patted Marushka on the head. A surprising thing for her to do, Lenore thought with a smile.

* * * * *

The man on the hilltop watched as Dixon helped the ladies carry groceries into the house. When Dixon unloaded a suitcase, the man tossed his binoculars onto the seat beside him. He got out and began pacing. How in the hell could they welcome *him* into their home? Why would the Commie allow it?

He then began to laugh. Yes, they were all ignorant when it came to Lenore. John Dixon wouldn't have the nerve to attempt anything. Hell, Dixon orchestrated getting that Soviet spy out of the prison he deserved and back to take Lenore for himself. Dixon stood by and let it happen. He could have had her for his very own, but he blew it.

It was becoming so vitally important to get Lenore out of that situation, before she became brainwashed any further. Surrounded by Commies and fools, she would be so grateful once he got her out of there. She would be with someone who would show her respect, and teach her how to respect herself. He didn't know if he would be able to wait much longer.

The family had been an expected inconvenience. Lenore mentioned those plans weeks ago. He planned to wait until the holiday crowd left before making his move. He knew that would probably be the best plan of action. She would go for one of her drives after that, and he would be the agent following her this time. He would use whatever means necessary to eliminate anyone who got in his way.

He laughed and got back into the truck, picking up the binoculars to watch the windows.

"Soon, Lenore. Very soon," he whispered as her face came into view.

* * * * *

Inside the house, Lenore and Leah were putting groceries away while John received a briefing from the agent surveilling Lenore and Leah on their outing. He told John of the reckless driver and that he had already radioed the Colorado state patrol about the Jeep. He also expressed to John his admiration of Lenore's driving. John thanked the agent and turned to go back in the house while the agent returned to his position to surveil the residence.

John unpacked and settled into the comfy, familiar guest room. He walked back downstairs and into the kitchen, where he caught an apron tossed by Lenore, much to his surprise.

"What's this for?"

"It's to keep that nice sweater clean," Leah offered.

"I know how handy you can be in the kitchen." Lenore answered as she pulled her hair into a pony tail. "See, you could have been on a slope chasing snow *rabbits* with Alex and the boys, or skiing black diamonds with Gregor and JD, but you didn't bother to call. You're stuck here doing kitchen duty."

He tried to feign insult, but couldn't suppress a grin. He put on the apron and pushed up the sleeves of his sweater, ready for action.

"What shall I do?" He clapped his hands together.

"We need for you to peel apples. Lots of them," Leah said. "Just peel, core, cut in half and put them into the bowl of water there. You can put the peels in this one." She moved a metal bowl closer.

"I'm baking an apple pie, and I need some for a fruit salad. Just need to save a couple for the turkey dressing." Lenore informed, as she plucked two apples from the pile and sat them on the counter behind her. "Grab a fresh lemon from the fridge to squeeze into the water bowl, to prevent the apples from turning brown."

John began opening drawers to locate a knife, then accepted one from Leah, who had pulled it from the knife holder sitting on the counter. She also handed him a melon baller to remove the core, and demonstrated with the first apple. John located a lemon, sliced it, and squeezed the juice into the bowl. Soon the trio worked like a fine oiled machine, with talking and laughing interspersed in generous doses.

Lenore prepared pie dough and Leah stirred the makings for two pumpkin pies together. John peeled and cored apples, half listening to the chatter between the two women. His mind went back to the lodge, replaying the conversation with the clerk, wondering if it might be something to be concerned about.

"I need to make a phone call. I have quite a few of these apples ready, have I earned a break?"

With teasing from the two women about making up excuses to get out of work, he laughed, but only until out of sight. He was all serious when he closed the door of the quiet den and picked up the phone. The number he fed into the phone put him on a secure line to headquarters, surprising his boss.

"John, I thought you were taking a few days off. I'm just about to leave. What's up?"

"I hope nothing. Just making sure we have plenty of agents around here. I've got a strange feeling something's not quite right."

"If anyone else said that, I'd tell them to quit bothering me and hang up. Tell me what's got you edgy?"

John related the story regarding the lodge, and waited for a response. He wasn't pleased with the words from his boss, but they were expected.

"What the hell were *you* doing checking into that lodge? You sure you're just not having a little trouble letting go of Lenore?"

"I suppose I am, in a lot of ways, but the fact remains that someone wanted that particular room enough to make threats" He twirled a pencil found on the large wooden desk. "I'm out of the loop for the holiday, so could you have her ex-husband checked out for me? Make sure he's being a good boy. I wish we could confirm the operative who snatched Lenore from the airport has indeed, gone back to the USSR." He paused, tapped the eraser end of the pencil on the desk, then added, "I owe you a steak dinner, in the location of your choice, if this turns out to be nothing." After a beat he added, "The lodge *is* one of the nicest in Glenwood Springs, you know."

"Dixon, all I can think about is a big turkey dinner tomorrow with my family. Just don't make me miss that or you'll have one pissed Director, okay? I'll put surveillance on the ex. If there's anything you should know, you'll get a beep."

"Great. I'd feel better if Frank could be in on this with me. I might have wrangled a diner invitation for him here." He leaned back in the chair and admired the new bookshelf on the wall to his left; a new addition since his last visit. No doubt Lenore had filled it with her favorite reads. He smiled.

"Can't help you there, I'm afraid."

"Frank's never taken a day off since I've worked with him," John opened a drawer and put the pencil inside. "He didn't want to elaborate on his decision to take off."

"Surprised me, too. Anyone else you want? I'll pull in the extra, since you are *officially* off duty yourself"

"I appreciate it. There's none that I'm as confident in as Frank. He's been with me from the beginning, and seems to have a built-in radar when it comes to Lenore." He straightened a note pad on the desk. "I have Pete Kelly, and he's a damned close second. Let's hope it's nothing, but I'll still need someone in from the Utah sector."

"John, try to relax and have a good Thanksgiving holiday."

"That's the plan for all of us. Guess I'd better finish peeling those apples now. Have a happy Thanksgiving and give my best to the family."

* * * * *

The Director hung up the phone. He sat for a moment, muttering *apples*, as he looked at the illuminated screen in front of him. There were currently three agents in the area, rotating shifts of surveillance on the Parishnikov household. Pulling in an extra agent from Utah would undoubtedly ruin someone's Thanksgiving plans. In their line of work, holidays were a luxury. They'd get over it. John Dixon was seldom wrong in his hunches.

* * * * *

John walked back into the kitchen, still wearing his apron, and sat down at the table to continue peeling apples. "Sorry if I took too long. Doesn't look like you're ahead of me yet."

Lenore plucked the last three peeled apples halves from the bowl.

"I think we just got ahead of you. Better do some fast peeling. Is everything alright?"

John lied as he avoided Lenore's eyes, apparently intent on his chore. He knew she would read something different in his eyes. "Sure, everything is fine. Just had some business I forgot to take care of before I left and happened to remember it. How many more of these things do I have to do?"

"At least five. Are we working you too hard?"

"If I break a sweat, I'll protest." He pushed up a sleeve of his sweater. "How did I get stuck with this job anyway?"

"We thought it would *appeal* to you," Leah replied with a wry smile.

John and Lenore both groaned at the corny pun.

The trio continued to work until pies were baking and the fruit salad was chilling in the refrigerator. Lenore made sandwiches and they sat at the table eating and talking. John wondered how he could question Lenore without raising suspicion. Leah managed to turn the conversation in the right direction without his help.

"John, do you think Lenore and Gregor will ever be able to live a normal life?"

Lenore looked at her best friend, then at John, not quite sure what Leah meant.

"How do you mean, *normal?*" he replied, knowing exactly what she meant.

"Oh, you know, without surveillance and all."

Lenore chewed and listened intently to the conversation between Leah and John.

"I'm sure that will happen one day. Maybe soon. We just need to be sure there isn't someone lurking around, trying to disrupt their lives. There are quite a few people who resent the hell out of any Russian, whether he's defected and becoming a citizen, or not." He then seized the opportunity. "Lenore, have you had any problems? Have anyone following you or bothering you when you're out?"

Lenore swallowed and took a sip of water before answering. "No, at least not anyone other than agents. I get tired of it, but I realize it's necessary if I'm to have any life outside this house at all." She tore part of the crust of her bread off and nibbled it. "Today I thought we were followed by an old Ford pickup truck. Sharp looking '48 or '49. It went straight when we turned for the pool. It caught my eye because I love old Fords. I also saw it parked across the street from the grocery store later." She said as she dabbed her mouth with a napkin. "Our agent followed us everywhere and right back here to the house. If anyone else would have been following, he would have noticed, right?"

John felt anything but calm when he answered. "Right!"

"Lenore, you didn't say anything to me. Why didn't you tell me you thought someone followed us?"

"Because, Leah, if I would have said a word about it, you would have been turned around backward in the seat, trying to see it, which would have caused me to have a wreck. Besides, I knew a good old agent had to be nearby. There always is." She rolled her napkin into a ball. "We had Barnes today. Haven't seen Dennis for a couple of weeks."

"Dennis?" John asked.

"You know, Dennis *Halvorson*. I bought his lunch one day when he surveilled me. We talked for a while."

"Yes, Halvorson has been reassigned."

"Reassigned? Why?"

"Lenore, it's not appropriate behavior for an agent on surveillance."

"Don't be such a stickler for rules." She stared at him. "If I remember correctly, you bent a few of them with me."

"She's definitely one up on you there, John," Leah observed.

"That was different." He folded his napkin and laid it across his plate.

Lenore didn't accept John's reply and her eyes showed it. Tiny specks of green were getting more prominent.

"Different how, John?"

John looked into the dark lashed green eyes, but he didn't give an answer. Leah looked from one to the other, wondering how far the discussion would go.

"Answer me, John. Why is it different? Why is it so wrong for me to get to know who's following me? My God, these men are everywhere I go." She flung her arms out in exasperation. "They know absolutely everything about me; about Gregor and Alex. Why should I not know them? What are you afraid of?"

John stared at her in silence, which infuriated Lenore. She stood and walked to the sink, tossing her plate into the less than hot water. Leah watched as John stood and walked to Lenore, taking her by the shoulders, turning her toward him.

"Do I really have to say it, Lenore? Do I have to say that I'm afraid someone else will fall in love with you the way I did, knowing they can't have you? What if they aren't as gracious as I am about stepping aside? What if it clouds their judgement for only an instant, and in that instant, something happens to you, or to Greg or Alex?" He tilted his head, staring into Lenore's eyes. "It was wrong to get involved with you. I know that." He shook his head. "I know it, but I wouldn't have missed it for the world, hurt and all."

Lenore's eyes were wide and blinking back tears as John continued. Leah listened to the man still so in love with the woman before him.

"I'm trying very hard to be your friend, Lenore. If I seem overly cautious, it's because I do care so very much for you." He tilted her chin up to meet her eyes. "Greg's my best friend and it would kill him if anything were to happen to you or his brother, so I need to make sure my agents are clear-minded. They must be the best, because they're protecting the best. Do you understand, Lenore?" He took his fingers from her chin.

"Y-yes, John. I understand. I'm so sorry. I didn't think any further than the moment. I don't want to hurt our friendship, ever." She shook her head. "I promise to be more cautious. Please don't be angry with me."

"Did Gregor know you were becoming friends with Halvorson?" Leah asked.

"I wanted to talk about it one evening and something else came up. I just forgot about it after that. I didn't think it was important." She frowned and turned back to John. "How did you find out?"

"One of the other agents told me. Halvorson talked about you a lot and the agent who told me thought it unprofessional and potentially dangerous, so he contacted me."

"Then, I guess I should tell Gregor?"

"It's been dealt with. That's not necessary," John confirmed. "Now, do you think we should check on the pies?"

Lenore and Leah raced to the ovens and opened the lower one first. The apple pie was done. No doubt about it. The two women juggled oven mitts until Lenore stepped back and let Leah take the pie from the oven and put it on a trivet. A quick check of the two pumpkin pies in the upper oven showed them cooking nicely, but not ready to test.

Lenore sat down at the table and began to cry, leaving Leah and John watching in bewilderment. Leah put her arms around her best friend.

"My goodness, what are the tears for?"

"It's my first holiday dinner with Gregor and I've burned the pie."

John walked to the counter and looked at the apple pie he had contributed a little effort to, trying to detect a flaw.

"Doesn't look burned to me. Aren't they supposed to be brown?"

"Sure, they are, but not black!"

Lenore continued to cry, and Leah walked over to the counter. She and John looked at the pie, then at one another, then back at the pie. John pointed to a spot where juice had bubbled to the surface and over the edge. It had indeed turned black. Leah used her glossy index fingernail and lifted the spot off the pie and threw it into the trash.

Leah turned to the bewildered brunette, "Lenore, I want you to come here and look at this pie. Show me where it's burned."

Lenore sniffed and wiped her tears with the heels of her hands and walked to the counter. She looked at the pie, then to her friends. She started laughing and crying at the same time. Leah and John laughed at first, then got concerned when tears overtook laughter.

"What's wrong now? The pie is just fine," Leah said.

"I'm sorry. I don't know, really. I'm just so afraid the dinner won't be nice and Gregor will think I'm a lousy cook and it's Alex's very first American holiday and I might have jeopardized our safety and I hurt John." She looked at the bewildered agent and a spastic sob escaped, "and John I never wanted to hurt you, not ever. Excuse me, I'm going to throw up."

As Lenore ran from the room, John watched her go then turned to Leah.

"Wow."

Leah sat down at the table and smiled.

John sat down beside her. "Did I really upset her, or is this dinner thing too much stress? I hope she isn't coming down with something."

"No, John. Lenore's pregnant."

"Excuse me." John shook his head as if to clear it. "Did you say Lenore's *pregnant?*"

"Pregnant. With child. On the nest." She giggled.

"She told you that?"

"Not exactly. She said they were trying, and if this morning is any clue at all, I'd say there's no way they could have missed her fertile time. He's been back since late September." She chuckled, then added, "That, along with the emotions and the nausea are pretty good signs, too."

"Is that a good idea? I mean, given her age?"

"Oh, Lenore's very healthy. She's had confirmation from a doctor that she could handle it. Anyway, it's a little late for concern now." She sipped the last of her Diet Coke. "I'm not sure she realizes, she's already pregnant. I wouldn't bring it up to her or Gregor just yet."

John sat quietly, staring at his fingers as they drummed to an unknown beat. His silence confused Leah.

"John, aren't you happy for them? It's what they both want."

John met Leah's eyes.

"I suppose I'm happy for them, but now it means we'll be protecting a pregnant woman. Guess I'm overly protective of Lenore anyway, and now, well, I'm concerned."

"Is that all it is, John?"

"What else?" He shrugged.

"Well, their having a baby sort of makes it all pretty permanent, doesn't it?"

"Was there ever any doubt?"

John got up from the table and walked to the kitchen window. He put his plate in the sink and stared at the landscape. Leah joined him and patted his back, as if soothing a troubled child.

"I wish you could both have her. I know you love her, maybe as much as Gregor. It's okay, you know, if you love her."

"Leah, through it all, you've been the only one who knew how I felt about her. I knew it would be hopeless from the start, but I just couldn't help myself." He turned and leaned back against the sink. "Yes, the baby changes things, but for some reason, it just makes me want to protect her even more. It makes her seem even more special. Does that make any sense at all?"

"Absolutely. Although the way I love Lenore is different from the way you love her, I know exactly how you feel. She's a strong person, but there's something about her that makes you want to protect her. She needs us both, John, as much as she needs her sons and Gregor. We'll just be here for her … in whatever capacity she may need."

"Uncle John and Auntie Leah, huh?" He sighed and dropped his shoulders.

"Something like that." She hugged him.

"You'd better go check on her. I'll wash up these dishes."

Leah left to check on her best friend as John drained the cool water out of the sink and filled it with hot, soapy water to clean the few remaining dishes. He stared out the window at hills beyond the cleared valley as he worked. The shadows were getting longer as the sun neared the hills on the western side of the valley. Something in the trees on the rise to the east caught his attention and he squinted to try to identify the source of light.

* * * * *

The man standing beside the truck lowered his binoculars. It appeared that John Dixon looked straight at him. The unaided eye would never be able to detect him from such a distance. He looked toward the sun, just barely above the horizon now, then back to his truck. A glint of sunlight reflected off the windshield.

He quickly brought the binoculars back to his eyes and focused on the window of the house. Dixon wasn't there. Could he have gone to get his own binoculars? A rush of adrenalin spurred him to run for the driver's seat of the truck. He started the engine and pulled away slowly from his position on the hill, back onto the old logging road. He stopped, after driving through the opening of a far less traveled trail, to get out and pull limbs and brush back across the entrance. He walked back to the logging road and swept over his tracks with a piece of brush, then tossed it aside, and got back into his truck. He drove further into the folds of mountain, timber, and brush, losing elevation as he went. He went slowly on the familiar path, but soon needed headlights in the dwindling light. The path ended at a driveway. Once again, he took care to eliminate any indication of his presence, then continued down the long drive which intersected a county road.

Previous explorations of the area had just given him a decisive advantage. He relaxed his shoulders, continuing away from the area and back to his remote cabin. He turned the heater on high as the trickle of perspiration running down his back chilled him.

* * * * *

Lenore and Leah returned to the kitchen to find John standing at the window with binoculars to his eyes.

"What are you doing with those? Do you see deer?" Lenore asked.

Not wanting to alarm the ladies, he muttered, "Uh-huh." He scanned the area that had caught his attention earlier. The sun had gone down behind the rise of hills west of the home, leaving only shadows where he had seen light reflecting. Whatever had been there only moments before was gone. He lowered the binoculars and turned to see a freshly scrubbed Lenore, smiling at him.

"What?"

"If you wait a few minutes, you'll see deer right here close to the house. Gregor has taught the dogs to leave them alone, so they come through at dawn and just after sunset."

"That's right. I guess it's been so long since I visited, I forgot. Are you alright?"

Lenore sat down at the table and John stood beside her. He let concerns about what he saw on the hill fade to the back of his mind as he sat the binoculars aside.

"I'm fine, John," Lenore assured. "I guess it's just all the excitement of having everyone here for the holiday. I'm sorry I got so upset."

"I just hope this isn't too much for you. Am I making things awkward for you?"

"Absolutely not! I promise."

"Great! Now what else needs to be done? I still have this silly apron around me." He lifted the front of the apron as if posing.

"I guess we can remove your apron, although I thought you looked quite stunning in it," Leah said, with a little giggle.

"Yep, you're free to go!" Lenore replied. "I won't be doing any more prep for tomorrow until morning. We'll eat early afternoon."

John turned and Leah assisted him in removing the apron.

"I need to start fixing something for the skiers to eat when they get home." Lenore glanced at the clock on the range. "They probably just finished their last run, so it'll be an hour or so before they get here." She grabbed a box of tea from a cabinet and tossed it onto the counter. "Leah, would you help me make some of your magic potato soup?"

"I'd be delighted, but I can do it all by myself. I think you have enough to do without having to fix that as well. I'll just get it started. You two go ahead to the living room and build a fire. I'll join you as soon as the potatoes start cooking."

"How 'bout I help you peel potatoes?" John offered. "I'm pretty experienced with peeling you know."

"You want the apron back on?" Leah asked.

"You're right, we need a fire."

John sprinted from the room and Lenore took a tray from the cabinet. She prepared the carafe of hot tea while Leah began peeling potatoes.

"Chicken stock?" Leah asked.

"Almost forgot." Lenore pulled two cartons of chicken stock from the cabinet and put them on the counter next to Leah, "anything else?"

"Nope, I'll join you in a few."

Lenore carried the tray of tea and cups to the living room to join John. She settled on the sofa and filled two cups with tea, watching her good friend work until flames began to lick at the fuel provided. As the glow began to reflect on his handsome profile, he turned to look at Lenore.

"What's magical about Leah's potato soup?"

Lenore laughed and held out a cup of tea to John. He rose long enough to accepted it, then returned to his position on the floor near the fireplace.

"I don't really know." She shook her head. "All I *do* know is that every time I've been sick and ate her soup, I felt better. I just started calling it *magic* potato soup."

"Maybe we should patent it and only give it with prescriptions." John suggested.

They grew silent as they watched the fire caress and consume the logs. Lenore drew her feet under her and nestled into the softness of the sofa, mesmerized by the flames.

John moved to a chair, as heat radiated from the fireplace, making his location nearer, uncomfortable. He watched Lenore, wishing he could hold her. Wishing that the baby she carried could be his. Ultimately, wishing he could stop feeling the way he did about her. Leah came into the room, breaking the hypnotic spell.

"The potatoes are cooking. Are you two about to fall asleep?"

John and Lenore both turned to look at Leah, who sat down on the sofa next to Lenore and poured herself a cup of tea.

Lenore sighed. "I think the fire had us in its spell. It got warm and cozy, didn't it, John?"

Though certain the warm feelings he had were not totally induced by the fire, he agreed. The three friends talked and laughed about past experiences and topics that, perhaps, would not have been enjoyed by the balance of the household. It would be their only time alone and they filled every moment. In just over an hour, with the potato soup prepared and warming on the stove, Marushka and Nicolai signaled the return of the skiers. Lenore bounded off the sofa and scooted into her shoes before Leah and John were aware of the reason for her quick movements.

"They're back! Gregor and the guys are going to be so excited to see you, John."

Leah and John waited inside for the group. Lenore ran out the door and into the arms of her husband as soon as he got out of the van. They embraced and kissed as if the absence had been unbearable, and were the subject of teasing from everyone, except for the two people standing inside the house. They knew that the absence had been nearly unbearable for Lenore and Gregor.

With equipment put away and ski clothes changed out of, in favor of jeans and sweaters, Leah ushered them all into the kitchen for a bowl of hot soup. Lenore set the makings for ham sandwiches out for everyone to help themselves. She stood close to Gregor, listening to the various interpretations of the day's adventures. Gregor's attention soon turned to John.

"John, it is good that you are with us for this holiday. You are a good friend to us all. When did you arrive? You flew into Aspen and rented a truck, yes?"

"I arrived yesterday. I stayed in Glenwood Springs last night. When I ran into the girls at the "springs" today, I was ordered to move my things here."

"Of course. We planned for you to be here. However, ..."

Gregor turned to look at Lenore, who smiled and kissed him on the nose, knowing she was probably not going to get away with her adventure without a scolding.

"Lenore, you did not tell me of your plan to go to the water today."

"We just couldn't resist. Do you really mind?"

His stern demeanor melted into a smile and he shook his head.

"No, I do not mind. I just prefer you do not vary from your plans. It is for the best." He hugged her, then kissed her on the forehead. "I hope you had fun."

Joel had listened to the exchange between his mother and new step-father, looking anxious, then relieved.

"Gregor, do you ever get angry with Mom?"

Gregor looked surprised at Joel's question, then answered with a smile.

"Joel, when I look upon the face of your mother, I can feel nothing but love. Do not ever be concerned that it will be different."

Grant tried to explain the feelings he knew his brother had.

"We can see how much you care, but you remember that Joel lived in a very hostile environment. Mom's last husband was very different from you."

Gregor nodded and answered Grant, "Yes, I know this. I wish that I could take those years away from you all, but I cannot. I can only assure you of my love, not only for your mother, but for you and Joel as well. You are a part of her, and my love extends to you also. I am your mother's husband, yes. I know you already have a father, but I am your step-father. I will not let you down in this role."

Alex looked from one to the other before inserting his own assurances.

"And I am the Uncle Alex. In this I will not let you down also."

He smiled, very proud of his new title and took it very seriously. He had also successfully lightened the mood.

"We think you are positively the greatest Uncle Alex in the world!" Joel announced as he and Grant patted Alex's back. The meal continued with a delighted uncle glowing in the attention of his two nephews.

Everyone helped clear and clean and put food away. Several unsuccessful attempts were made to get into the pies. With the task finished, they all eventually gathered in the living room where the fire was stirred back to life. Sometime later, amid the hum of friendly conversation, Gregor roused Lenore from sleep with a kiss on her forehead.

"You have worked and played hard today. You should go to bed."

"I'm sorry. It's just so comfortable and warm, I couldn't stay awake."

The boys planned to stay up to teach their Uncle Alex how to play poker, the rest decided to call it a night and went upstairs to their separate rooms after hugs and kisses. With nightly routines completed, Gregor settled into bed beside his sleepy wife and nestled her close to him.

"I love you, Gregor. Thank you for this holiday gathering. It means so much to me."

"My precious wife, it is I who thanks you. If it were not for you, there would be no family to gather. You have given my life so much meaning, so much love. Sleep now. Tomorrow will be here soon."

She snuggled against his chest, lulled to sleep by the strong beat of his heart, her fingers curled into the thick hair on his chest. He continued to stroke her hair and caress her, long after she had fallen asleep.

* * * * *

There were two agents who did not find sleep quite so easy to achieve on this night. One sat in a bedroom of the house that two very special friends had invited him into. The other sat in a remote cabin going over again and again his plans to take Lenore. Both men were thinking of how they could best protect her.

John's feelings were so far, unfounded. He wondered if there may or may not be anyone to protect her from, or if the confused love he had for Lenore blew ordinary things out of proportion. He turned off the light and wished that he could turn off his feelings as easily.

The man in the cabin had an unstable desire to protect Lenore from what he perceived to be a dangerous entrapment. He convinced himself that she was being held against her will, as she most certainly would be in days to come. Something had snapped when he was taken off assignment to protect and surveil Lenore. They had become friends, and who better to protect her than a friend, after all? No, he convinced himself it had to be some sort of plot to keep her prisoner of the Communist. Not only had Dixon brought Parishnikov back and handed Lenore over to him, he had brought along the brother. The man's duty to protect had clouded and now became an obsession. He knew Lenore would be *so* grateful she would love *him*. Lenore would be his.

He turned off the light, but he did not sleep.

CHAPTER 6

The natural clock inside Lenore's head awoke her early on Thanksgiving morning. She quietly got out of bed and slipped into a robe, trying to keep from waking her husband; always an impossibility. Gregor raised himself upon one elbow.

"Why do you leave our bed so early?"

"There's so much to do! I need to get the turkey ready to bake and I need to prepare breakfast for everyone."

"I will help you. The turkey is very heavy and awkward. I do not want you to do this by yourself."

Gregor hauled himself out of bed, then pulled on a pair of sweatpants from the closet and stepped into slippers. He followed Lenore to the kitchen and poured them both a glass of juice as she put a kettle of water on the burner for tea. He took the giant turkey from the refrigerator and placed it into the deep kitchen sink, then helped Lenore clean the bird and discard packaging. Amid laughter at the awkwardness of handling the giant fowl, they managed to pat it dry and place it onto a cutting board. Gregor helped his wife with accruing pans and adjusting racks in the oven. Lenore mixed an assortment of herbs and spices into butter before pushing it under the skin of the turkey and rubbing it over the surface. Onions, garlic, celery, and a few sprigs of rosemary, preserved in the freezer from a trip to a farmer's market in early October, were put into the bottom of the roasting pan. Oranges and lemons were sliced into wedges and added to the nest. A rack came next and then the huge turkey.

"Gregor, the lid is *not* going to go on this pan. I'll need parchment and foil."

Lenore successfully crafted a makeshift lid of aluminum foil with parchment between it and the skin of the turkey. They both smiled at her resourcefulness.

Gregor put the assemblage back into the refrigerator until time for it to begin roasting. Then he sat down in a chair and pulled his wife onto his lap. She giggled and kissed him on the neck and nibbled at his ear.

"You are giving me turkey skin." He laughed.

"Goose bumps, darling," she replied, giggling.

"Now, my precious wife, I will take you back to our bed. You need your sleep."

Lenore ran her fingers through the hair covering his chest and kissed him deeply. "You should have covered your chest if you wanted me to sleep." Kisses deepened as he softly cupped her breasts. Their kisses became more urgent.

He led her up the stairs to their room, kissed her gently as he eased her back onto the bed. He stepped easily out of his sweatpants, and the silky robe covering Lenore did not hinder his intent.

"Wait!" She said after a very intense kiss.

"Why must I wait, Lenore?"

"Make love to me on the balcony." She got out of their bed.

He raised his eyebrows. "My precious wife, it is very cold outside this morning."

"Please?" She tugged his hand.

He knew her passion for making love beyond the confines of their room. He also knew the brisk November morning air would not cool their passion. They pulled the comforter off the bed and abandoned the warm room for their private balcony. With the satiny comforter beneath her, Gregor looked at his wife laying naked, reaching out for him. He laid beside her and began kissing and gently tracing lines from her erect nipples to the feathery softness between her legs. He had always hoped such passion and desire could be his one day, but this far exceeded his imagination. He had married a woman so beautiful, so full of love for him, so responsive to his touch. Their bodies met and their passion for one another was soon satisfied.

"You have enjoyed our lovemaking this morning?"

"My wonderful husband, I am always satisfied with our lovemaking." She smiled and softly kissed him. "Isn't the morning sky beautiful?"

"It is a little difficult to see from this position, but what I see is indeed beautiful."

His eyes were full of Lenore, and he kissed her lightly on the forehead and nose. The morning light glowed on her face. She looked at the handsome face of her husband, and traced the line of his trimmed beard and his soft lips.

"You are so handsome. I hope our child looks just like you."

"Our child will be beautiful like its mother." Gregor pulled the edge of the comforter over them and moved to her side. They cuddled together in the early morning light.

"What have you told Leah?"

"Only that we were trying." She smiled. "She knows me too well and believes I am pregnant for sure. She's just concerned because of my age, but I think accepts the fact that we are going to have a child."

"I am also concerned, Lenore. You must take care of yourself. You will eat broccoli and fresh fruits and drink milk. I do not want you to lift things like the turkey. You must wait for my assistance, or ask Alex to assist."

"I promise to take care and not take chances, but this does not make me an invalid. It's a pregnancy."

"This is a new experience for me. You will tell me if I am being over-protective. Perhaps there is a book I should read."

"No! You're going to go through this the hard way. You will learn from experience," she advised.

They laughed and kissed again before Lenore threw the cover off, exposing their warmed bodies to the crisp air. She jumped up, ran inside and directly to the bathroom. Gregor closed the door to the balcony behind him and tossed the comforter onto the bed. Lenore had started the shower and he joined her.

* * * * *

They were clean and dressed, standing in the kitchen with freshly brushed smiles, as one-by-one, their guests ambled into the room. Lenore had prepared an offering of fresh fruit, croissants, yogurt and an assortment of juices, hot tea, milk, or hazelnut coffee. Scrambled eggs were an additional offering, kept in a warming tray. John was the first to join them.

"Happy Thanksgiving! Did you sleep well, John?"

"Yes, I did Greg." He accepted a cup of coffee. "Thanks Lenore. This food looks great!"

"Please, help yourself," Lenore urged.

He filled a plate and sat at the table in the large kitchen.

JD entered next. Gregor greeted him with a cheerful, "Happy Thanksgiving! Did you and Leah sleep well?"

"Happy Thanksgiving to you Gregor, John, Lenore. In fact, we slept so well, Leah is still sleeping. Don't expect her soon." He laughed.

"She may sleep, as long as she wishes, although we will awaken her for turkey, if necessary. Please help yourself. I will pour your beverages."

"Thanks. Coffee and orange juice, please."

JD seated himself across from John with his breakfast choices as Gregor sat coffee and juice in front of him.

"John, these two people are obviously meant for one another. They're both morning people."

John smiled and took a sip of coffee before he could manage a reply. "Yes, they are." He absolutely wanted to get off *that* subject. "Tell me, JD, how's business since your star employee deserted you?"

"Terrible! We may just have to close the doors."

"If you think I'm going to feel guilty, you're probably right, but I'll get over it." She walked over to where JD sat, and hugged him. "I always told you to open a store here."

"Well, believe it or not, the board told me they would check out this area. I told them you would possibly consent to going back to work for us if we did open here. Would you?"

Lenore looked at her husband to answer.

"How soon would this take place, JD?"

"If we did find a suitable location, it would take a year, maybe more."

"If this would make Lenore happy, then I think it would be great."

John wondered how she would manage a full-time job with the responsibility of a new baby? He didn't voice his concerns, knowing he was not supposed to be aware of her condition. He changed the subject to Gregor's employment.

"How about you, Greg? You still plan on going back to work for the company you were with before?"

"I have been in touch with them and they have a position for me. I would be away from here several days each month, but I could take Lenore with me. I would conduct my business by telephone and computer link for the most part."

"You're both welcome to stay with us when you're on the Front Range," JD offered. "Fort Collins may not be as convenient as staying in Denver, but I know Leah and Lenore would enjoy it."

"We appreciate the offer, JD. We will be happy to accept your hospitality from time to time."

"You know I have plenty of room. You're always welcome to stay at my place, too," John added. "Lenore, you just have to promise you won't try to re-arrange furniture or anything."

"I'll try to restrain myself." She laughed.

"While we have a minute Greg, I wanted to let you know there could be a position in Denver at a television station for Alex. I wanted to run it by you first."

"What would be the position?" Gregor sipped his tea.

John swallowed and wiped his mouth. "For the time being, they would have him mostly in the background, tracking storms, forecasting; that sort of thing. Eventually he could be on air. I put his name in and they seem pretty interested."

"I appreciate knowing this before you present the idea to my brother. I believe we need to make sure he is ready to be on his own."

"I agree. He could live with me, of course. I think that would be best for him and for your peace of mind." He shook his head. "I did not make any promises to the station. They understand the circumstance and think he could be a great asset, but only when things are right."

Gregor looked at Lenore, who offered her own thoughts. "You will know when Alex is ready for such a change. I think it sounds interesting, but I also know how you'd feel about having him live apart from you."

"This is something we will discuss together after the holiday."

Alex came in from feeding the dogs, hung his jacket by the door from the garage and washed his hands. Joel and Grant came from upstairs into the kitchen and all three began grazing on the breakfast fare. Leah was the only one still missing from the gathering.

"Alex, did your nephews teach you how to play poker?" JD asked.

"I do not think I am ready for the Vegas," he shook his head, then added, "although my nephews are great instructors. I do not understand the straights and flushings so well yet."

Joel and Grant corrected in unison, "Flushes!"

"You see what I mean?" He laughed and shrugged.

"Yes, but he has a terrific poker face, doesn't he, Grant?"

"Show them, Alex!"

Alex could manage to hold his expressionless gaze for only a moment before breaking into his charming smile; a family trait shared with his brother. Everyone agreed he had a great *poker face*.

Lenore looked from Alex to Gregor. There were familial similarities between the two brothers, but they were distinct individuals. Alex chose to be clean-shaven. His hair, several shades lighter and straight, compared to the dark, natural wave of Gregor's hair. She looked at her own two sons. They were similarly different. Grant's hair was dark and full of body, compared to Joel's straight, light brown hair with sun-streaked highlights. She wondered what the child she carried now would look like. A smile settled on her face.

Joel interrupted her thoughts. "Mom, do you think we could watch the parade? Can you get it on your TV?"

"What a great idea! Yes, you should be able to get it with the satellite dish." She turned to her brother-in-law. "Alex, the Macy's Thanksgiving Parade is very much something you should see. You guys can take your plates with you to the living room to watch."

Joel and Grant were explaining about Macy and the traditional parade as the trio left the kitchen. Lenore began washing dishes, with Gregor's assistance. John and JD joined the parade watchers. When they were alone, Gregor encircled is wife with loving arms and kissed her on the neck.

"I saw your smile. What was it for?"

"Oh, just thinking about how much the boys are like you and Alex in many ways, and wondering what this child will look like."

"It makes me happy to see your smile. I know you are communicating this happiness to our child. I intend to keep you so happy and full of peace for all your life, but especially now. It is very important for our baby."

"I'm very confident there will be no interruption in my happiness now."

As Lenore hugged Gregor with sudsy hands, Leah walked into the kitchen with a sleepy, "Hello."

They greeted her with offerings of coffee and juice and settled her at the table when she had made her breakfast choices. The trio soon migrated to the living room to enjoy Alex's wonderment at the traditional Thanksgiving parade.

* * * * *

Nearly an hour's drive from the Parishnikov home, Dennis Halvorson ate his own breakfast. He had taken the time to scramble an egg and sipped coffee at his small wooden table. The single light bulb did little to defeat the darkness. The dense growth of trees and brush, along with the mountainous terrain, provided the necessary seclusion he desired, but filtered the sunlight. He would need privacy and seclusion. There must be no interruption in his efforts to de-program Lenore from the Commie influences of her life in captivity. He knew there would ultimately be success. After all, he and Lenore were meant for one another.

Dennis felt a chill in the cabin and got up to stir the embers and add a log to the small wood stove in the living room. The crackle and spark of the fire accepted the offering and began to consume the log. He eased the stove door closed and stood near to get warm. As the warmth began to defeat the chill, he admired his surroundings.

The old hunting cabin, for all its rustic charm, remained sturdy and comfortable. A well, from which crystal-clear water flowed with abundance, could even provide Lenore with occasional bubble baths. He had seen a bottle of bubble bath in her shopping bag and had purchased the identical brand. A toilet, sink and small clawfoot tub left no room for a cabinet in the tiny bathroom, but he had filled a shelf with soft, thirsty towels in the confined functional space. She would be pleased with his thoughtfulness and knowledge of her preferences.

Lenore would have to bathe thoroughly. She would also need to cleanse herself inside as well. He had douches for her use to rid her of the Russian's semen, before he would want to penetrate her and fill her with his own.

The kitchen pantry had been filled with food, and he stocked a cache of assorted meats in freezers. Those freezers were inside a shed near the back door of the cabin. The colder temperatures negated the need of electrical power to keep things frozen. The generator could be connected by a simple flip of a switch if temperatures warranted.

He had purchased many cases of Diet Coke and they were stacked in a corner of the kitchen. She once told him of her love for it and her decision to not drink it anymore. The Russian had forced her to give up something she enjoyed. She would be free to consume as much as she wanted now. He laughed and shook his head. Yes, he knew Lenore so well and she would appreciate his kind gesture.

The table sat in the kitchen area and provided the only separation from the living room. It was a small, but comfortable part of the two-room cabin. For warmth, a wood stove and generators were available.

He finished his breakfast and washed his plate, fork and cup and the small skillet. He put the clean wares away and wiped down the entire area before he put on a jacket and went outside to check on the generators. No electrical power grids were in the area. He preferred it that way; wood heat for now, and space heaters would run on generated power after Lenore arrived. He had a huge supply of fuel for the generators and plenty of batteries and candles. Connections to outside power grids would risk detection. The fact that he did not have actual ownership of the property also prevented connection to any utility. He didn't like the term *squatter*, but accepted the fact of being one.

Halvorson walked to the bedroom. The small bed had been fitted with a soft mattress, clean sheets, and plenty of blankets. Her bed. Soon to be *their* bed. He shuddered with the thought of laying with Lenore. Theirs would be the perfect life.

He admired the clothes he had hanging on pegs. He wanted to buy more clothes for her; sensible clothes. Certainly, no form fitting, slutty garb. His Lenore would always behave as a lady; *his* lady. Halvorson stared at the framed photograph on the wall beside the bed and sighed.

Returning to the kitchen, he took a small gun case and cleaning set from a cabinet, and sat at the table. He carefully cleaned and polished his stainless Walther PPK .380 and made sure the suppressor fit well on the barrel. He admired the fit and aimed the Walther at a spot above the cabinet before removing the suppressor and stowing it and the weapon in a case. He had test fired the Walther with the suppressor and knew it would in no way hinder his aim. The case and cleaning set were placed back in a cabinet near the back door. He would soon keep the weapon loaded at all times

As Lenore enjoyed a comfortable holiday with her dearest friends and loved ones, Halvorson busied himself with cleaning and dusting, straightening, and organizing. When evening came, he dozed on the sofa, not wanting to lay in the bed until he could lay beside Lenore. His plan to stay in the room at the motel had been ruined, but the urge to teach the clerk a lesson had passed. Although it would have been far more convenient to stay at the motel, and be in the room he knew Lenore had enjoyed, he took it as a sign for him to stay at the cabin, out of sight. He would be patient. She would be with him soon.

* * * * *

"My precious wife, you have outdone yourself today. I believe our family and friends are adequately satisfied. You need to rest now."

Gregor led Lenore from the living room where the remnants of a football game were being watched by the other men of the house, and Leah napped with her head on JD's lap. The sounds from the game were defeated with the close of their bedroom door upstairs.

"I should at least offer everyone a sandwich or something, don't you think?"

"I believe everyone is well-aware of the way to the kitchen, and they are very capable of preparing their own sandwiches. You will rest for a while." He gently led her to the bed.

"Will you lay with me until I fall asleep?" She yawned, "I guess I am tired, after all."

"Yes, but you will sleep." He kissed her softly.

She snuggled down into the covers, knowing it would take little effort to change his mind, if she wanted to. He took his place beside her as she unbuttoned his shirt and rested her hand on his chest, flexing and curling her fingers into the hair that grew in abundance there. He hugged her and kissed the top of her head.

"Would you ever be able to sleep if I were to shave the hair from my chest?"

"Never again." They both laughed quietly.

He stroked her hair and caressed her with the tenderness she could not resist. Soon the sound of her steady breathing assured him she was asleep. Quietly, Gregor eased himself out of the bed and found everyone except John still watching the game. Evidence of spontaneous snacking proved they could, indeed, find their way around the kitchen. He knew Lenore would be pleased.

Gregor pulled on his jacket and stepped outside. The two Great White Pyrenees stood beside John, watching Gregor as he joined them. John scanned the surrounding hills through binoculars.

"What do you look for?"

"Nothing in particular, I guess. Is there a road up there?" John indicated with a nod toward where he had seen the reflected light.

"There is an old logging road, though it is rarely used. Why do you ask?"

"I thought I saw something up there last night about sundown. Light reflected off something. By the time I'd gotten the binoculars, the sun had gone down far enough, it wasn't reflecting."

"Perhaps we should explore. It is too late tonight. I know the way to this road. We will go tomorrow morning," Gregor said.

"It's probably just some glass or something, but it wouldn't hurt to see."

John lowered the glasses and looked at Gregor, who continued to view the suspected area. When he looked at John, there were no further words necessary. Their minds connected on the same thought. They didn't expect to find a piece of glass, but they both hoped they would just find evidence of a passing four-wheeler, exploring new territory. They went back inside and to the kitchen and fixed themselves sandwiches before re-joining the others.

As promised, Gregor woke Lenore after she had slept an hour. Leah had also roused from her nap and the two women met in the kitchen. Remnants of what five men could do to a kitchen in the throes of a snack attack were evident, but they chose to ignore the mess long enough to satisfy their own hunger.

"Who's winning the game?" Lenore asked.

"Are you kidding? Who's playing? I fell asleep on JD's lap just about the first inning, I think."

Lenore replied, "Innings are baseball."

"Whatever. Lenore it's so relaxing here. Gregor must have had you in mind when he had this place built."

"Gregor says he had me in his dreams, but didn't know it until he saw me that night. Can you pass the cranberry relish?"

"Sure." Leah handed the festive mix to Lenore. "You know, I think you probably had him in your dreams, but didn't know it until you met him, too. You knew it from the first glance, but you didn't want to admit it."

"Why do you say that? Potatoes?"

"No thanks. Because it bothered you so much when he could read your eyes. You knew right then and there you had been waiting for Gregor all your life. Your souls merged, right there on the spot." Leah stared at Lenore's plate. "What on earth are you eating?"

Lenore looked down at her plate, swallowing a mouthful of mashed potatoes and cranberry relish mixture before answering. "It tastes wonderful."

"Well, it's colorful. The green and black olives add a lovely contrast. The sweet potatoes and green beans on your dinner roll looks tasty. No turkey?" She laughed as Lenore then reached for a slice of white meat. "How far along are you?"

"At least a month and a half, is all. Maybe two. I go to the doctor on Monday, I didn't want to tell anyone until we had confirmation."

"Well, call me psychic, but your emotions, throwing up and eating habits give you away. Gregor knows?"

"Yes, that's why he's so insistent about my naps and eating well. He's so excited, Leah."

"Then I'll be excited with you. You must call me after your appointment on Monday."

"I promise! Can you hand me the gravy?"

"Only if you promise you aren't going to put it on your pie." She grimaced.

Lenore accepted the bowl of gravy and hesitated over the pie, paused as if the idea had crossed her mind, then both women laughed. Alex walked into the kitchen with several empty plates and stacked them on the counter.

"Thank you, Lenore, for your wonderful cooking and yours as well, Leah. I am very full."

"You're very welcome, Alex. What do you think of this holiday?" Leah asked.

"It is a good thing to be giving thankfulness. I have much to be thankful for. Such food and such family and friends. There will be more of these holidays?"

"Yes, we are big on holidays in this country."

"I will be happy for these holidays to come. I will wash these dishes to be helping you."

"I appreciate that, Alex. We will work together and get it done."

Eventually, everyone migrated from the living room, back into the kitchen. It took over an hour before the last of the food was put away and the counters cleared, due to spontaneous outbreaks of nibbling. The joyous noise of conversation interspersed with hearty laughter delighted Lenore.

Alex, Joel, and Grant were planning to ski on Friday. Lenore and Leah would shop on the traditionally busiest shopping day of the year; something Lenore had never enjoyed, or even had the opportunity. Working in retail always necessitated working on *Black Friday*. She only got to experience it from the other side of the counter, so to speak. Extra money couldn't be wasted anyway.

With the guys needing the Pathfinder for ski equipment, Lenore and Leah would be left with the Saab. Lenore assured Leah the agent of the day would be happy to allow them the use of his vehicle's trunk to hold their bounty.

Gregor, John, and JD would use John's rented truck to traverse the mountainous area beyond the valley where the home sat. Gregor and John knew the real purpose behind the needed exploration. Others assumed Gregor wanted to introduce JD to the area.

They all went to bed that night looking forward to what the coming day would bring.

CHAPTER 7

The eastern sky above the valley warmed with color as Lenore stood at the window, sipping her first cup of coffee. Gregor closed the door from the garage, returning from feeding the dogs and joined his wife where she stood, transfixed on the glow of an impending sunrise. He washed his hands and dried them before he wrapped his arms around her and kissed her temple.

"It will be a beautiful sunrise for my beautiful wife."

Lenore turned from the window and snuggled into his arms.

"It's a perfect day for all of us." She looked up at her handsome husband with concern in her eyes. "I must remember to send sunscreen with Grant. His nose sunburned Wednesday. Do you think I should make lunches for them to take?"

"No. They will prefer to eat in the lodge, I am sure. It will provide them opportunities to meet girls." He laughed.

"Oh, that makes sense. I need to give them money for lunch."

"I have already given them each money for their day. In fact, they would have enough to rent a room and have it catered if they chose to do so. You worry like a mom." He hugged her.

"Old habits, you know?"

"These are habits you will continue to find very useful for the rest of your life, especially with our new child."

They both smiled and kissed as the skiers came into the kitchen, ready for a quick breakfast before they left for a day on the slopes.

"You two sure kiss a lot. I think it's *pretty neat.*"

"Thanks Joel. We think it's *pretty neat,* too." She slipped from her husband's arms and walked to the range. "I want you to sit down and have a good breakfast before you go. There's juice, coffee, tea, and milk. Your oatmeal will be ready in a very few minutes." She gestured and added, "There are croissants and muffins, too."

The trio assembled at the counter as Lenore cooked. They wore a varied selection of turtlenecks and festive winter sweaters, and their ski bibs were already in the Pathfinder. They filled glasses and cups and then plates with muffins and croissants. They accepted bowls of Lenore's oatmeal and checked out options of blueberries, peanut butter, chocolate chips, pecans, or maple syrup to top it. With a couple of trips from the table to the island, their choices were moved to the table for them to begin eating.

"Grant, I have some sunscreen I want you to use today. I noticed your nose got a little red on Wednesday." She laid the tube beside Grant's plate.

"Thanks Mom. I'll use it. I don't understand why my nose always gets burned. Is it that big?"

"No silly, it's not big at all. You have fairer skin and, you never wear hats."

"Maybe I'll buy a hat today."

Gregor smiled as the conversation continued. He loved the way Lenore and her sons found communicating so easy. She was the perfect mother for their child and would teach him how to be a good father. He hoped he would never let any of them down.

Gregor had been surprised at the acceptance Grant and Joel had shown him. Lenore took time and explained how she had met him and some of what had transpired because of it. They had questioned him extensively about his intentions toward their mother, and once assurances were given that he would not disappear from their mother's life again, they accepted him without resentment or animosity for what she had endured because of him. Joel told him it looked as though his mom had just emerged from a dark cloud. He had worried about the changes in her personality and the sadness. He had attributed it to her being divorced, and his graduating from high school. He had no way of knowing it had been due to Gregor's disappearance.

Curiosity fueled many questions regarding his former profession, his time in the Soviet prison and his relationship with the CIA. The most serious questioning centered around whether their mother could be in danger. Gregor had assured them he would always do everything in his power to keep their mother safe. He had chosen to not tell them there would be protective surveillance for a time on all of them. They were, after all, a part of the beautiful woman he would give his life for, if necessary.

* * * * *

John entered. He filled a cup with steaming hot coffee amid greetings. He accepted a bowl of oatmeal and grabbed a croissant before moving to the table to sit with the three men very intent on consuming breakfast.

JD and Leah entered together. Everyone seemed anxious for the day's activities to begin. Lenore teased Leah about her obvious break in routine.

"You never get going this early. You're dressed and everything. Holey buckets!"

Leah wore camel-colored corduroy jeans and a deep burgundy sweater. Her small waist was accentuated by a gold belt, and a cascade of gold chains hung from her neck.

"She's been up for over an hour. I think it has something to do with shopping. That's the only thing she likes better than sleeping."

"Well, not the only thing." Leah wagged her eyebrows at her husband.

He hugged her. "I won't even ask the order of importance."

John sipped his coffee and listened to the flow of conversation as he ate. He tore a piece off his croissant before asking his question.

"Where are you girls going to shop; Aspen or Glenwood Springs? Is a trip to Grand Junction any possibility?" He popped the piece of croissant into his mouth.

Leah and Lenore looked at each other for the answer, but neither had it.

"I guess we really hadn't discussed it. We could go to Aspen, which may provide us a glimpse of some celebrities, but I think there would be more bargains in Glenwood." Lenore refilled John's coffee. "I can't see wasting shopping time driving to Grand Junction. What do you think, Leah?"

"Well, let me *pondercate* this a minute." She appeared deep in thought, sipped her coffee then replied. "Let me get this straight; you're telling me we could buy more in Glenwood Springs, or blow two hours driving to Grand Junction and back or we could pay more in Aspen? Who needs to drive or see celebrities? I say we should go for quantity."

Lenore nodded and turned back to John. "Guess we're going to Glenwood Springs. Did you need for us to shop for you?"

"No, just curious."

"Hey, you're on vacation. Leah and I won't vary from our itinerary, I promise. You three old guys have exploring to do and we have shopping to do." She put her hands on her hips. "These three younger guys over here, *who are eating entirely too fast*, are anxious to get to the slopes." She made sure to speak loud enough to get their attention.

Joel, Grant, and Alex looked up at Lenore. They had nearly finished breakfast. Grant had the only mouth empty enough to reply.

"Sorry Mom, but Alex says we need to get there as soon as possible. It's going to be packed, and unless we want to park three miles from the slope, we need to get there early. The breakfast is great, though."

Joel and Alex nodded in agreement.

"Go if you need to, just drive carefully. I'd rather you walk further than have a wreck."

The trio carried plates and glasses to the sink while swallowing final sips of juice. Each grabbed an extra muffin for the road.

"I promise you, Lenore, that I will be a most careful driver with my two nephews." He gave his sister-in-law a quick hug. "Thank you for the breakfast. I must start the Pathfinder now." He grabbed his jacket from the peg and went out the kitchen door connected to the garage.

Joel and Grant were right behind Alex with their hugs and thanks.

"Thank you, Gregor, for the money. Is it okay if I buy Kim a gift with it?"

"Joel, it is your money to do with whatever you wish."

"Thanks!" He gave Gregor a hug, kissed his mom on the cheek, grabbed his own jacket and bounded out the door after Alex.

"Thanks, Gregor. It's appreciated." Grant chose to shake Gregor's hand, with thanks every bit as sincere as his brother's. He hugged Lenore, then followed Joel and closed the door behind him; his jacket and sunscreen in hand.

The five people remaining in the kitchen looked at one another as if waiting for the "all clear" siren to sound.

JD spoke first. "If those guys go at this skiing the way they did the last two minutes, they're going to be exhausted tonight."

"JD, don't you move that fast anymore?"

"John, I don't think I ever did," his slight Texas drawl slipped out. That produced laughter from everyone.

As the conversation continued, Lenore moved to Gregor's side. Joel's hugs always surprised and touched him. The former Soviet spy had moist eyes as he smiled.

"Lenore, I hate to interrupt, but should you start getting ready to go?" Leah questioned.

"Leah is right." Gregor nodded to his wife. "I will clean the kitchen. Perhaps I can talk John and JD into assisting me."

"Sure, it's the least we can do for all the good meals you've fed us. I understand there's an apron somewhere that fits John." JD noted.

"I'll never live it down, will I?"

Lenore went to a cabinet. "I think you will if I can find two more aprons."

The ladies left the room with three men in aprons, laughing at one another while they cleaned the breakfast clutter. After a quick shower, Lenore went to her bedroom to finish her routine while she and Leah discussed their schedule.

Lenore chose practical jeans and a dark blue turtle neck sweater. Her light denim jacket would provide plenty of warmth, and comfortable black leather boots would be great for lots of walking. They would begin shopping at the mall and work their way back through town. With a final check of cash and credit cards, they were ready to go.

Gregor, John, and JD were in the dining room looking at topographical maps of the area when the ladies entered for their good-byes.

"Anyone need anything from town?" Lenore asked.

Gregor answered, "Perhaps you should pick up a bottle of wine and more milk. I cannot think of anything else."

She scrawled a quick note on a piece of paper and tucked it into her purse. After a lingering kiss for her husband, Lenore was gently pulled toward the door by Leah.

* * * * *

Gregor watched them pull out of the driveway, a smile still on his lips as he returned to the maps.

"They will have an enjoyable day."

"The town of Glenwood Springs will never be the same. My wife is a champion shopper, Gregor," JD noted with a chuckle.

"I just hope your wives don't change their minds and take off to Grand Junction or Aspen."

JD looked at John with raised eyebrows, "They didn't say they would, but why are you concerned, John?"

"Because it's going to be difficult enough to keep track of them in town, given the increased holiday traffic. The agents won't be prepared for a variation from the plan."

"You're telling me they're going to be followed?"

John looked at Gregor, then back to JD before answering.

"Of course. Lenore is followed everywhere she goes. I assumed you knew."

"Leah told me that at one time they were both followed, but I just figured that was over now. Should I be concerned here?"

"It is merely a precaution. John feels that since I am a former Soviet citizen, there may be those who would be less than friendly to my wife."

"I see. Well, I hope your agents are good, because when my wife goes on a shopping trip, she could wear out a triathlete."

"That's why I assigned two agents today instead of one." John's eyes didn't convey the amusement in his voice.

The momentary tension eased and the men began scanning the maps again. Gregor pointed to a spot on the map.

"This is where you told me you saw a light. This road is accessible from the highway a few miles north of our drive, though it is gated. It's rough, but it follows the tree line and then comes out near the entrance of our driveway."

JD and John watched as Gregor indicated the route on the property he knew. Once again, JD questioned them.

"What light are you looking for?"

With a nod from Gregor, John began to tell JD the purpose of their intended excursion.

"JD, when I stood at the kitchen window just before sunset night before last, light reflected off something. It could have been just about anything but we want to make sure it wasn't a vehicle of some kind. There shouldn't be anyone up there." He rubbed the back of his neck. "By the time I got my binoculars, the sun no longer reflected on anything. We're just going to go up there and check things out."

"Do the girls know about this?"

"No, we didn't think it necessary to worry them. Headquarters says there's no known threats in the area. They aren't aware of anything out of the ordinary." John walked to the window and stared at the area. "I had them check on Lenore's former husband. He's, evidently, not causing anyone grief except for his current spouse."

"So, it could have just been someone exploring?"

"Yes." John turned to JD.

"You *are* a cautious man, aren't you, John?"

"It's my job."

"It is also his nature. We should be going. I trust we have not upset you, JD?"

"No, Gregor. In fact, I'm feeling very safe right now."

"Good! We will also show you other areas. It is a beautiful valley and surrounding forest."

The maps were rolled and put back into their containers. The three men got into John's rented truck and drove away from the house. They would not encounter any strangers on their tour.

A person, who was certainly no stranger, headed toward Glenwood Springs from the opposite direction.

CHAPTER 8

With one load delivered to the agent's trunk, the two shoppers headed back inside the crowded mall accompanied by agent Mills, whose professionalism never suggested he could be inconvenienced by the shoppers. He headed for a coffee shop after confirming a time to meet. The shoppers walked away as the agent watched, keeping track of their movements from a seat near the coffee shop's front door.

"Lenore!" Leah shouted as she grabbed Lenore's arm, startling her.

"What?" Lenore jerked, expecting a thundering avalanche about to carry them off, at the very least. She checked their surroundings quickly.

"This store. Look!" Leah squealed as she pointed. "The store where you bought your beautiful jacket. You know, the one you wore the night you first met Gregor."

* * * * *

Mills stopped halfway to them when he realized the situation was benign. He returned to the coffee shop just in time to reclaim his table as two teenage girls were ready to grab the vacancy. He picked up his untouched piece of pie and cup of coffee, then gestured to the girls. They settled at the table in a giggly flurry, thanking him. He stood near the door, balancing the plate atop his cup, always aware of Lenore and Leah's route.

* * * * *

Lenore peeked inside the door of the store and agreed. "Oh, it is, isn't it? Do you realize you scared me half to death?" She gently shoved her shopping companion.

"Oh, sorry, but when I saw it, I got excited."

"Obviously."

"Do you still have it?"

"Yes. I had nearly donated it to a clothing drive once or twice before Gregor came back." She sighed. "Something kept me from doing it. It felt too special."

"Think you'll ever wear it again?" Leah pointed to a festive sweater in the window display.

"Oh, I already have." Lenore gave an approving nod. "We went to the dance hall a couple of weeks ago and Gregor insisted I wear it. It felt just as special as it did the first time."

"The jacket or the dance?"

"Both," she smiled, then added, "We enjoyed our first dance since that night."

"Did you go alone or take Alex?" They walked into the store and Leah headed to a stack of sweaters drawing her like a magnetic force.

"Oh, we enjoyed taking Alex." Lenore stood beside Leah as she searched through the stack. "He loved it and danced with several *lovely ladies* and his shyness was no defense with those girls." She chuckled at the memory.

"He already knew how to dance *country/western* style?" Leah abandoned the stacked sweaters and approached another display, with Lenore following close behind.

"Well, only after I gave him a few lessons at home the week before we went. He's a fast learner."

They meandered through the store without making a purchase, and continued to the next. The crowds were growing and it became a challenge to talk above the clamor.

"Did Gregor have any old girlfriends there?"

Lenore shook her head. "No, if you recall, he never had any girlfriends before he met me. There were a few old dance partners that were a bit disappointed in not getting to dance with him. No animosities though."

"I'll bet they really chased after Alex."

"Oh, you bet." Lenore stopped at the seasonal choices in a window display. "I think we need to go in here."

"Yes, maybe we'll both find nice sweaters for our families."

"I still need to find one for Alex and something for Joel to take back to Kim." Lenore turned to a tall blond lady looking back, annoyed, and unfamiliar. Catching sight of her friend walking through the door, Lenore offered an, "Oops, excuse me." and dashed to catch up, while Leah continued talking, unaware of her proximity to Lenore.

"Shelly needs a fabulous red sweater for the holidays."

"Oh, she should celebrate in style *this* Christmas." Lenore was well versed in catching up with a conversation already in progress with the always in motion Leah, "I'll add a pair of very special Christmas earrings for her."

"Oh, Lenore, she will be absolutely delighted. You're her hero, you know."

"Silly girl!" Lenore shook her head.

"Not at all," Leah assured her.

The two women entered the store and separated, each in search of the perfect gift. Lenore had no intentions of trying to keep track of Leah, when her friend disappeared behind racks of clothes taller than she. The dark-haired lady continued her own quest, knowing Leah would find her when she was ready.

With two sweaters across her arm, and struggling to keep her small purse's strap on her shoulder, Lenore bent over to pick up a shirt someone had dropped and not bothered to pick up. Having worked in retail most of her life, picking up and straightening products always felt like a natural thing to do. A pair of wing-tip shoes could be seen under the hanging clothes, so she stood, hung the shirt back up, and walked around the end of the rack. A familiar face surprised her.

"Dennis? What are *you* doing here? I thought they reassigned you." She stared at him.

Startled, he dropped the sweater he held.

"Whoa, I didn't mean to scare you," she said. "Let me find Leah. I want to introduce you to my very best friend."

"Wait." He looked quickly around the store and touched her sleeve. "I didn't expect to see you. Are you and Leah alone?"

"Yes, Dennis. As alone as I ever get. You know that," she frowned. "Why do you ask?"

"I mean, well, I'm not on assignment at this time. I'm just here buying clothes for my sister for Christmas. I'm sort of on vacation."

"All the better! Want to bring your sister to the house for dinner?" She regretted the invitation as soon as she said it.

"No!" He waved her off with his hand. "I mean, I … I really can't." He smiled, hoping it would help. "She lives away from here."

"Oh … where?" Lenore was genuinely interested.

Leah emerged from behind racks and shoppers and moved to Lenore's side. She stared at Dennis Halvorson without smiling. "Leah, here's one of my shadows." She gave a curt nod towards Halvorson. "I guess, former shadow. Dennis, this is Leah Chase."

"Hello." Leah greeted the man with a little less enthusiasm than Lenore thought normal for her best friend. "Must be quite a challenge keeping track of this one." She glanced over at Lenore.

The agent looked flustered and struggled to reply. "It has, no, I mean, uh, it had its moments, for sure." He continued to glance past the women toward the doors leading out to the mall.

She turned to Leah. "He's shopping for his sister." Then she turned back to Dennis. "I guess I never knew you had a sister. What's her name and where did you say she lived?"

"Lenore, I'd really rather no one know anything about my sister. She's very private."

Both women look at one another, then back to the agent, waiting for an explanation.

"She prefers it that way, don't you see? No one knows of her. If they did, they could intrude on her life. I hope you understand."

"Sure Dennis." Lenore nodded. "I understand the *need* for privacy. I miss it myself sometimes." Lenore glanced at Leah, who continued to scrutinize the agent. "If you don't want us to tell anyone you have a sister, we won't tell a soul." Lenore noticed beads of perspiration forming on Dennis' forehead.

"Please. I would also appreciate it if you didn't tell anyone you even saw me here today. I'm supposed to be on vacation, don't you see, between assignments." He smiled but continued to glance toward the door. "If they know I'm here, they could call me back into service. This may be my only opportunity to shop before Christmas."

Leah piped in, "Well, if that's the way you want it … we are good at keeping secrets, aren't we, Lenore?"

"Right!" Verifying their security detail, Lenore added. "Um, well, we left our agent of the day at the coffee shop. We promised to be back or at least check-in at two." She checked her watch, as did Halvorson. "We'd best be getting back then, before he comes looking for us and sees you."

Lenore picked up the sweater the agent had dropped and peered closer at the shoes he wore. She stood and shook the sweater, positioning it back onto the hanger.

"This is a very pretty sweater."

"It's for my sister," he replied as if cued. "She likes turquoise just like you, Lenore."

"It's beautiful!" She held it up to see better. "Your sister should love it." She handed it to Dennis. "You have very good taste and your sister is very lucky to have a brother who is so thoughtful."

"I try to take care of her."

"How kind." Lenore noticed Leah seemed a little quiet. "Well, I guess we need to be getting our selections paid for and on to the coffee shop. Busy *girl-day*, you know." She gestured with a wave of her hand.

"Yes, that's probably a good idea. Nice meeting you, Leah." He glanced quickly at Leah, then back to the brunette. "Wonderful to see you again, Lenore." His comment brought a chill to her, and she wondered why.

"Nice meeting you, Dennis," Leah said, but her eyes didn't reflect her words.

Dennis turned and directed a comment at Leah. He wasn't smiling. "Don't forget, Leah, you need to keep my secret, okay?"

"Sure Dennis," Leah said, then took Lenore by the arm, walking quickly to the cash register.

The two women paid for their selections and walked out of the store as Halvorson paid for his own purchase. They walked directly toward the coffee shop where agent Mills waited. Leah took a quick glance behind them and saw Dennis peeking from the door they had just left, watching their retreat. He then ducked his head, turned, and headed swiftly in the opposite direction.

"Lenore, I don't like that man."

At that moment, she didn't like the feeling he had generated. She wanted to hear what Leah had to say.

"What about him don't you like?" Lenore tried to not impart her own thoughts.

"Isn't he the one John talked about?" She stopped and took Lenore by the arm. "The one you were getting too familiar with?"

"Yes. One and the same. Could that be the reason you don't like him?"

"I don't know, he just gave me the creeps." She looked behind them again. "I also don't think he even has a sister. I think he was following you!"

Lenore nodded. Leah had nailed it.

"Maybe so, but what do we do about it?" She glanced at Leah as they continued their walk to the coffee shop. "Do we give in to our intuitions, tell someone and possibly piss him off or trust that *maybe* he really is on vacation and buying a Christmas gift for his sister and we just surprised him?"

"Kind of awkward, isn't it?"

"Or dangerous," Lenore mumbled.

"Don't go there." Leah nudged her.

"Sorry." Lenore cringed.

"Do we casually mention it to someone?"

"I don't like keeping things from Gregor, but …."

"I can understand that, but how about John?"

Lenore gave it some serious thought before she stopped once again and turned to Leah. "Oh, I just don't know." She shifted her packages to one hand and ran her fingers through her hair with the other hand. "They both tend to be over-protective of me anyway. It could turn into something more than it needs to be."

"True, but this will take some very serious pondercating."

"At the very least."

The two friends were quiet as they arrived at the coffee shop and agent Mills greeted them. He noted the seriousness in their normally cheerful demeanor.

"Is everything alright? Is there a problem, Mrs. Parishnikov?" He looked behind the women, narrowing his eyes.

Lenore glanced again at Leah and answered, affirming her decision to keep it between themselves. "Oh, we're just deciding where next to stimulate the economy of Glenwood Springs. I think we're going to head downtown before we go home." She smiled, disarming his concerns. "I hope you brought your walking shoes, Mills."

"Always." He smiled, then patted his very flat tummy. "I need to walk. I had a piece of pie. Just let me contact Johnson to let him know our itinerary. He's been waiting outside."

"Johnson? I didn't know there were *two* of you today." Lenore's eyes were wide.

"I suppose it's due to the increase of holiday traffic and people," he said, as he took a radio from his pocket.

After a quick and quiet conversation with the other agent via radio, Mills preceded them toward the exit. Leah grabbed Lenore's arm and held her back.

"You may not have to mention it to anyone. Maybe the other agent saw him."

"If Johnson did see him, how do we explain not telling Mills?" Lenore asked. "Shit!"

"You really don't think we should tell?"

"Okay, to be honest, he made me uncomfortable enough, I'm halfway *afraid* to tell."

"Okay, I can agree with that. He made me uncomfortable too, especially the way he said to *keep his secret*." Leah scanned the crowd and shuddered.

"What will he do, if they don't know, and then he finds out we told?"

"I hope we figure it out before we get home," Leah reasoned. "I need to whiz."

"That way." Lenore pointed then caught up to Mills. "Time out. Leah needs to make a necessary stop first."

The agent simply smiled, the vision of patience. When Leah returned, he held the door for them as they walked out and headed to the Saab for the journey downtown. The two shopper's packages were put into the trunk of agent Mills' sedan. Agent Johnson pulled up next to Mill's car, ready to follow.

As Lenore started the Saab, she tapped the steering wheel and glanced at Leah. "I don't know about you, but I don't feel so much like shopping anymore."

"Me either, but won't it make them wonder if we just suddenly head on home?"

"Probably. Let's just wander through a couple of stores, then tell them we're tired."

"Sounds like a good plan," Leah agreed. "Now I don't like him even more. He put a dark cloud over a very fun day together."

"Well, it'll still be fun. We'll have quite a job sorting packages when we get to the house."

"Yes, we won't let him ruin our time together." She turned to Lenore. "He really has weird eyes, don't you think?"

"Well, I can't say I've ever seen any like them, but then I've got weird eyes, too." She fluttered her lashes.

"Your eyes aren't weird, they're little barometers," which made them both laugh.

*****

They found a parking space a couple of blocks from the main street of downtown Glenwood Springs, and waited in the car for the agents to appear. With the men close behind, they began wandering through the crowds and a great variety of stores the town had to offer. Soon Halvorson seemed to slip to the back of their minds and laughter returned, punctuating their efforts and conversation. Lenore found several toys to send home with Leah for Dustin and Danny. In a large book store she purchased a leather-bound American dictionary with an accompanying thesaurus for Alex. Leah agreed, Lenore had chosen the perfect gift for her brother-in-law.

Even the ever-present agents were forgotten as they added to their packages from several stores. They both spied an artisan jewelry store, and upon entering, the soft music and gentle scent on the air greeted them. The din of holiday shoppers and assorted Christmas carols playing up and down the streets were shut out behind the heavy glass doors. They separated on their own private quests.

"Look at these, Lenore. I love these little heart rings," Leah called out.

Lenore walked to the counter and stood beside her best friend who pointed to a display of rings inside a glass display case. A well-dressed fine jewelry employee appeared on cue, ready to assist.

"Would you care to try something?" Her practiced greeting was genuine. She sported many pieces of expensive jewelry. Employee discounts were no doubt a factor.

Leah looked at Lenore, who nodded, and the employee used a key to unlock the case. Several trays of small rings were lifted out and placed atop the counter. After a bit of discussion, they each decided on a favorite and weren't surprised to find it to be the same style.

"We need to get these. It'll be like our best friend rings." Leah held out her hand and admired the silver heart ring on her right pinky finger.

Lenore admired hers, viewed the selection once again, then said, "Yes, I agree!"

Both women handed the friendly clerk their rings. Lenore added a pair of ruby and emerald Christmas earrings for Shelly. The delighted clerk efficiently rang up the sales and allowed the rings to be worn by the duo. The earrings were nestled into a festive box, then gently tucked into a tissue lined bag.

Once they were settled inside the Saab, they clicked their rings together as if christening their importance.

CHAPTER 9

While JD enjoyed the view, Gregor and John walked up and down the road, eyes fixed on the ground. They looked for indications of frequency or purpose of someone being there.

"Greg, take a look at this." The former KGB operative walked to where John stood, eyes focused down at the ground. "See the grass here? Someone has been here often enough to mat grass down under the tires."

Where they stood, Gregor could see a clear view of the home he shared with Lenore and Alex. "There is no question of what this person is looking at. I want to know why."

"Greg, we also need to know who. Then maybe we'll know why. I'm stepping up security." John checked the view, then at the old logging road where they stood. "We'll position agents at both ends of this road. If he *or* she, should try to drive up here again, we'll have our answers."

"Nice view of your house, Gregor," JD noted as he joined the two men.

"Evidently, we are not the only ones who appreciate it, JD. See here," Gregor indicated. "Someone has been parking here often. I need to find out who and why they are watching my home."

JD turned from the view to John. "Couldn't it just be your CIA agents?"

"No, I wasn't even aware this road existed before now." He shook his head. "Not us."

JD turned to Gregor. "Do you think it's because you're Russian?"

"That would be the most obvious reason."

"I don't see why people would hold that against you. After all, you've given up your homeland and your former profession. Hell, they should welcome you with open arms." He crossed his arms and tilted his head. "Don't we have some pretty good, or at least better relations going with the Soviets, too?"

"Doesn't matter to some," John explained. "There are some who continue to hold grudges and fail to consider all sides. He's run into it a few times."

Gregor walked away from the two men and continued scanning the ground. He offered no further discussion.

JD watched Gregor walk away, then turned to the CIA agent and spoke quietly, "John, has his life or Lenore's been threatened?"

"No, nothing like that, so far." He wished he hadn't added that. "They just do some name calling and there's been a little property damage on the fence near the house. When we've tracked them down, he's spent a little time talking to them, and that's been the end of it. I'm not sure what he says to them, but they never bother him again." John rubbed the back of his neck and watched Gregor. "This is different. They're not approaching him or the house. He doesn't like being stalked. It might be nothing, but it's best to know for sure."

JD simply nodded and followed John as he scanned the ground. They met at Gregor's side to see what he focused on. As neatly as a cookie cutter in rolled-out dough, an impression of the sole of a man's shoe was preserved in the recently frozen earth.

* * * * *

Dennis Halvorson turned off the heater in his truck, yet rivulets of perspiration continued to find a path down his face and he could feel the wetness under his clothes. How could he have been so stupid as to believe crowds would make a perfect cover for his shopping excursion? He had come face-to-face with Lenore. He sighed. She was more beautiful than ever. Surely, she would keep their encounter a secret.

His delight faded. It would be a secret *until* he rescued Lenore, then this Leah woman would tell them. She wouldn't hesitate to mention seeing him, shopping for clothes for a sister that didn't exist. The Company knew he had no sister. Their background checks were more thorough than anyone's ability to hide a sister. Leah Chase just became a liability. He hit the steering wheel in frustration. He hated killing, but what else could he do? He needed to cover his tracks. Lenore would eventually understand. If there were any other way, he wouldn't kill her best friend. She would need to understand there is sometimes collateral damage in order to reach your goal; a matter of simple logic.

With a quick check of the rear-view mirror, Halvorson turned off the highway onto a gravel road. He would be at his cabin soon.

There, at the sanctuary he had prepared for himself and Lenore, he could relax and think. He needed to decide what fate would befall Mrs. Leah Chase. It had to be something quick and painless; at least as painless as any death could be. If she suffered, Lenore would certainly have trouble forgiving him, or accepting his reasoning.

Ruts in the edge of the road formed by the freezing and thawing of the late November temperatures, jerked the steering wheel in Halvorson's hands. He slowed a bit, which returned control of the vehicle in time for him to negotiate a turn onto a far less traveled road. A mile further over an old Forest Service Road, he stopped, turned off the engine and got out to pull an assortment of broken limbs and brush aside, allowing the truck access to a trail. He listened to the quiet for a moment before getting back in the truck and pulled forward enough to get out and cover the opening. He started the truck again to continue his journey.

Halverson followed the trail toward a rustic cabin. Before approaching further, he stopped, turned off the engine and once again got out to listen and survey the area. It would take much closer inspection for someone to mistake the area as being inhabited. He prided himself in being very good at camouflage. He noted tracks of the deer who journeyed past morning and evening. An occasional creak of tree limbs and a soft hush of wind far above were the only sounds. He took a deep breath and let a plume of foggy air escape slowly in the cold, trying to force himself to relax.

So peaceful. So private. So perfect for his Lenore.

He drove the truck nearer the cabin and parked it behind a dense growth of trees and bushes. The gray color made it nearly imperceptible in the forest shadows.

The cabin's white clapboard siding was filthy and covered with lichen on most surfaces. Many of the boards were missing and Halvorson had made attempts to cover the spaces with new lumber. The repairs were in stark contrast to the ancient clapboard, but necessary. The roof had a nearly solid mass of debris from the surrounding trees. Necessary patches had been made, and the autumn shed of leaves had the newer shingles well-disguised.

A fire in the wood stove would warm the cold cabin up quickly, but first he hurried to put Lenore's things into her room. Eventually it would become *their* room. He had worked very hard to make it just right. It had to be perfect for his lady. No ruffles. He knew her *that* well. The yellow walls and disturbing pattern on the old worn linoleum floor couldn't be helped just yet. He decided it would be a fun thing for them to do as a couple when they could remodel it to Lenore's liking. For now, the abrasive colors would remain, but a simple turquoise quilted comforter would please her.

The room had no functioning window. He had covered it first with plywood, then a poster of an outdoor scenes of snowcapped mountains and a waterfall. It would have to suffice until Lenore could be de-programed and trusted to have an open window. He gently closed the door and went to work warming the cabin.

It took time for the heat produced by the woodstove to penetrate every corner of the rest of the cabin. It could not be used after Lenore arrived; at least for a while. No sense in trying to attract attention. Even a tiny tongue of smoke could invite closer inspection by those looking for Lenore. Electric space heaters, powered by generators, would provide necessary warmth. The generators were close to the cabin, but he was sure the noise would not be much of a factor. He had built a shelter for them and insulated it well with a makeshift cave of dirt and rocks.

Two lights would also be lit by generators or batteries. One light for the kitchen area and the other on the ceiling in the bedroom would both be operated by switches on the wall outside the bedroom. He would leave the one for the bedroom lit 24 hours a day for a time, perhaps until she became sleep deprived enough to be more cooperative in his efforts to deprogram her. The mesh covering for the fixture was a precaution in the event there could be a struggle. Training taught him to prepare for variables.

The small rustic bathroom provided functioning fixtures, but a camping toilet would be in the bedroom along with a camping sink for Lenore's use until she accepted her situation.

Yes, he had thought of everything. He would keep Lenore comfortable. She would learn to be grateful and to rely upon him for everything.

He sat down on the sofa in the dark room and untied his wingtip Florsheim shoes. They were still damp from walking through remnants of crusty snow between the truck and cabin. He slipped out of them and flexed his stockinged toes in the warmth of the room. He would clean and polish the shoes later. He smirked. If anyone ever saw his footprints, it would be assumed they belonged to

Frank Gillespie. Unless Leah Chase mentioned she saw *him* wearing wingtips.

With a deep sigh, Halverson stood and began pacing across the worn flooring. So many plans to make in eliminating Leah Chase and rescuing Lenore. Dennis assured himself he was intelligent and a very good problem solver. He looked forward to this challenge.

* * * * *

"JD, you're an expert on shoes." John turned to Lenore's former boss. "What's this imprint?"

JD knelt on one knee, took a pair of glasses from a pocket, and slipped them on. "Oh, this is an easy one. Florsheim Royal Imperial. Nice shoes. I'd say about a ten wide, give or take a half size. The freezing and thawing could make a difference."

"Frank Gillespie," John said. "That's a relief."

Gregor and JD were waiting for more.

"Has to be Gillespie. He wears Florsheim wingtips." He gestured toward the valley. "Must have kept an eye on things from this vantage point."

JD accepted the theory, but Gregor disagreed.

"John, it has been nearly two weeks since Frank has been assigned here, and this imprint is less than two days old. We had snow covering this area only a week ago. An impression this clear could not have lasted." He gestured to their surroundings. "Also, what about the light you saw in this area? Whatever reflected the light has been moved, or driven away."

"Could Frank be here and neither of you be aware of it?" JD asked the question and Gregor waited for John to answer.

"Actually no. In fact, Frank is on holiday right now. He's been out of communication since Monday." He gestured to Gregor. "The agents always check in with Gregor when they come on duty."

Gregor nodded, his eyes narrowing. "So, there is someone else who wears such shoes, and likes to keep an eye on my home."

"I guess if surveillance happen to stop someone, we'll have them check their shoes." John turned to Leah's husband. "JD, are you sure this is the imprint of a wingtip Florsheim shoe?"

"No." JD shook his head, making the other two men look questioningly at their expert. "I mean, it's certainly a Florsheim Royal

Imperial, but not necessarily a wingtip. They make a wide variety of Imperials; smooth toe, cap toe, slip-on. They'll have to look at the shoe itself, I'm afraid." He glanced back down at the impression. "I'm certain of the size. Been doing shoes for a lot of years."

John turned to Gregor. "How do you want us to handle it, providing we can find the person?"

"I would prefer to speak to them myself." Gregor's eyes met John's. "Privately, of course."

"As usual." John nodded.

"Tell me, Gregor, what do you say to them?" JD asked. "Do you simply talk to them and try to make them understand, or do you scare the curiosity out of them?"

"Whatever will work the most efficiently, JD."

No doubt the former Soviet KGB operative would be effective, as the serious, eyes softened to match the smile now in place. The shoe store owner was very glad to be the recipient of the friendly part of his personality.

The trio walked back to John's truck, with questions and concerns not far from anyone's mind.

* * * * *

By four-thirty in the afternoon Lenore and Leah were ready to head for the house following a quick stop at the grocery store, no doubt much to the relief of two agents who had accompanied them. The merchants of Glenwood Springs would smile a little broader when they counted the day's receipts.

The late November sky faded to a washed out blue with a few clouds moving in.

Leah looked up at the sky. "Are those snow clouds?"

"Nope. Just some high cirrus clouds. Nice and fluffy," replied Lenore.

"I guess you're learning a lot about such things with a meteorologist in the family," she teased.

Traffic on the southbound highway remained steady. With fatigue setting in, Lenore didn't bother to pass many vehicles.

"Yes, Alex keeps us informed of the weather conditions. It's great." She yawned. "Leah, I don't know about you, but I'm exhausted! I've never shopped like this before in my life. Those poor agents have packed trunks and we have stuff here in the back. Wow!" She shook her head. "I'm almost ashamed."

"Ashamed of what?" Leah chided. "Being able to do what most people do? You bought some very nice gifts, but I wouldn't say you were extravagant at all. I know for a fact you hardly purchase a single item unless it was on sale and a good sale at that!" she assured her best friend. "Now, let's just go home so you can lay down and rest. The little package you're toting round inside takes more of your energy then you think."

"Guess so." Lenore gently caressed her lower abdomen and smiled. "I struggled to not buy baby things, but until I get the official word on Monday, I just feel like I shouldn't."

"I would have indulged the urge. The doctor's confirmation is merely a technicality. You know you're pregnant." A familiar old VW microbus passed and Leah pointed at it, "Apparently even an old hippie shops on Black Friday. Don't you just wonder what they bought?"

Lenore snickered, nodded, then announced, "We have to plan another shopping excursion when Gregor and I come to the Front Range for him to work, that would be a good time for us." Lenore's eyes twinkled. "I think this baby's daddy is going to enjoy buying things for it, too. He's already designing a nursery."

"Big difference from when we were having our babies, isn't it?" Leah recalled. "I remember JD and I could barely afford formula. We got hand-me-down baby furniture, clothes, and blankets. I imagine it was the same for you."

"Yes," Lenore agreed. "Grant's nursery consisted of a baby bed crammed between our bed and the wall of the bedroom in our tiny apartment. I didn't sleep the first year. I woke every time he moved or squeaked." She passed a vehicle, knowing the agents were having no trouble following. "By the time we had Joel, we'd moved to a two-bedroom apartment, but we still had to keep Joel's baby bed in our room." She smiled at the memory. "Grant always wanted to play with his baby brother in the middle of the night. He just knew Joel had to be a great new toy acquired just for him."

"Well, you probably won't get any more sleep this time either because you'll keep this baby in the room with you and Gregor." Leah patted Lenore's arm. "I doubt if you *or* Gregor will get much sleep."

The lively conversation continued as Lenore maneuvered the Saab around familiar curves that took them home, with two agents following at separate distances.

* * * * *

Gregor paced between the front door and the large picture window. John and JD glanced his way as they talked, occasionally drawing him into the conversation, but his eyes never left the view from the front window. When the Saab pulled into the drive, he stopped mid-sentence and bounded out the door. A few moments later, John and JD followed.

Lenore and Gregor embraced and kissed as though the absence had been unbearable. Leah smiled as JD gave her a quick peck on the cheek. John stood awkwardly to one side with hands jammed into the pockets of his jacket, watching Lenore and Gregor, then turned his eyes to Leah. She closed her eyes and nodded, knowing he felt anything but comfortable at that moment. He squared his shoulders and walked to the car. JD opened the door on the other side.

"You two were gone all day and this is all you bought?" JD asked.

John opened the door on his side and looked inside, shaking his head. "This can't be right."

Lenore had turned from Gregor, though their hands were still connected. "Well, you see, the two agents shadowing us all day have these really *big* trunks in their old non-descript sedans." She gestured up at the road. "There they are, with the rest of the bounty."

Two very professional agents passed various packages to the three men with the skilled proficiency of handing off secure documents to awaiting diplomats. The ladies took some of the goods and offered sincere thanks to the tolerant agents. With the task completed, they stood aside and listened to what John asked them to do before returning to their respective vehicles. One agent stayed near the driveway on the road. The other disappeared from view, but he would not be far.

"Leah, I sincerely hope at least half of these packages are Lenore's." JD pointed at the mound of bags in the center of the living room, shaking his head.

The petite blonde stood beside her husband, proudly surveying the day's bounty. "Probably about half. Why?"

"Did you forget we came on public transportation?"

"If there's too much, maybe Gregor and Lenore can bring it when they come to the Front Range. Maybe even before Christmas time." She tilted her head. "I really don't see a problem."

JD turned to John and spoke quietly. "She never seems to see a problem. *That's* the problem."

John laughed as Leah punched her husband soundly in the arm. "I heard that!"

As the harmless teasing continued across the room, Gregor hugged Lenore. "I am glad you had an enjoyable day and I am glad you are home. You must be tired."

"A little. I've never enjoyed shopping before. I suppose because I either worked or just couldn't afford it. I hope I haven't been extravagant."

"My precious wife, it is not in your nature to be extravagant." He touched her cheek. "It gives me great pleasure that you can do these things. Where would you like to have the packages until you can sort them? I will do this for you because you must lay down for a while."

Lenore started to protest, but knew he would have his way. Instead, she hugged him. With apologies to her friends for leaving them for a nap, Leah said she would be taking a nap as well. The guys assured the tired shoppers their packages would find the way to Lenore's art room where goods could be sorted later.

In the quiet of their room, a weariness overtook Lenore quickly. Gregor helped her out of shoes and clothes and nestled her into bed.

"I didn't feel that tired until I saw this big old comfortable bed. Will you hold me for a bit?"

"Of course. I would never have you go to bed alone. Do you need anything?"

With a yawn, she replied, "Only you!"

With that, he settled her into his arms. With feathery soft caresses, her even breathing let him know she was sleeping. He watched her a while longer, then quietly moved out of the bed. With one soft kiss, he left the room to join the others.

"Lenore will rest for a while." He spoke to JD as he entered the living room. "She tires easily lately."

"Leah headed for bed as well. She got up a whole lot earlier than usual, so I knew a nap would be needed." JD voiced concerns to Gregor, "I hope there's nothing else going on with Lenore."

"No, JD, I do not believe there is anything wrong, but she has an appointment on Monday for a check-up. We want to be sure she is healthy."

"Might not hurt. Probably just reacting to a major lifestyle change."

"I'm sure that is it."

Gregor knew JD was unaware of Lenore's condition. He didn't know another person in the room *did* know. Someone who had once loved her in the same way that he did. Someone who ached for her and wished the child that grew in her could be *his*. Neither man knew there could be a third who planned to take her away from them both.

CHAPTER 10

Saturday would be a quiet day at the Parishnikov home. Friends and family enjoyed the last full day together. No skiing or shopping would interrupt. The train would be leaving Glenwood Springs Sunday morning with Joel and Grant, Leah, and JD, heading for the Front Range of Colorado to school and work and grandchildren. Lenore tried to push the thought of their departure from her mind as she listened to the precious sounds of laughter and conversations surrounding her.

John had suddenly decided to extend his visit, stating the need to use up some vacation days which delighted Lenore. Gregor and Alex would have someone to ski with. Though she felt physically healthy enough to ski, Gregor had dissuaded her from taking a chance of risking the pregnancy. She hadn't attempted to argue. She knew the ensuing months would take a lot out of her.

Leah opted for a nap while Lenore and her sons took an afternoon walk. The bright Colorado sun warmed the valley, where not long ago there had been the first snow of the season, fueling the ski industry. Warm Chinook winds had melted most all the snow in the valley. A few traces could be seen in the protected areas and higher elevations were pristine with new snow.

Two large white dogs accompanied the trio on their walk. Nicolai enjoyed an impromptu game of fetch with Joel, but Marushka refused to leave Lenore's side, walking between her and Grant, which he found interesting.

"Does she think I'm going to hurt you?"

Lenore smiled and patted Marushka's large white head beside her. "Oh, not at all. She knows you are part of the family. I think she just likes me. Us girls need to stick together, don't we Marushka?"

A wagging tail and nuzzle of Lenore's hand confirmed it.

"Why doesn't she play with Joel and Nicolai?"

"She takes her job very seriously, Grant."

Grant stroked her soft fur and a slobbery lick assured him of her favor. "Guess so. Does that mean Nicolai doesn't?"

Lenore laughed. "Don't let his playfulness fool you. He's keenly aware of everything going on around us."

They watched the magnificent white male run to retrieve the stick then chase the laughing young man to give it back. Joel would tire long before Nicolai. Hiking boots were no match for leathery pads toughened on rocky terrain. Joel finally sat down in the dormant grass, allowing the pursuing animal to give him the stick, and a generous face licking.

"Aw, geez, Nick, enough already!" Joel scolded, wiping this face with a jacket sleeve. Nicolai wagged his tail, circled the protesting human, and gave another slobbery lick to the top of Joel's head before ambling away. "Not my hair, for cryin' out loud!"

As Grant teased Joel about his new "*do*", Lenore noticed Nicolai sniffing the air, circling the group. Joel tossed the stick again, but Nicolai offered only a glance. His nose probed the breeze and his tail had stopped wagging. Marushka stepped in front of Lenore, stopping her from walking further; clearly not an accidental movement.

"Boys, I think we should go back to the house."

Joel got up, dusting the debris from his pants, and stood beside Grant. "Why? It's a beautiful day," he extended his arms. "Besides, I hoped we could spend more time alone with you, Mom."

"We can talk on the porch back at the house."

Grant had noticed the action of the dogs. "What do you think it is, Mom?"

"I don't know, Grant, but I've learned to trust their instincts."

Joel looked at the dogs and back to his mom. "They see something or smell something, don't they?"

"Yes. Let's start back." She took their hands. "I have no idea what they see or feel but it's probably not something we need to experience." She squeezed their hands to reassure. "Maybe a skunk or porcupine. Could just be deer or elk moving through."

"Or an intruder," Joel offered.

Lenore stopped and turned to Joel dropping both her sons' hands. "Why did you say that?"

Joel raised his eyebrows. "Just a thought. I overheard a conversation between Gregor and John."

"Like what?" Grant asked.

The younger man shrugged his shoulders. "They were saying something about whoever they found watching the house would get caught in the act by the agents."

Lenore bit her lower lip and stared at the ridge where Nicolai continued to focus. Marushka walked a few paces ahead of Lenore, Grant, and Joel, then turned back, as if urging them to continue their retreat to safety. So, John wasn't burning vacation days. He was on duty! "Let's go."

She grabbed her sons' hands again and began a deliberate pace toward the house. Perhaps by the time she got there she would be able to ask logical questions. Right now, anger fueled her steps.

Joel and Grant had been told nothing of what had really happened to her in Kansas City. They believed Lenore had sustained her injuries by falling down an embankment, when she went to dinner with John.

They didn't know how close Lenore had come to being taken to the Soviet Union or that only after they threatened to take Joel, her survival and *mom* instincts had kicked in. She clobbered one abductor in the face with her briefcase, shoved a burning pipe down the throat of another and knocked a gun out of the hands of a third, giving her the precious seconds needed to run from the vehicle. She had slid down an embankment and dodged cars on the southbound side of an interstate, before falling face down in the median. She had twisted her ankle, received numerous cuts and scrapes, and became impaled with filth from wet road debris, but fueled with fear and adrenaline, she got up. She ran across traffic, to the northbound side of the interstate from her abductors.

Lenore flagged down a truck driver who graciously agreed to take her back to the airport. After having his truck shot up by the one lone, still functioning abductor driving the airport van, the trucker used the size of the semi to his advantage, nudging the van into a massive concrete overpass support. Hours later at the airport, John and Frank appeared. She rescued *herself*. Not the CIA! No, she wasn't a helpless female and she didn't like being kept in the dark! Damn it, someone needed to get a piece of her mind!

Lenore released her sons' hands as she mounted the steps to the house, Gregor stepped out the door and immediately surrounded her with loving arms and a kiss before she could unleash her frustrations. The battle ended before it began. How could she resent this wonderful man for trying to protect her? She decided to question her husband and John after their friends had left.

"Are you alright?" He kissed her forehead. "You have not been gone long on your walk."

Joel sat down on the steps beside Marushka and smoothed his hair. "The dogs started acting weird, so we had to come back."

Gregor looked from Joel back to Lenore. "What is he saying? What did they do?"

"Probably just a skunk or elk alerted the dogs." She tried to sound casual as she searched Gregor's face for a hint of stress.

"Marushka wouldn't let Mom walk any further," Grant added.

Gregor's eyes scanned the mountainside. "I think it should be checked out." He smiled at Lenore, but his eyes didn't convey it.

Lenore heard the door open behind her. John had been listening to the conversation and had his jacket in hand. "I've got the radio. Let's go." He handed Gregor a jacket and started off the porch. She saw John's service weapon strapped across his shoulder before he put on the jacket.

Gregor donned his own jacket, gave Lenore a quick kiss and turned to leave.

"Wait!" Lenore grabbed his arm. "What's going on? You don't usually react this way over a possible skunk." She turned to John, who had stopped and turned back to her. "John, I think you need to let me know why."

"Lenore, we'll explain everything when we get back, I promise. Right now, we need to get up there and see what alerted the dogs."

Joel stood and stepped forward. "Can I go?"

Lenore, Gregor, John, and Grant answered him simultaneously with a firm, "No!"

"Okay, okay! Geeze!" Joel said, ducking his head as if dodging a blow.

Gregor put a hand on Joel's shoulder. "I'm sorry. I would just feel better knowing you were here with your brother to protect your mom if necessary. I understand you and your brother are most capable in that position."

Joel puffed a little with pride. "You bet we are."

Alex joined the group on the porch and a few words were exchanged in Russian. The only word Lenore recognized was *rifle*. Alex turned and went back into the house.

"Very well then, we will go." Gregor turned and touched her cheek. "Wait for me, Lenore. I will return."

A quick kiss on her lips produced a chill. Those same words had echoed in her head for nearly a year, when Gregor had disappeared from her life to go back to Russia. His plan had been to bring Alex back with him to the United States. She tried to shake it off and watched as he jogged to catch up with John. He wasn't going to Russia; no Soviet prison. Chances were great he would not even be leaving the boundaries of their property.

Joel sat back down on the step and Grant stood beside him. They watched Alex, Winchester lever action rifle in hand, exit the house and take off in a different direction than Gregor and John. He would be watching the house from a secure vantage point. Marushka would remain and keep guard on the porch.

Lenore turned and walked into the house, leaving her sons on the porch. "Leah! Leah, where are you?" She walked through the house, up the stairs to the hall, where Leah appeared at the door of their guest room.

"Lenore, what is it? You sound upset." She gave Lenore a hug, then held her at arm's length. "We're just getting things packed."

"Leah, something's going on."

"Where? What?"

"I don't know."

Satisfied with that response, Leah led her back into the guest room, where JD stood with clothes ready to go onto suitcases. "Do you want me to leave?"

"No!" Lenore answered before Leah could. "I think you may know something."

* * * * *

Nicolai preceded Gregor and John across the valley toward the eastern ridge. John communicated with two agents by radio, as Gregor jogged quickly ahead.

"You're certain no one has passed you? You didn't leave to go take a piss or something, did you?"

"Negative! Negative!" crackled from two different voices on his radio.

"Okay, move out. Take it slow and easy. Head toward one another. I have a feeling one of you is going to meet someone besides the other of you. Keep your radios on. Stay silent unless you find someone."

"Confirmed," replied the two agents.

John slipped the radio back into his jacket pocket and sprinted to catch up with Gregor, who intently followed Nicolai.

"They're moving in from either end of the road. See anything?" John asked quietly.

"No, but Nicolai does. He has not altered his course." The large white dog continued to run ahead. "He does not run toward skunks."

As Nicolai entered the thick underbrush of the slope, they lost sight of him. Several minutes passed as they began climbing, skirting rock outcroppings, juniper, and dormant scrub oak. The sound of Nicolai's growl brought them both to a halt.

"This way," Gregor whispered, moving toward the sound. John moved as quickly as he could, but the Russian man seemed to defy gravity as he quietly leapt from rock to rock and over deadfall and underbrush. Nearly a year in a Soviet prison had not affected his physical abilities, John thought, or he had a hell of a shot of adrenalin fueling his agility.

"Nyet! Sidet Nicolai." John heard words spoken as he cleared the last obstacle, drew his Heckler and Koch P7M8, stood next to Gregor and pointed at the bare ass of a teenage boy laying atop his equally naked girlfriend.

"Please don't shoot us." The young man pleaded as the young girl underneath him sobbed and attempted to disappear under her boyfriend's naked body lying prone atop her.

Gregor turned away and shook his head.

John holstered his weapon and cleared his throat. "Do you two realize you're on private property?" He crossed his arms over his chest. "How in the hell did you get up here anyway?"

"We left the car down by the highway and hiked in for a picnic. I guess we didn't think anyone would know we were here," the young man replied.

"You have the first part of your statement correct. You didn't think." John glanced around. "Where did you leave your clothes?"

"Between here and the car where we had a picnic. I sort of chased her up here after."

John turned to look at Gregor, who bit his lip to keep from laughing. Nicolai cocked his head to one side and then sniffed the foot of the startled teenager.

"Is he going to bite?" He pulled his foot away from the snout of the curious dog.

"Probably not," Gregor said, with a wink at John, who turned away, trying to keep his amusement under control.

With a steadying breath, John turned back to the couple. "I'm going to help you kids out this time." He glanced at Gregor who still struggled to stay serious. "Gregor, if you would loan this young lady your jacket, we'll see if we can locate the rest of their clothes."

Gregor slipped the leather jacket off and handed it to John who, in turn, handed it to the young man. The two men turned away from the couple as they got up and the young lady slipped the jacket on, clenching it around herself. Then he decided a dose of humility was in order. "I'm afraid my jacket isn't going to do you much good young man. I suggest you walk quickly to where you left your clothes, if you can figure out how you got here."

Two agent vehicles pulled up to the scene seconds apart. John approached with his hand up and shaking his head. "Everything is under control. Go back to your posts."

"Affirmative," and, "Yes sir!" were the replies. Both vehicles turned back toward the Parishnikov driveway.

The young man led his girlfriend down the road and indicated some brush piled in an unnatural way. "We followed this road, or I guess it's just a trail." The cold air did nothing to slow him. "Then we got up here and saw the valley and thought it was so beautiful. We decided to have a look."

Gregor stepped beside the young man and walked with him. "I would like to tell you to please consider what you have done. You have shown your lady disrespect by your actions today. Such lovely ladies are always to be treated respectfully." The young man, though intent on his journey, paid attention.

The kind-hearted Russian continued. "Also, where you are is my property. It is private. If you would like to come here, please, first come to my home and we will decide if it is a good day or not. It is indeed a beautiful valley and I would be honored to share it with you."

With that said, Gregor let the couple continue their trek and they began picking up and donning assorted pieces of their abandoned wardrobes. Nikolai followed, intently tracking them.

John fell behind the group, intent on surveying a trail they had discovered. Emerging near the highway, the young man shook Gregor's hand and apologized for trespassing and said he would enjoy coming to visit. The young lady returned his jacket with a hug and her own thanks for helping them.

New friendships had been created from chaos. Gregor turned to walk back, and the large white dog bounded up the trail before him until they were beside John.

"Greg, did you know about this trail?"

"I did not. I have walked this area many times, but I see it has been uncovered recently. I wonder by whom?"

"I hope we find out." John replied as they both surveyed the path and tire tracks indicating recent and frequent travel.

* * * * *

"They think someone has been watching the house from up there?" Lenore asked JD.

"They're pretty sure. They found tire tracks and a footprint," he replied. "They've assigned extra agents at either end of the road."

Lenore paced around the guest room as Leah and JD watched. "I just don't understand why they didn't say something to *me* about it." She pointed to her chest. "I should be made aware of any situation that comes up." She turned back to JD. "What kind of footprint?"

"Maybe Gregor didn't want you to get upset, considering," Leah offered.

JD glanced at his wife. "Considering what?"

"Lenore's pregnant."

Both women watched JD's reaction. His eyes immediately focused on her abdomen, then back to her face. "You are?"

"Well, I have to go to the doctor on Monday for confirmation, but it looks that way."

He reached out and gave Lenore a huge hug. "I'm happy for you, Lenore. Gregor, too."

Lenore smiled. "Thanks JD."

"What do the boys think?"

"We haven't told them, yet. I want to make sure, first." She waved her hand. "Now, what's this about a footprint?"

The sound of Grant's voice pushed the discussion of footprints down once again. "Mom, where are you?" He called from the stairway.

Leah and Lenore emerged from the guest room. "What is it, Grant?"

"I just want to sit down and talk to you about some concerns. Leah, I have no problem with you and JD being a part of the conversation. I'm going to grab Joel."

Soon, Lenore, her two sons and her best friends were sitting around the kitchen table.

"Okay, Grant, what are your concerns?" She intended to be honest with him, no matter how uncomfortable it might be.

Grant glanced at Joel first, then his mom. "We've been talking and we really don't think we know the whole story. Why did John and Gregor react the way they did? Is there part of this whole situation we don't know?" He glanced again at Joel, who nodded. Then he asked, "Mom, are you in danger?"

Lenore drew in a deep breath. She hoped there would never be a need to discuss it, and yet, knew it would surface someday.

"I guess it's time to tell you everything." She glanced at Leah, who nodded and patted Lenore's hand. JD sat quietly, ready to listen to more than he had been told, as well.

"Things didn't exactly happen the way you've been told when I got injured in Kansas City. Truthfully, it's far from what you've been told." She searched their eyes for indications of fear or anger that they had not been told all of it from the beginning. "Please don't be upset that I didn't tell you. I thought it best at the time."

"I think I understand, or will. Joel?" he asked his brother.

"Mom, we love you no matter what, but I think you need to believe we can handle it. We're your sons."

With that assurance, Lenore began telling them of the abduction. She told of the Russian operative who held her at gun point, forcing her to leave the passenger waiting area and get into a van. She explained that the CIA agent surveilling her was distracted when a man had a medical emergency. Lenore still didn't know the man who fell had been shot by the Soviet operative and didn't survive.

Lenore's sons and JD listened with keened interest. Leah watched their reactions.

Lenore filled in the missing parts of how she had been taken from the airport, how she had affected her own freedom and the vision of her arriving at the airport, thanks to Jerry the trucker, before John and Frank had even arrived.

"Way to go, Mom!"

Grant shushed. "Let her continue."

She explained the injuries, which Joel had always believed were from falling at dinner with John, were in fact from falling in the median in her escape. She even admitted that the hole in her briefcase was a bullet hole and the only casualty of the event.

Their eyes were wide. They had a lot to take in. She searched their faces for reactions.

JD sat quietly beside Leah. She knew her husband would be asking a lot more questions when they were back home, but for now, he simply listened.

"Did that truck driver, Jerry ever come for a new pair of boots?" Joel asked.

Lenore smiled at her youngest son query. "As a matter fact, yes, and also the CIA handsomely compensated him for damages to his semi." She nodded her head at the recollection of his bravery on her behalf. "I couldn't have made it without him."

"I recall that young man. You were so adamant about paying for his boots," JD noted. "I thought you had a long lost relative there."

"Nope JD, Jerry saved my life," she assured him. "He's been here twice to visit. He's a great guy."

"If I'd known, I'd have paid for the boots myself!" JD said. "He'd have even gotten some new socks!"

His remark lightened the mood.

"Gregor didn't know about this, did he?" Grant asked. Lenore knew her serious older son would have deeper concerns. She would address each one.

"No, Son, he sat in the Soviet prison and the operatives were going to take me as leverage to make him repatriate and return to being a KGB operative. He had no knowledge of the incident until John told him, after he and Alex were safely here in the United States."

Grant frowned. "Could there be more Soviet operatives?"

"We don't think so. A point was made and the two governments were involved. It would *literally* cause an international incident if they tried anything again."

"Wow!" replied Joel. Grant needed more assurance.

"Then, why are Gregor and John so intense about a possible trespasser."

Lenore didn't have an answer for them.

Leah offered a point of view. "Boys, you must remember who we're talking about here. They're both very intent on keeping your mother *and you* safe and protected. I think it's their nature to *first* suspect the worst, then be relieved when it's not. Don't you?"

Both young men thought about it for a minute and agreed with the logic.

"Wow, Mom, I'm proud of you! You were your own rescuer. Bet those dudes never dreamed you'd do *that!*"

Lenore assured him, "No Joel, they had no idea what would happen if they told a mother they intended to bring harm to one of her children."

"I'm glad we have you on our side," Grant said with a chuckle and Joel nodded in agreement.

"We're proud of you, Mom, and very glad that Gregor and John are the way they are." Joel added. "We're also glad you know how to shoot a revolver and anything else you need. I guess we won't have to worry about bears, either."

Her youngest son had proudly pointed out benefits.

At that moment, Alex walked in the front door with a rifle slung over his shoulder. "They return now. I do not see captives." He headed to the gun safe to secure the weapon.

Lenore ran out the door. Marushka followed her toward the two men and Nicolai. Gregor's arms opened to receive her and they held one another and kissed. John continued toward the house. Both Great White Pyrenees dogs stayed by the embracing couple and moved only when the couple resumed their trek toward the house.

"What did you find?" Lenore asked.

"Certainly not what we were expecting," Gregor said, chuckling. "I believe this is a story best shared with everyone after dinner."

Satisfied there had been no danger encountered, she would wait patiently for the story to be related. It was obviously going to be interesting.

Lenore, Grant, and Joel resumed their walk, relaxed and enjoying the time together. Both dogs accompanied the trio and never focused on anything other than enjoying their human companions. Nikolai managed to find the stick Joel had been tossing for him earlier, and dropped it at his new human friend's feet. The game commenced, much to the delight of the energized male dog. Lenore absorbed every moment and every sound of laughter; so many precious memories accumulating.

After dinner, everyone gathered in the living room to be enfolded in their final evening together, treasuring the coziness of a fire and companionship. Gregor and John shared the story of the two young lovers interrupted by a large white dog and two men; one of whom had a gun pointed at a bare rear end. It brought the expected reaction and Lenore enjoyed watching as Gregor and John had so much fun relating the encounter. It was such a delightful end to a great visit between friends and family. Soon, everyone said their good-nights and hugs were exchanged. Morning would bring the departure of guests, but these sweet memories were now a part of Lenore's new family and truly, a precious gift.

Lenore didn't know the frequently used trail they had discovered had little or nothing to do with the young couple.

* * * * *

Dennis Halvorson drove toward the front range of Colorado. He would be there to greet Leah Chase when she returned home and one loose end would be eliminated. He had hours to go before he would sleep.

CHAPTER 11

Kisses, hugs, tears, and promises boarded the train along with Joel, Grant, Leah, and JD, just after noon. Gregor tenderly held on to Lenore as she waved at the retreating train, knowing no one could see her or wave back. She turned and buried her face in his chest and cried for a bit as he soothed and assured her.

"It will not be long until Christmas time with them." He gently touched her cheek, wiping a tear. "We will have much news to confirm upon that visit."

His gentle reminder brought a smile to Lenore, thinking of the impending confirmation they would be getting on Monday.

"I know. I just miss my boys so much, and Leah and JD." She wiped her eyes with one of the never-ending supply of tissues Leah had produced when they were saying their good-byes. She looked up at her handsome husband. "Please don't ever think the sadness would mean anything else. I love my life with you."

"Of course not, my precious wife. It makes me happy to know you have so much love inside for our sons. Our child will also know this love. We are both blessed to have friendships with Leah and JD and John. They are as much family as our sons and Alex."

Lenore realized it was the first time Gregor had referred to Joel and Grant as *our* sons. She hugged this man who held more than her body. He held her heart.

"Gregor, thank you for being so strong and coming back to me. I love you so very much."

He gave her another hug and a kiss, then they turned and walked toward their vehicles. The drive home in an empty car would be difficult, but she knew Gregor would be within sight of her in the Pathfinder.

*****

The train passengers were silent as they separately reflected on the holiday. Sweet memories were made and new traditions took root. They each needed to see Lenore at peace and happy. They also needed to see Gregor in the role of husband, stepfather, friend, and protector. He far exceeded expectations. A deep love and respect had taken root along with new traditions.

Tears soon dried and Leah settled back to enjoy Lenore's sons and hear their thoughts on the time spent together. JD joined in the discussion. He considered Grant and Joel part of his family as well. Recollections of the fun pushed away sadness, and they realized Christmas was not that far away. Lenore, Gregor, and Alex would visit the front range side of the Rockies, for that holiday.

Leah delighted in knowing she would be making an abundance of purchases for the baby her best friend carried. This child would always be surrounded by love *and* the latest fashions, naturally. She rubbed the silver heart atop her new pinky ring. *Best friends.*

Eventually, the cadence of the train lulled each into a quiet place. Grant and JD both napped. Joel and Leah watched the speeding visions of the Colorado landscape pass by the window.

Leah finished a Diet Coke from the supply of several Lenore had sent along. She reached out and patted Joel's arm, speaking quietly.

"Want to join me in the club car for some cocoa?"

"Sure," Joel said as they quietly got up and left the two men sleeping.

With cups of steaming cocoa and a necessary muffin to accompany the fare, the two settled into a familiar visit. They certainly weren't hungry. Lenore had prepared a huge brunch before taking them to the train station.

"Are you comfortable with your mom's situation, Joel? You know I'm the one you can be perfectly honest with on *any* subject."

Joel nodded. "I know that, and it's appreciated more than you could imagine." He nibbled at the muffin, then swallowed and spoke. "To answer your question; yes," he assured Leah before continuing. "I think it's the happiest I've ever seen Mom. Ever!"

"I hear a hesitation there Joel."

"Well, I wish she lived closer of course, but then …." He shook his head. "I think about the whole incident there with the guns and the seriousness. It's kind of got me concerned. What do you think?"

Leah sipped her cocoa and nodded, studying her table partner for a moment before answering.

"Joel, I've been with your mom through some incredible times. I know you're concerned and I can see why, but I assure you, that lady is not going to let anything happen to her or anyone she loves. She's so strong, Joel." She patted his hand. "There's that new step-father of yours to consider as well. He will always take good care of her, and would move Heaven and earth to make sure she stays safe and loved."

Joel nodded, and Leah saw moist eyes.

She spoke softly to the young man feeling not quite as grown up as he thought. "Your *"Uncle John"* is always going to be there, for both your mom, and Gregor."

Joel nodded, then cocked his head and asked, "Do you think it hurt John to see Mom go to Gregor? They dated a long time."

"Oh, I'm sure, but he is a professional and knew, when the situation changed, he had to step aside. He will always love her, but he also loves that Russian man. Their friendship will never be betrayed."

"He's a great guy."

"One of the greats, for sure." Thoughts of Dennis Halvorson produced a chill, but she kept smiling for Joel. She knew she would tell JD about the encounter when they were alone.

The two continued to sip cocoa and nibble on muffins, finding lighter subjects to discuss. Soon Grant and JD joined them. The family of four were content and enjoyed the return to Denver and Fort Collins and normal lives. They were all at peace.

＊ ＊ ＊ ＊ ＊

With the Pathfinder and the Saab parked in the garage, Gregor pushed the button to lower the garage door. Lenore waited until he stood beside her before opening the door to the house. The lingering odors of a delicious brunch made the house feel even more warm and comfortable. Lenore walked to the living room where Alex had the fireplace glowing and welcomed them home.

"It is sad to see the rest of our family leave, but what a wonderful time we had." He hugged Lenore. "I am grateful that you have given me this family to be part of, which makes it the wonderful time."

Lenore patted his back. He was becoming more comfortable with expressing himself in his new language. Perhaps conversing with Joel and Grant had helped.

"Yes Alex, everyone had a wonderful time. Thank you for being such an outstanding uncle to Joel and Grant. I believe you three have a lot in common." Her assurances produced another hug from Alex. "Thanks for warming the house. The fire makes it even cozier."

Gregor came into the living room after hanging coats in the hall closet.

"I do not see John's truck."

Alex shook his head. "He has asked to convey the regrets. He has assignment and cannot stay. He will be in touch."

"Kind of a sudden decision, don't you think? I thought you three could get some skiing in." Lenore raised her brows and looked at Gregor. "What happened to taking some vacation time?"

Gregor felt certain he knew what the assignment was, but did not want to upset Lenore. "It would appear we will have to ski another time," he assured her. "Would you like for me to make tea while you relax and warm by the fire?"

"No. I can do that. I do have some questions about a footprint JD told me about."

Alex retreated to his favorite spot on the sofa and picked up an abandoned paper.

Gregor followed Lenore to the kitchen, where she filled the kettle and set it on the burner, gathered three mugs and tea, before she stood beside Gregor at the counter and said, "You have heard about the footprint."

"Yes. Tell me about it please."

She met his warm brown eyes, knowing he would. "We found the print atop the hill east of here. Someone had been parking there often enough to make an imprint in the ground with a vehicle. The imprint of the shoe JD called a *floor shine imperial* of a size ten wide. We believe it most likely is from Frank." Gregor didn't want Lenore to know Frank had not been in the area for two weeks and the imprint most certainly had not been made by him. Lenore confirmed it.

"That is not the size Frank wears. He is a 13 narrow. An unusual size. In fact, I teased him once. I told him it looked long and skinny like a raccoon foot, and he nearly smiled." She shook her head. "No, not Frank's footprint." She bit her bottom lip. She had a decision to make. With the thought of Halvorson watching their home, the decision was easy.

"When Leah and I were shopping, I saw a pair of wing tip *Florsheim* shoes on the other side of a rack of clothes. At first, I thought it might be Frank." She shrugged. "When I walked around the rack, it happened to be Dennis Halvorsen. I looked back down at his shoes again and noticed the size difference. They were much wider and shorter than Frank wears."

With the secret out she felt both relieved and troubled.

"Why did you not mention this?" Gregor asked.

Lenore hunched her shoulders a bit. "I guess we were just all so busy I didn't have a chance." She hoped it would appease her husband. It did, for a bit.

He narrowed his eyes. "I wish John had not left. This is something he should be aware of."

"Why Gregor?"

"The CIA reassigned Halvorson because he had become too familiar with you."

"You knew?"

"My precious wife, of course I knew." He pulled her close. "John discussed this with me prior to the reassignment." He kissed her on the forehead and then the tip of her nose. "He felt the familiarity could be dangerous. Halvorson could make an error in judgement because you were becoming a friend, instead of an assignment. He was told to report back to Langley."

"This means he's been watching the house, and not as an assignment, right?"

"It appears so."

"I know Leah absolutely did not like him and for the first time, he made me uneasy." She took a deep breath and nestled into the comfort of her husband's embrace. "He claimed to be shopping for his sister, but Leah thinks he just followed us." She leaned back and looked at her husband's face; A face far more serious than she wished it to be. "He told us not to tell of seeing him so he wouldn't be called in to work," she frowned. "He knew he wouldn't be called in to work here. Do you think he could be dangerous? Should I be afraid?"

Gregor pulled her close again, searching for the right words. "I do not want you to be afraid. It seems if he is still in the area, John should know and we will all be more cautious. Due to the holiday, John put extra agents on duty even before discovering the footprint.

We will not let anyone harm you, my precious wife." He hoped he could keep that promise.

The tea kettle whistled and Lenore turned off the burner and prepared a pot of tea. Both were deep in thought and quietly took cups and tea to the living room to share with Alex.

"I will see if I can reach John." He smiled and touched her cheek. He took his cup of tea and went to the office, closing the heavy oak door, preventing Lenore or Alex from hearing the conversation. She had no desire to hear it.

* * * * *

John Dixon sat in front of the sturdy log building headquarters of the US Forest service. He had called there to speak with Dale Conover about unused or abandoned service roads in the area. The maps he had didn't show the old stuff. He needed Dale's memory. Unfortunately, the automated call noted the hours of operation and asked him to leave a brief message and someone would get back to him, explaining the calls were monitored 24 hours a day. He only then remembered it was Sunday.

The call from Greg on his mobile phone had confirmed the feeling growing in the pit of his stomach. He could now be certain Halvorson continued to surveil the Parishnikov house. He wished he hadn't left there. His mobile phone chirped again.

"Sorry to keep you waiting Mr. Dixon" a man's voice spoke. "Conover is in Iowa on vacation, but I have someone who could help you, maybe more than Conover if it's regarding maps and this area in general. I have a law enforcement ranger, Will Davidson, heading your way. Maybe ten minutes out."

"Looks like I'll wait." He felt anything but patient.

A Colorado Forest Service law enforcement truck pulled up in less than ten minutes. John watched as a woman got out and walked toward his truck. She was tall and trim, dressed in a well-fitted pair of jeans and a brown leather bomber jacket. She sported a brown leather, fleece lined cap with ear flaps pinned up. It might have looked comical on anyone else. She gave John a cursory nod without breaking stride.

Her beauty was accentuated by her dark, sharp and observant eyes. Her face glowed in the late autumn sun with a touch of Native

105

American duskiness. She radiated a self-assurance of someone who knew where they were going and a no-nonsense attitude. It brought to mind another beautiful lady who always walked with such self-assurance. John got out of his truck.

"Mr. Dixon, I'm Will Davidson." She extended her hand to John, who took it and was impressed with the firmness of her handshake. The badge on the jacket identified her as a Colorado Law Enforcement Forest Ranger. "I understand you're seeking information on abandoned roads in the area. May I inquire as to why you may need this?"

Her directness left no question of her authority. John took his identification out of his pocket and handed it to her. She glanced at his credentials and handed them back.

"Same question. Why are you seeking this information Mr. Dixon?"

He tucked the leather case back into an inside pocket. "There is a local family who seems to be under surveillance from an unknown. We are needing to investigate."

"Would this by any chance be the Parishnikov family?"

"As a matter of fact, yes." John's eyes narrowed, wondering how she knew.

"Given the fact you're CIA, Gregor is a former Soviet operative and his brother also lives there, it's an obvious deduction." She maintained a professional seriousness. She crossed her arms and shifted her stance. "I've been there to introduce myself. They're good people. As a matter of fact, Lenore and I have met for lunch a couple of times as well." She looked hard at John. "What's going on?"

"We found evidence of surveillance and then discovered an abandoned road. Hardly more than a path, really. It's been used often and attempts to disguise it were evident. Since you're acquainted with them, you know it would be of concern."

"Absolutely. Let's go inside and we'll dig out the old stuff."

She led the way to the building, unlocked the door and then re-locked it when they were inside. In a sparse office, Will removed her cap and jacket, before going to a locked cabinet. John mentally chastised himself for the unprofessional admiration he felt, as he watched her graceful movements and the way those jeans and the uniform shirt graced the curves of her body. Her black hair was knotted at the back of her head and he wondered, for an instant, what it must look like out of that knot.

"Dixon!"

"Oh, yes, sorry. What was the question?" Did he detect a smile forming at the corners of her mouth?

"I said, give me a hand with these." She held one long cylinder out to him and a second as he took the first. "These should cover all the surrounding area of the Parishnikov place." She carried a third map tube and he followed her to the conference room. The large table would provide ample space to check the topography of the area.

"These *are* old, aren't they?" John noted as they carefully removed the first set from the protective case.

"Yep. Probably the only set in the state." She caressed the old paper with obvious affection. "Not all the information they contain has been copied to newer maps, given some of the roads or trails have been abandoned or overgrown. Some have also, unfortunately, been built on or paved over. We'll see what we can find."

The first set of maps imparted information for the area west of the property. There were two roads indicated on that map of which John hadn't been aware of. Will assured him they were non-existent now, due to building in that area. The area of concern appeared on the second set of maps. There were old roads indicated, east from the valley. John confirmed the more traveled road, running north and south on the east edge of property, which agents were now patrolling. It had been an old logging road. The path discovered, which attempts had been made to conceal, was clearly marked on the old map. It forked off the existing road, meandered east over a ridge, down alongside and eventually crossing a small stream. They compared the map to a current edition. The path didn't exist, but they noted property near the east end, where the path would now intersect a driveway. The driveway led to a homestead.

"Mystery solved." Will noted.

"Well, it explains the trail we found, and where it comes out." John agreed. "Now it really concerns me that someone is using this trail," he indicated it on the map. "They're trying to keep it hidden, and more than likely, using it to surveil the Parish house."

Will looked directly at John. "Why do you call him Parish instead of Parishnikov?"

John looked back into the Ranger's eyes. "When we first accepted him into the United States for political asylum from the Soviet Union, we assigned him a more *American* sounding name. We figured it would be easier to assimilate into society."

"They don't use it though."

"No, not anymore. Lenore won't hear of it." He shook his head. "If you've spent any time with her, you know she is very proud of her husband and what it took for him to be here with his brother."

"Yes. We are becoming friends. She's explained some of their past challenges."

John wondered if he might be one of the challenges discussed.

"I'm glad she's making friends." He liked knowing Lenore was getting acquainted with people in the community. He got back on subject with Will. "Do we know who owns the property where the path ends?"

"We will soon." She wrote numbers on a small notebook pulled from her back pocket with a pen offered by John. They returned to her office where she opened a large book and ran a finger down a ledger page, stopping at a listing.

"The property belongs to the Billings estate. Bunch of brothers bought it forty or forty-five years ago. Most of the original brothers are gone, but the kids and descendants still use it for family gatherings. Always busy there in the summer, but they close it down around the end of October." She closed the ledger. "Nice folks and respectful of the land. I can contact them and see if they've noticed anything or anyone in the area; unless you'd rather do it." She handed the pen back to John which he slid back into an inside pocket of his jacket.

"I think it would be better if you made contact. Tends to put people on edge when the CIA calls to chat."

Her smile brought a smile to his lips.

"You might let them know we will also be checking the property to make sure it is secure."

"I can do that."

"Right now, I'm going to head back to the Parish place. Excuse me, that would be the Parishnikov place."

There it was again; an amazing smile.

"Okay. Let me see what I can find out. Give me your mobile number. I have Lenore's home number. Give me a call when you get there." They walked together to the front counter.

"Will do." He raised his eyebrows. "That raises a question if I'm not being too nosey. Your name is Will? Short for …?"

The lady's dark eyes turned to the ceiling and then back to John. "My full name is Willow Breeze Davidson. And no, it isn't a Native American thing. Although my father's people are Ute, I suspect marijuana may have had a bit to do with my name. My folks were hippies." She shook her head. "I don't tell everyone I meet, so keep it kind of quiet, okay?"

"It will be held in the strictest confidence. I'm a professional secret-keeper, after all," he joked. He couldn't help it. She even laughed at his silly joke.

They stood near the desk, staring at one another until John reluctantly broke the spell.

"Oh, my number. I have a business card, but the mobile isn't on there." He took a business card from the small leather folder encasing his ID.

"Oh, yes." She grabbed a pen from the holder on the counter and took John's card. "Shoot."

With the number in hand, Will raised her eyes, meeting John's.

"Nice meeting you, Mr. Dixon. I hope we meet again."

"I think we should, and please call me John." He kept the leather case open, "it's also necessary that I have *your* personal number." He raised his hand as if taking an oath. "Strictly business you know."

Willow wrote a number on a piece of recycled notepaper and handed it to John. He put the paper alongside his ID and business cards. This was, after all, pertinent information.

With an exchange of handshakes, Willow unlocked the door for John. She relocked the door and watched him get into his truck and pull out of the parking area.

She replayed the conversation as she returned to the office, carefully replaced the maps into the tubes, and then the tubes back into the cabinet, locking it. She signed the duty roster and made a note of the encounter, before donning her coat and cap and closed the building.

"I need to ask Lenore more about this guy," she mumbled as she started her truck and headed home. She could make her calls to the Billings descendants from there.

* * * * *

Lenore sang along with a favorite tune on the radio while preparing a salad for dinner. Alex got her attention and she turned the radio down. "Sorry, what?"

"There has arrived the truck of John. Gregor has gone to greet with him."

"Oh? Looks like I'll need to get another piece of salmon from the freezer." She dried her hands.

"I will get the salmon for you Lenore."

"I'd appreciate it, Alex." She headed for the front door, as Alex went to the garage to access the freezer.

Gregor and John were standing on the front porch, deep in conversation as Lenore joined them.

"Change your mind about staying John?" She hugged herself against the cold. Her teal-blue plaid flannel shirt and blue jeans were just not quite enough for the chill.

John and Gregor exchanged a look that did not go unnoticed by Lenore.

"John has information on the roads of this area and would like to explore further."

Lenore tilted her head. "This is because of Halvorson, isn't it?"

John looked squarely into Lenore's eyes. He knew better than to avoid answering anything but the truth.

"Yes. Gregor has told me of your encounter when you and Leah were shopping. We need to ask him why he's still in the area but trying to cover his presence." He shook his head then tried to put her at ease. "May just need to know we have the routine surveillance under control. He may just be feeling over-protective."

"I'm not comforted by that, John." She expected a lecture about not informing the agents of her encounter, and relieved when it didn't follow.

"Let's go inside to discuss," Gregor suggested.

"Of course. Sorry John. Please do come inside." Lenore turned toward the door and called over her shoulder. "Bring your bags back in, too."

John turned to Gregor. "I'd planned to stay somewhere else to give you a break from all the company."

"There is much to discuss. I prefer your presence here."

John's decision to stay had been made before the invitation. He had already called Willow from his truck phone to let her know he had arrived at the Parishnikov home and planned to remain. His bags were taken to the familiar guest room where Lenore busily changed the sheets on John's bed.

"I hadn't gotten bedding changed yet. It'll just be a minute." She smoothed and tucked sheets then settled the down comforter into place. The guys assisted where they could. She and Gregor folded the extra blanket to lay across the foot of the bed, fluffed the freshly covered pillows and turned to leave. John picked up an armload of sheets to carry to the laundry.

"I'm sorry to put you to so much trouble, Lenore."

"Nonsense! You know we think of you as family. It will never be any trouble to have you here."

She was sincere. She also felt a little more comforted by his presence. One more good guy around could never be a bad thing. She knew Gregor mirrored her thoughts.

"She is right. Please get comfortable." He took the bundle of bedding from John.

Lenore went back into the kitchen as Gregor carried the sheets to the laundry room.

"It *is* good to have him here, isn't it Gregor?" She asked, when her husband entered the kitchen. "We need to get this Halvorson thing under control."

"I believe it is best as well." He stepped behind his wife and encircled her with his arms. "I hope it does not cause you too much work or concern."

She turned and put her arms around Gregor and kissed him, then leaned back. "You know, if we can take one little worry off our minds, it is a good thing. Now, unless you want kitchen duty, go talk to your friend about these roads he's discovered."

He laughed and kissed her again before leaving the kitchen. She noticed the package of salmon retrieved by Alex, who now focused on reading his stack of newspapers in the living room.

Lenore had subscribed to several newspapers and assorted magazines when she moved to the area with her husband and brother-in-law. She knew the more Alex could read and learn about what went on in the world, the sooner he would feel a part of his new country. Alex absorbed the reading material, often bringing an article or even advertisements for explanations from Lenore, and it became an enjoyable bonding time for them both.

Lenore turned up the volume of the radio up. She no longer sang as she worked on dinner preparations. The situation being discussed between Gregor and John intruded her thoughts.

Further exploration of the area John and Willow had found on the map would wait until tomorrow. During their dinner of grilled, maple-glazed salmon, the subject did not get discussed, though Lenore knew it couldn't be far from any of their thoughts. She mentally chastised herself for having put them all into this situation by befriending an agent. Lesson learned. She hoped it wasn't a lesson learned too late.

CHAPTER 12

It was after 7 pm by the time passengers gathered belongings, exited the train, and entered Union Station following the 6:38 on-time arrival. Grant said his good-byes with assurances of staying in touch and headed for the taxi stand. His Cherry Creek condo wasn't far.

Leah, JD, and Joel waited for Leah's luggage and packages, then headed to the secure parking area for the Chase's van. With familiar effort, luggage and packages were fitted into the confines of the vehicle and the trio got comfortable for the hour drive to Fort Collins. The journey seemed short as lively conversation filled the time.

Joel confirmed plans to have dinner with Leah and JD later in the week when he got out of the van, and then walked toward his dorm. It would be a short time before semester break.

Just after 8:30 JD used the remote opener to access their garage, pulled in next to Baby, their '72 Chevelle convertible, and turned off the engine. He got out and headed for the inside switch by the back door to close the overhead door, turn on the garage lights and open the door to the house. He half-listened as Leah talked about what she needed to do before going to bed while she gathered a few items to bring inside.

As JD pushed the switch, the slats of the door began to close noisily and he heard a loud *ping* and Leah shriek. He looked toward the back of the garage and flipped on the overhead lights.

"Leah?" He asked, wondering where she had disappeared. Surely, she hadn't gone outside.

Silence.

"Leah, where'd ya go?" He walked to the back of the classic convertible to see his wife laying on the floor.

"Did you trip on something? What happened?" He stepped closer, ready to help his wife get up off the floor.

Then he saw blood seeping from beneath Leah, her arms still full of her jacket and purse and an empty Styrofoam coffee cup clutched in her fingers. He ran back to the house door and fumbled with keys to open it. He ran inside, grabbed the portable phone, then ran back to Leah. He dialed the numbers and knelt beside his wife.

"Leah, what happened? Leah, can you hear me?" He shook so hard he nearly dropped the phone.

A voice on the phone asked what his emergency was.

"My wife. She's been hurt." He paused to listen. "No, I don't know what happened. There's blood and she isn't talking."

To some, the fact that his wife didn't talk would have been a minor point. He listened to the calm voice on the phone.

"Yes, I think so. Hold on." He leaned down to Leah's face. "Yes, she's breathing. Oh my God, please hurry. There's blood coming from somewhere."

* * * * *

The man standing in the shadows across from the Chase home cursed silently. The interruption of the door closing had startled him as he shot. He needed to verify the kill. He hated loose ends, especially with so much at stake.

As he started across the street, a vehicle came from around the corner. He remained in the shadow as headlights momentarily swept across the area. He could hear sirens and knew if they were coming to Chase's house, the area would soon be crawling with activity and police. The risk was too great and he needed to get back to Glenwood Springs. Lenore would be waiting, after all.

Halvorson removed the suppressor from the stainless Walther PPK .380. He slipped it into his coat pocket and the weapon into the holster beneath his jacket, then walked as quickly as he dared to avoid drawing attention to himself. By the time he had gone three blocks to his waiting truck, the pounding of his heartbeat had become deafening. He checked the area to be sure no one paid attention to the guy getting into the old pickup truck.

"Damn, damn, damn!" He banged the steering wheel. He took a deep breath and closed his eyes for a few seconds, getting himself calmed. He removed his brown leather gloves and slammed them to the passenger side floor with force, upset that he, a professional sharp shooter and agent of the CIA, had possibly missed the kill shot. He had seen her drop and hoped he had succeeded. He knew he'd hit her.

He started the truck and drove slowly away. Perspiration permeated the flannel shirt under his black jacket. He met a police car with lights flashing as it turned into the neighborhood when he got to a major intersection.

He had a long drive ahead but adrenaline would fuel his wakefulness for the journey.

*****

JD continued to listen to the calming voice on the line as he soothed Leah and recited their address and names.

Leah's eyes fluttered open.

"JD? What happened? My side." She gasped. "It hurts so bad."

"Sweetheart, I don't know what happened." He softened his voice and added. "Just lay still."

He listened to the voice on the phone.

"Yes, she just woke up, but she's really hurting bad. Please hurry." He could hear sirens in the distance getting closer.

"Leah, I gotta open the garage door for the ambulance people. I'll only be a second." JD laid the phone down next to Leah and ran to the front of the garage. He slammed the opener with his palm and turned to run back to Leah. Nothing happened. He stopped, turned back to the opener, and pushed the button with his finger. The garage lights blinked and the door started opening as he ran back to his wife.

"JD, why am I on the floor? Help me get up. It's dirty down here JD and close the door. I'm cold." She started to move, shrieked with the effort, and again lost consciousness.

JD cradled her as the pool of blood got bigger. "Oh God, let those sirens be the ambulance." He picked up the phone. "Please, is that the ambulance I'm hearing? She's out again and bleeding so bad." His tears mingled with Leah's blood as he continued to hold her in his arms.

A police car arrived first. The officer ran to the garage to check the situation. His dark blue jacket was emblazoned with FCPD on the back and his name, Armstrong, engraved on a small brass plate opposite his badge.

"Sir, the ambulance is close. Do you know what happened here? Did she hit her head?"

"No! I don't know. Possibly." He shook his head. "We just got home from a trip and I had gone to the front of the garage to close the door and heard her cry out. I came back here to see where she'd gone and found her. I don't know what's wrong." He smoothed her hair. "She's hurt bad and the blood isn't from her head. She's bleeding so much. So much!"

The ambulance backed into the driveway and two paramedics exited the vehicle. They ran to the garage after retrieving equipment.

"Sir, please move aside so we can help her." The paramedic patted JD on the shoulder, assuring him they were there to help. "Tell me her name."

Reluctantly he gently settled Leah's head back onto the floor and stood, moving next to the officer. "Leah. Her name is Leah Chase. I'm her husband, JD Chase."

"Mr. Chase is there anything she could have fallen on?" one of the paramedics asked.

JD shook his head. "No, I can't think of anything. I never saw anything. The door started closing and she screamed and then she wasn't talking. Leah is always talking. Always," his voice broke "always."

The paramedics gently removed the articles Leah had been clutching and began working to find the source of the blood and assess her injuries.

The officer began checking the area for anything that may have caused her injury. JD's eyes never left the paramedics. What the officer found provided more questions than answers. He stepped closer to the back of the convertible, squatted down, and peered closely at the license plate. In the center O of Colorado, he noticed an indentation.

"Mr. Chase, let me show you something. Has this always been here?" He gestured to the license plate.

JD stepped carefully around the paramedics to stand beside the officer, then leaned over to see the license plate of *Baby*.

"What the hell is that?" He started to put his finger into the indentation and the officer grabbed his arm, stopping him.

"Don't touch it, please." JD stopped before his finger found its target. He stepped aside as the officer stood, walked back to his patrol unit, and keyed his radio.

"Possible gunshot injury. May have evidence of bullet on scene. We need an investigative team here."

"What did you say? Gunshot?" He walked to the officer. "Someone shot Leah?" He turned back toward his wife, barely visible as the paramedics worked.

"Mr. Chase, we can't be sure until we investigate. That's what it looks like to me."

"That can't be right." JD ran his fingers through his hair, then stopped as he realized his hands were covered with Leah's blood. "Who would shoot Leah? Why?" He looked to the police officer for an answer neither had.

"Mr. Chase, we're going to transport Mrs. Chase to Poudre Valley Hospital now," the paramedic said to JD. "They'll take good care of her. You can meet us there."

JD looked momentarily confused. He stared at the blood on the floor as they brought a gurney in and lifted Leah onto it, securing her down with straps. He stepped to her side and kissed her softly, "It'll be okay, Leah. It just has to be okay." He gently took her hand and kissed it, holding it to his cheek until the paramedics began to move the gurney to the ambulance. He followed them down the driveway and waited until they closed the door with his wife secured inside, then watched it pull away from the house. The lights and siren added to the commotion around him. He walked back into the garage and back to the side of the officer.

"I need to get to the hospital but I'm not sure I can even drive." He stared again at the blood beginning to coagulate on the garage floor as the sound of the siren receded.

"Sir, I'd prefer you didn't move anything from this garage, including a vehicle," the officer said firmly.

The gathering crowd parted as a neighbor spoke. "JD, I'll take you to the hospital. Liz can watch the house and close everything up when they're done."

"Do you need me to stay here?" JD asked the officer.

"No. Go! We can talk to you later."

JD and his neighbor ran across the street, got into a car, and headed out of the neighborhood.

* * * * *

The Eisenhower Memorial Tunnel lighting had an irritating strobe effect and Halvorson couldn't wait to exit.

He replayed the event in his head again and again, chastising himself for letting the closing door of the garage startle him. He knew he shot Leah; she went down, but he couldn't confirm a kill shot. He should have taken a chance and checked, but that may have necessitated killing her husband as well.

He took a deep breath and blew it out fast. It didn't matter. They didn't matter anymore. No one would be able to connect him to the shooting. Kill shot or not, it would put her out of commission long enough to get Lenore securely into his safe place. His Lenore.

Exiting the tunnel on the west end, he settled into the drive and relaxed again. He checked his fuel gauge and decided to make a stop in Dillon. With a fill, he would have plenty of fuel to get to his destination without further delays or detours.

At a brightly lit 24-hour gas station, Halvorson filled the truck and went inside. After scrubbing his hands in the less than pristine restroom and air-drying his hands for lack of towels, he grabbed a cup of coffee and a sandwich of questionable vintage, paying in cash. No need to leave a paper trail of any kind, he reasoned. The heavy middle-aged clerk had puffy bags under his eyes, no upper teeth and a jutting underbite that reminded Halvorson of an abused bulldog. He had greasy, straggly hair and needed a good shave and shower. He hadn't been cordial which suited Halvorson just fine. He hated chit chat, especially with people who didn't matter.

When he got back into the truck, he looked in the rear-view mirror at himself, checking his own teeth. He was sure they could do with a good brushing, but they were sound and even and white. He smiled at himself. He and Lenore were going to make a very handsome couple.

Dennis Halvorson had very light hazel eyes. Childhood classmates had called him *"old cat's eyes"* because they were so light in color. He hated those boys. They should have been friends. Friends didn't point out your differences.

Lenore had never made fun of his eyes. She had even told them they were interesting and nice. Lenore, always so thoughtful and kind. His Lenore.

He got excited at the thought and started the truck, pulled away from the station and maneuvered back onto Interstate 70 westbound. He encountered little traffic, other than an occasional semi. He sipped the weak coffee and took generous bites of the sandwich, knowing he needed to fuel his body. That would be the only thing the stale, tasteless sandwich would provide.

Halvorson hated litterbugs with a passion, but as he tossed the debris from the window, he smirked. No one would connect him to the shooting with a cardboard cup and a sandwich wrapper in his vehicle. He knew what and how to look for evidence, so don't leave any.

It would be nearly four hours before he would arrive at what he now referred to as his *staging area*. The operation had begun. He needed to stop thinking of the event in Fort Collins and concentrate on what came next. That was tangible; something he had control over and he loved control.

The remote cabin, chosen because of its seclusion, looked shabby and uninhabited. He spent every off-duty hour working to make the inside comfortable, without disturbing its outer appearance. He had purchased several generators from towns as far away as Grand Junction, Rifle and even one from Gunnison. They wouldn't connect him to Glenwood Springs. Cash bought silence and bad memories. No point in advertising his intent.

He knew people would start looking for Lenore, but he hoped she would be so appreciative of his efforts, she would tell them to go away because she had finally met her one true love. He shook off the reality of it not being as easy as he hoped.

He turned on the radio, listening to static. It provided a distraction for his busy mind.

* * * * *

Lenore slipped quietly from the bed and grabbed her robe.

"Why do you leave our bed my beautiful wife?"

She turned back to the bed. "I'm sorry to wake you. I'm just restless and can't stay asleep." She sat back down on the edge of the bed, letting go of the robe.

"Are you anxious about the appointment today?" He placed his hand on hers. "Or what Halvorson said to you and Leah?"

"I don't think so. I mean, I know I'm pregnant. It's a simple confirmation," she reasoned. "As far as the other situation? I know the best are handling it." The faint glow of a nightlight from the bathroom created enough light for her to see her husband's concern.

"Is there something else, Lenore?"

She squeezed his hands. "I'm pretty sure a little cuddling would help."

Gregor pulled back the comforter and sheet. "I would love to cuddle."

Lenore nestled back under the covers with her handsome husband. He settled her hand on his chest where her fingers naturally flexed into the generous hair. She was comfortable and safe, secure, and undoubtedly loved. She just couldn't let go of the anxious feeling and sleep remained elusive.

* * * * *

JD gratefully accepted the clean clothes from his daughter, Shelly. She had come to the hospital when her dad phoned and as soon as she had assurance that Leah was stable, she went to her parents' home to retrieve clean clothes for both and the case of what Leah considered her most vital necessities. She knew as soon as her mom awoke, she would want to check her hair and make-up.

"Thank you, Shelly." JD started to hug her and stopped, looking down at his clothes. Leah's blood had dried and stiffened the material. He had washed his hands several times, but blood remained under his nails. "Sit with your mom. I've got to shower."

He closed the door of the bathroom, shutting out the beeping sound of the monitor beside Leah's bed. He stripped and put the soiled clothes into the "patient's personal belongings" bag provided. He looked at his reflection and saw blood on his cheek and in his hair. He shuddered.

The hot water and antiseptic soap felt cleansing as tears washed down the drain along with the pink tinge of blood. When the water ran clear and no blood remained under his nails, he shut the water off and started drying with what the hospital had provided; a towel scarcely larger than a dishtowel that would never be considered plush. He was thankful to have it. He dressed and ran fingers through his wavy blond hair for lack of a comb.

Antiseptic hospital odors and the beeping of a monitor assaulted him upon exiting the bathroom. He closed his eyes and breathed deeply to control the nausea.

"You okay, Dad?" Shelly asked, noticing his hesitance.

"I'm fine. Any change?" he asked his daughter, stepping closer to the bed to look at the monitors. He knew absolutely nothing more after checking them than he knew before.

The young lady peered up at her dad with tears glistening in her eyes as she sat, holding her mom's hand. "No change. You look better though."

"Feel better, too. Thanks for getting us some clothes." He rested his hand on her shoulder. "I could sure use a hug now. How about you?"

Shelly released her mom's hand and stood to be surrounded with her dad's arms.

CHAPTER 13

Lenore awoke, sat up and wondered how she had managed to sleep through her husband leaving their bed. The light from the balcony door signaled a sunny day already well underway. She tossed the covers aside and headed to the bathroom for a shower to not only wake her, but in preparation of her doctor appointment in a few hours.

With towel dried hair and wearing comfy jeans and a soft blue sweater, Lenore went to the kitchen to find Gregor and John quietly conversing at the table. Alex poured coffee into her favorite mug.

"Thanks Alex!" She accepted the offering, along with his slight bow and hug.

"Good morning, Lenore. I hope you have slept well."

"Yes, I did." She smiled, then took her first sip. "And you?"

"I too have slept well. Thank you for asking." His language skills were improving and Lenore was proud of him.

She sat in the chair next to her husband and noticed their silence.

"What? Why'd you stop talking? I've interrupted something." She looked from one to the other for a reply. John answered.

"We've just been discussing the Halvorson situation. He appears to have either left the area or for some reason, is avoiding us. Interesting, your encounter on the shopping spree." He drummed his fingers on the stoneware mug. "What I find interesting is that Leah didn't like him. She likes everyone, except your ex."

"He also really made *me* feel uneasy, especially the way he glared at Leah when he said she had to be sure to keep his secret." She mimicked a glare. "I don't know what that was all about, but we didn't like it."

"That's why we're trying to locate him, to just see how he's doing. One thing to be over protective. Quite another to make you or Leah feel uncomfortable." He took a sip of coffee. "We believe that more than once he's watched the house by using an old trail to get to and from the area undetected."

Gregor explained further, "This is why we are interested in the maps of the area. John has met and spoken to your friend, Willow."

"Oh! Don't you just love her?" Lenore suddenly became giddy. "We think she is *the* best and I've been planning on introducing you two!" Lenore noticed the smile settling on John's mouth.

"She seemed very adept at her job," he offered.

"Adept, huh?" She laughed. "I'm glad you two met. You're both very adept you know." She added, "maybe I'll sleep better tonight knowing the whole possie is on the job." Lenore stood. "Right now, I'd better get some breakfast made."

Gregor tilted his head at John, who raised his hands in surrender as the delighted Lenore got busy. They both knew she had decided there would be a connection and indeed, a connection had been made. John's initial interaction with Willow was only a beginning.

Following breakfast, John and one of the agents would check out the trail. John would then find out what Willow had learned from the property owners. He looked forward to the meeting for more than just information.

* * * * *

Gregor and Lenore traveled toward Glenwood Springs with hands entwined. They would soon receive the confirmation of Lenore's pregnancy and were looking forward to telling their loved ones. Merely a step that Lenore insisted they complete before it would be made known to Grant and Joel.

They were assured in the doctor's waiting room that their wait wouldn't be much longer. Lenore still tried to shake an uneasy feeling in her gut and fervently prayed it had nothing to do with the pregnancy. Gregor soothed and spoke quietly to her, sensing her restlessness and knowing she couldn't voice it.

"I hope waiting for your appointment is not much longer. You are anxious, as am I. There will be much to celebrate this evening."

She leaned her head on his shoulder. "You're right, Gregor. I'm just uneasy about something and don't know why." She sat back and took his hand. "We need to decide how to tell the boys; in person at Christmas, or a phone call?"

"Of course, it would be best in person. We will see how the weather will be for the next few days and perhaps drive there to tell them. Would you like to do that my precious wife?"

"Oh, Gregor, that would make it perfect, don't you think?" Her eyes were wide, and twinkled at the idea. "It really is a big deal."

"Then we will make the plans to do this, if you are feeling well enough."

"Oh, a little morning sickness won't stop me." She sat up straighter.

"No. You will not let such a thing stop you from being a good mom," he teased.

"Mrs. Parishnikov, we're ready for you." A tired looking nurse stood at the door with a crisp white cap pinned firmly on frizzy, over-permed gray hair. White support hose covered heavy legs, and very worn, practical white oxfords were on her feet. She gestured with the manilla folder in her hand to the pile of assorted colorful magazines stacked haphazardly on a nearby table and addressed Gregor. "She won't be long. There're magazines to read," in an emotionless, practiced statement to those who waited.

Lenore and Gregor stood and she kissed him and squeezed his hands before entering through a heavy door. Only a small narrow vertical window with wire mesh glass provided any view beyond the door. He sat down and stared as it closed. There would be no magazine interesting enough to distract his focus on the door.

* * * * *

"He's taken time to remove deadfall and bigger rocks. He's used this trail more than a few times, that's for sure." Agent Pete Kelly made note of their route.

Dixon mumbled in agreement as he continued to scan the ground for any clues. The trail provided nothing; not so much as a discarded gum wrapper. Someone that careful and cautious made them more dangerous. They had checked the home and outbuildings on the Billings property. That provided no evidence of anyone disturbing the area for quite some time.

Kelly and Dixon made their way back to the top of the trail where it intersected the perimeter logging road now familiar with agents.

"I guess we know about all we're going to find about this trail. I have an idea Halvorson, or whomever, will be aware we know about it now and won't be using it again. Maybe discovering it will be sufficient," Kelly offered.

John Dixon knew he couldn't dismiss it quite as easily as that.

"Be vigilant in your patrols. Far as I could see from the old maps, there are no other such trails or paths, so he may take this route anyway, possibly challenge you guys. Be on your toes."

"Yes, sir."

Again, Dixon wished Frank Gillespie could be reached. Perhaps not one to be in the great outdoors checking trails, but Frank had instincts; Instincts honed by decades of service in the CIA. The older agent spent years as an operative in Europe and could think like the perpetrator he pursued. He had the added benefit of knowing Halvorson. Frank was an expert at sizing up the people he interacted with.

The cranky older agent also had respect for Lenore, calling her a *tenacious little broad* who knew how to drive like a man. That was borderline affection coming from Frank Gillespie. He had been on the front line following her abduction in Kansas City. He also knew she could handle herself.

John had his next best agent at his side. Pete Kelly was sharp, eager, and efficient. Just under six feet tall, he kept his dark hair neatly trimmed. He had handsome features on an olive complexion, indicative of Mediterranean lineage. Most comfortable in denim jeans and Henley shirts, he dressed professionally when needed. He wore gold rimmed glasses, most often found sitting atop his head rather than his nose. His stocky build might have belonged to a professional athlete had he not chosen to be in his current line of work. His attention to detail impressed Dixon. The agent's relaxed demeanor cloaked a comfortable façade for the man who could immediately explode into action. John found Kelly a valuable second in the absence of Gillespie.

Dixon left Kelly at his car. The younger agent would head to Glenwood Springs in a couple of hours to provide back-up relief for agent Williams, assigned to surveil the Parishnikovs on their errands today. His own replacement would be briefed upon arrival at the Parishnikov home.

Dixon had the feeling something was about to break and he wished Lenore and Gregor could just stay home until they located Halvorson. It would certainly be easier to protect them, but practicality overruled logic. Gregor and Lenore were determined to live a *normal* life. He hoped one day that could happen.

He continued toward the Forest Service office to meet Willow. Serenity settled on his face.

* * * * *

Dennis Halvorson became intently focused. He considered the two syringes he had prepared earlier. One, he knew, would be necessary to get the assigned agent out of his way. The other, well he wished it could be avoided, but reality spoke otherwise. If needed, the stainless Walther in the holster under his coat could put both the agent and the husband out of the picture for good. However, it needed to go down, it would go down today.

He watched the sedan and its occupant. Though agent Williams, perhaps his own replacement, occasionally turned to check the surrounding area, he'd not honed-in on Halvorson's presence. Soon, this inept young man would be having a very long nap and Halvorson would be the agent driving the sedan following Gregor and his Lenore. He planned to rear-end the Parishnikov vehicle and take Lenore. If the husband became a problem, he would be shot. He got out of his truck and headed for the sedan. This agent he approached was no challenge.

Not very good at your job buddy, he mumbled to himself. Evidently no one expected him to be around, so why would they look for him? He stopped when he noticed a crowd of people walking from the building, including Lenore and Gregor. A sudden and very interesting development.

* * * * *

"Let's just go home." Lenore's voice wavered. "I'm just wrong."

"Lenore, what did that nurse say to you?" He opened the car door for her, closed it, and went to the driver's side and got in. "Why can we not wait until the power comes back on for the results?"

"Oh Gregor, I just feel like a fool and a failure at the same time." She sobbed as he held her against his chest. "I can't even give you a child of your own."

"But the doctor did not tell you this, correct?" He tried desperately to understand. "The test results were not presented."

"No." She moved back to her seat. "I gave a urine specimen just before the power went out. Then the nurse said they see this all the time. Women my age start going through early menopause and the symptoms can mimic pregnancy." She wasn't comforted by her husband's concerned eyes. "Oh Gregor, I was so sure." She began searching for a tissue. "She also said I shouldn't be embarrassed. I'm most likely just another desperate woman trying to convince herself she is still young and that a good dose of hormones will fix me right up."

"Lenore, you know your body. This cannot be."

"Let's just go home. They have all they need from me to confirm menopause. We'll just go home and wait for a call with a prescription." A spastic sob racked through her. "I'm just wrong, that's all. I can get over it, but it just hurts right now."

Gregor opened his car door. "I believe I need to speak with this nurse. I will be right back."

"Oh, please don't Gregor." She reached for his arm. "She's had a lot of experience and just knows these things."

"Absurd! It is not her place to say such things to you, whether she has seen such things from others or not." His powerful eyes flashed with anger and Lenore withdrew her hand. He stopped and his eyes softened. "I am so sorry Lenore. I just need to make this person understand what they have done. They have made you cry."

"You really don't need to Gregor."

She accepted a kiss from her husband. He got out of the car and walked back into the darkened medical office.

* * * * *

Dennis watched as Gregor returned to the building. This suddenly became an opportunity he could have only dreamed of. He quickly approached the open window of the agent's car. The younger man jerked when he became aware of Halvorson's presence and reached for his weapon. The needle pierced his neck, and as it emptied, the agent looked at his attacker with shock before slumping against the door. Halvorson sprinted to the silver-brown Saab parked near the entrance of the medical office.

* * * * *

Lenore continued to search for a tissue when she heard a tap on her window. She turned to see Dennis Halvorson.

Lenore reluctantly rolled her window down only two inches. "What are you doing here Dennis?"

"Lenore, you've been crying." He opened the car door and Lenore immediately regretted not locking it after Gregor went inside. She tried to reach the horn to alert Gregor and hopefully the agent monitoring them, but instead, Halvorson jerked her from the car, pulled her arm up behind her back and began leading her away.

"Stop! Ouch! What are you doing Dennis?" She struggled against him. "You're hurting me and scaring me, Stop it."

"Don't scream. Don't make this deadly. If you come quietly, I won't have to kill your husband." His voice was close to her ear, quiet and raspy.

She stopped struggling and began praying that Gregor did not come out the door. She allowed Halvorson to direct her across the parking lot and past the other agent's car. She gasped and stumbled to a stop when she saw the agent slack in the driver's seat. Halvorson hesitated, temporarily losing his grip on Lenore.

"Dennis, did you kill him?" She did not keep her voice quiet and he grabbed her arm once again and tightened his grip.

"Oh, I wouldn't do that, Lenore. He's just sleeping right now. Keep moving and be quiet. We don't need to attract attention, do we?" He pushed her, making her arm twist further up her back. Her shoulder screamed with pain but she did not cry out.

A half block past the parking lot, Halvorson shoved her into the passenger side seat by way of the driver's door on his truck. Lenore's every instinct keened to fight and escape, but the threat on Gregor's life held too much power. She would cooperate, for now.

Halvorson showed Lenore the syringe of fluid. "Will I need to use this on you?"

Lenore realized it must be what was used on the unconscious agent. "No Dennis, I'll cooperate if you'll explain what's going on." She shook hard and didn't feel at all reasonable.

He laughed as he closed his door. "Oh, my darling Lenore. Don't you see, I've helped you to finally escape." He reached out to caress her face. She slapped his hand away.

"Escaped from what? Escaped from who?" She shook her head and yelled, "What the hell are you talking about?"

"Them." He gestured to the sedan. "They've all been holding you against your will for that Commie. You've been brainwashed and I'm here to take you away from all that. You're free. Finally free!" His delight with himself faded when he realized Lenore didn't react as he thought she should. She plainly didn't understand the wonderful thing he had just done for her.

Her eyes were wide and dark green as she spoke slow and clear, "Dennis, I'm with Gregor by choice. I've not been brainwashed! We've talked about this." She put her hand out to open her door and found the handle missing. "Let me out of here, Dennis. You will not get into any trouble if you simply let me go now." She turned to face her abductor and raised her voice. "Now Dennis! Let me out of here ... *now!*"

"Oh Darling, I so hoped you would show more gratitude. It looks like I'll need to give you a little nap. This de-programing may take a bit longer than I'd hoped."

With a swift move, he plunged the needle into her thigh, through her jeans.

"You idiot! What are you doing?" She reached out to punch him in the face and found her strength fading along with her vision. "No. Please nooooo."

* * * * *

John contacted the Company to let them know what had been learned or suspected regarding Halvorson. They confirmed the agent had not arrived at Langly. John advised them of his intent to communicate with Willow before ending the call. He opened the door of the Forest Service building and went inside.

Willow looked up. "Nice to see you again, John. Any new developments?"

Oh, that smile. He walked closer and stood at the polished wood counter where the beautiful lady stood on the other side. "No, just wanted to check back with you and decided it would be better in person. Did you speak with the property owners?"

"Yes, I did; in fact, I just got off the phone with one of them. They all said the last family gathering was to sort of close down things for the season and as far as they knew, no one had been up there since the middle of October. They hadn't noticed anything unusual at that time."

"Well, that confirms that it wasn't any of them." He drummed his fingers on the counter. "Agent Kelly and I checked out the property, house and entire route and saw nothing to note except that the trail had been cleared and used repeatedly."

Willow crossed her arms across her chest. "That's not good. Do you have any ideas who it might be?"

"Yes. One of our agents, Dennis Halvorson, is at the top of the list. He got reassigned from the Parish, I mean Parishnikov surveillance. Doesn't look like he took it well."

Willow noted John's correction with a nod. "Why the reassignment? Has he been questioned?"

"He got a little too close to Lenore. Her kindness and openness evidently signaled something more to him than it should have." He met Willow's concerned eyes. "It can cloud your judgement when you're on a surveillance task."

"I can see how that could happen with Lenore. She's such a good person."

John didn't reply. He knew the consequences of surveilling Lenore all too well. "He's either left the area or is in hiding, so we haven't been able to question him. Wish I knew. He made Lenore and her friend Leah very uncomfortable last Friday when they ran into him. Leah really disliked him."

"From what I know of Leah, she likes everybody, except Lenore's ex. I don't think anyone likes *him*." She rolled her eyes, then got serious. "You need to find this guy John. How do I help?"

"I wish I knew. Do you have property listings that would tell us if Halvorson owns property in the area? That might be a start."

"Consider it done. I'll see what I can find out here with the other rangers and contact area county records as well."

"There is one more thing I need to ask." John looked directly into her serious dark eyes.

"Sure. Ask away."

"It's about your favorite places to eat in these parts. I thought perhaps you could allow me to buy you dinner one evening."

"I'd like that, John. There are myriad choices."

They both stood, searching for something to say, until one of the other rangers poked his head out of an office.

"Agent Dixon, you have a call. Sounds urgent." He pointed to the other end of the counter where John stood. "You can use that phone. I'll transfer."

"I told headquarters I would be here. Looks like they've forwarded a call." John and Willow walked to the other end of the counter where he picked up the phone.

"Dixon here."

"Dixon, you have a call from JD Chase. Says it's important he speak to you right now."

"Patch him through." After a series of clicks he heard JD's voice.

"Hello, John? John it's JD, are you there?"

"Yes JD, what's going on?"

"I think you need to know Leah's been shot."

John's eyes widened. "Shot? When? Where? Details JD."

As JD related the events of the last evening to John, the agent continued to glance at Willow. Willow knew of the close relationship between Lenore and the Chase family. This would devastate Lenore.

"So, she's stable? Is she talking? Do you know who shot her?" John ran his hand over his face.

"Well, she was unconscious overnight. They had to do some surgery to patch her up and extricate the bullet but she woke just a little while ago. The first words out of her mouth after she woke, and knew what had happened to her, were to get in touch with you."

"Interesting. What else can you tell me?" John observed Willow standing nearby, intent on listening.

"All she remembers is getting out of the car in our garage. The rest is fuzzy. She also hit her head on the garage floor, which gave her a concussion. I never even heard a gunshot. I heard a *ping* sound and didn't know about the gunshot until the police found an indentation in the Chevelle's license plate. I just knew Leah was bleeding and unconscious."

JD hesitated for a couple of beats, then continued, "One thing she said for sure is that you are not to tell Lenore, because of, well, I guess it's okay to go ahead and say it; Lenore told us she is pretty sure she's pregnant when we were there and Leah said you knew as well."

"Yes, they are currently at an appointment this morning to confirm, I believe. I can understand not wanting to upset her. Anything else?" John looked at Willow, knowing she wouldn't be aware of Lenore's probable pregnancy.

"Yes, she says she's sure its Dennis Halvorson because he was so threatening when she met him on the shopping spree. Now, I don't know if it's pain med or the concussion, but I've been ordered to report all of this to you."

"We'll need to get in to touch with the Fort Collins detectives." He pulled the phone away from his mouth and asked Willow for something to write on, and received a stack of recycled paper. "OK, I have some paper, give me all the details you can think of, JD; your address, the officer's name to start."

*****

The lights flickered on as Gregor spoke sharply to the nurse. She did not defend herself from his verbal assault. The doctor stood beside Gregor.

"You are very wrong in what you have said to upset my wife. It is not your place to say such things to her, whether it may be factual or not. You owe her an apology and I sincerely hope you will receive a reprimand from the doctor. You did a very foolish and thoughtless thing and you have no place in this medical environment." He knew his eyes were flashing with anger because she flinched more than once during his verbal rampage.

"Mr. Parishnikov, I assure you this nurse will be reprimanded. I wish to convey my sincere apologies to you and your wife." The middle-aged doctor put his hand on Gregor's shoulder; more to calm the infuriated husband than just a friendly gesture. "If you will wait a few minutes, we will have the results from your wife's pregnancy test. Please, ask Lenore to come back inside."

The nurse turned away and walked back through the door to the exam rooms. Gregor could detect a sob of emotion. He was glad. He turned to bring Lenore back inside when a young woman burst in through the front door, excited and out of breath.

"Someone needs to call the police. I think a woman's been kidnaped."

Gregor's heart began pounding as he pushed past the woman and ran outside to the vehicle. Lenore was not there. The passenger door stood open and her purse and jacket were still inside. He checked briefly around the area, then ran back to the building.

The receptionist had the police on the line and Gregor turned the young woman toward him.

"Please, did you see the woman in the Saab? A woman with dark hair right out there?"

"Yes, that's the one. She had on a light blue sweater. They didn't see me from across the parking lot and I was afraid to interfere. He looked dangerous. I watched and saw what they got into." She gestured. The panic in her eyes mirrored his own. "They headed north. It's an older Ford truck. Sorry, I couldn't get a plate number."

Gregor bounded out the door and got in the Saab. He started it, backed out from the parking spot, slammed it into gear and used the jolting forward momentum to close the gaping passenger door.

Turning onto the street and heading north, he did not focus on traffic. He strained to see as far ahead as he could for the truck and in his distraction, drove through a red light. A sound of screeching tires and the glimpse of a white delivery van, just before they collided, ended his pursuit.

The world spun for what seemed like eternity with Gregor's head shoved into the door window glass. A few moments later, he shook his head to clear his thoughts. The driver's side of the vehicle was impaled on the front of the delivery van, making the door inoperable. He climbed across to the passenger side of the vehicle and stumbled from the car. He thought briefly of continuing by foot, before he realized it was a hopeless situation. He needed to get to a phone.

As a police car pulled up to the collision, Gregor ran to it. He pulled his wallet from his pocket and handed it to the policeman exiting the patrol car.

"Please sir, my wife has just been kidnaped and I am in pursuit." He ran the fingers of his free hand through his hair in frustration, then pointed to the two vehicles, speaking quickly, "I accept full responsibility of this collision, but I must get to a phone."

The officer refused the wallet. "I need for you to stay here. Please take your information out of your wallet and hand it to me."

Just then, the officer's radio crackled with a voice stating an APB had been issued for a gray colored older Ford truck, possible kidnap victim inside, last seen heading north. He eyed Gregor, who held out his driver's license and registration.

"Your wife?"

"Yes. Please, I must call for help."

The officer held up his hand, then accepted Gregor's identification cards. "The police have already been called."

Gregor shook his head. "No, I must call the CIA. I must get back to the clinic."

Shock registered on the officer's face. He looked at Gregor with true concern. "I have your ID and you've accepted responsibility. I don't know what's going on here, but go. Good luck, sir."

Gregor ran the four blocks back to the clinic and pushed past two police officers and a growing crowd of onlookers.

Gregor reached behind the counter and took the phone from the receptionist. "Give me a line. I must make a call." His lungs were gasping for air as he dialed the number.

* * * * *

"Hold on JD, I'm getting another call. Stay on the line please." John nodded to the ranger who pushed a button to keep the call on hold and pushed another to connect John to the second caller.

"Dixon here."

"Lenore has been taken by Halvorson!"

John felt like the earth disappeared from under him and he held onto the counter. Willow put her hand on his arm.

"When? Where did this happen?" He tried to maintain professionalism, but it was wavering. "Tell me everything."

"We were at the doctor's office and I went back inside. John, I left her alone in the car. I simply did not think."

"Are you sure she's been taken? Could she have simply gone for a walk?" He shook his head. "Where's agent Williams?"

"I have not checked. I do not know."

Willow suddenly understood and mouthed *Lenore*. John confirmed it with a nod. She ran back to her office and took a key from her pocket to unlocked a cabinet, removing a Sig Sauer P226 and holster from within. She strapped the holster around her waist and checked the magazine of the gun to make sure it was empty. She went to another cabinet where the other ranger had already opened the door and handed her a box of 9mm cartridges. She began loading rounds into the magazine, keeping an ear on the conversation. John took note of her actions.

"Willow and I will be there as soon as we can. Don't touch anything. Make the witness stick around, too. Check on Williams and I'll meet you there."

Willow put her jacket on, pocketed the remaining box of cartridges and stuck the hat atop her head. "Let's go. We're taking my service truck. It'll have more authority around here than your rental truck. Besides, this just became a personal matter for one Colorado Ranger, as well as the CIA." She emerged from behind the counter. "I'm also an expert at search and rescue."

"I have to call CIA central and let them know what's up." He punched in the number he knew by heart. It seemed time moved in slow motion as he wove through the many connections necessary to relay the proper information and leave a message for the director. Dixon dropped the phone back into the cradle and turned to the door as Willow opened it.

They both ran to their vehicles. John unlocked his truck and grabbed his weapon, a Heckler and Koch P7M8, a shoulder holster and a box of 9mm cartridges, and sprinted back to Willow's truck. She had already started it and backed out, ready to drive out of the parking lot.

Then John remembered JD was on hold.

"Wait." He jumped out of the truck and ran back into the building. He grabbed the phone and signaled the ranger that he was reconnecting with JD. He steadied his breathing.

"Sorry to make you hold JD. We have a situation here and I need to let you go for now. I will be back in touch as soon as I can. Please call if there's any change with Leah. We're working on the Halvorson connection." He started to hang up and put the phone back to his ear. "Give Leah my love. I'll not tell Lenore what's happened."

As he ran to the truck, he wished the only concern he had would be to keep JD and Leah's situation to himself. Right now, he couldn't tell Lenore if he wanted to. He felt a lump in his throat and took a deep breath as he fastened the seatbelt. They were already out of the parking lot as he did. He tried to reach agent Williams, the assigned agent, on Willow's radio. No response. A sense of dread increased.

＊＊＊＊＊

Dennis Halvorson was pleased with himself and glanced at Lenore. He softly stroked her hair.

"So beautifully she sleeps." He struggled with the thought of it being drug-induced as his attention returned to the road ahead. "You are finally free my darling and we are going to have such a perfect life together."

CHAPTER 14

JD walked into Leah's hospital room and immediately noticed the absence of a beeping monitor. The IV bag was gone as well. Leah lay on her side and strained to turn her head to see her husband.

"You'll have to come to this side of the bed. This is my new necessary position."

He went to the other side of the bed, leaned over his wife, and kissed her.

"You look practically normal, except for the reclined position." He chuckled. "I got in touch with John. He won't tell Lenore and sends his love. He said they're checking on Halvorson."

"I take offense at the term *normal* you know. What did John say about my theory?" She pointed to the water glass on the table at the foot of her bed and wiggled her fingers. "Does he think Halvorson's the one who shot me?"

JD retrieved the glass, put in a new straw, and filled it with water from the small thermal carafe. He bent the straw, allowing Leah easier access to the drink. She drank deeply before handing it back.

"John said they were checking on the Halvorson connection. That's about it. He put me on hold for a long time, then came back and said they had a situation there he had to take care of. Kind of cut it short."

"JD, that doesn't sound right. Call Gregor and Lenore." She tried to reach the phone on the table beside the bed without luck, then sank back onto the bed with a pain induced grimace.

"Let's get some pain med in you before we do anything else." He pushed the call button.

"Oh, I'm fine. Let's call Lenore. I think something's going on."

"Leah, my first concern is you." He kissed her forehead. "You'll sound better to Lenore if you aren't in pain, right?"

"Oh JD, I just hate to admit it when you're right, but you're right. Tell those nurses to hurry!"

* * * * *

"What the hell? That's Gregor and Lenore's Saab. Stop!" John demanded. It wasn't necessary. Willow had already pulled to the side of the street.

John ran to the officer busily taking information from the driver of a white delivery truck. A tow truck was intent on hooking up the Saab.

"What happened here? Where's the owner of the Saab?" John took his ID from an inside pocket and showed it to the officer.

The officer looked at the ID. "He ran back that way." He gestured with his thumb. "Told me he had to make a call to the CIA. Evidently a call to you." He handed the leather ID case back to John. "What the hell is going on here? He said his wife had been kidnaped. What's the CIA connection, if you don't mind my asking?"

"With all due respect officer, right now I can't get into it. Please finish what you're doing." He handed a business card to the officer. "Here's my card. Take that car to the Parishnikov residence. I'll foot the bill."

"I can do that." The officer nodded, then stopped John by the arm as the agent turned to leave. "Agent Dixon, I'd appreciate it if you were in charge of this." He reached inside the car and handed Lenore's purse to the confused agent. "Evidently the purse was forgotten by her and her husband both. Good luck in finding this lady."

John nodded, grabbed the purse, and cradled it like a football as he sprinted back to Willow's truck. He got back in, pointed south, and said in a voice that sounded far more in control than he felt, "Go."

Willow drove around the wreck and continued south. John scanned both sides of the street and when he saw the clinic sign, he pointed. "There."

Willow turned into the lot filled with police cars and a large crowd of curious people just cruising through to check out all the excitement. She stopped the truck away from the crowd and they ran to agent William's car where Gregor stood.

"Is he dead?" John asked the attending paramedic.

"Who are you?"

John produced his identification again. "I'm his boss."

The paramedic raised his brows upon reading the ID. "He's still alive. We aren't sure what's happened, sir. There don't appear to be any injuries, but we're going to transport him to the hospital. They'll find out."

Agent Kelly pulled his vehicle in behind the incapacitated agent's car, jammed it into park and ran to John's side.

"Is he dead?"

"No. They'll transport him to the hospital. Stick around and process the vehicle for possible evidence. Clean out the car and secure his service weapon. Arrange for the vehicle to be transported to the house." Kelly knew John referred to the place agents called home while on assignment in the area.

"Yes sir."

"I want you at the hospital if and or when he gets lucid enough to answer questions."

"Yes sir," Kelly affirmed.

John walked to Gregor and Willow. He put a hand on Gregor's shoulder.

"We'll find her Greg. We'll find her." He tried to assure himself as well as his close friend. "When did the car wreck happen? Are you injured?"

"I am alright. I tried to pursue and had the collision. I should never have left her alone in the car. I did not think." He was beyond anger, beyond frustration. A very frightened husband whose whole world had been taken away stood in front of John. His eyes were huge and wet. He paced, hugging the purse Willow had given him to his chest. "John, what have I done to our wonderful Lenore? Why did I not protect her from this?"

"It shouldn't have mattered that you left her alone in the car. We've always had agents protecting you both. Unfortunately, Halvorson took Williams out of the picture." He gestured to the comatose agent being removed from the car and put on a gurney. "You had no one. We don't know yet what kind of poison could be involved." He shook his head and looked at his friend. "Not your fault Greg. Not your fault. Halvorson caught us with our pants down."

Willow agreed and assured Gregor, "That's right Gregor. You had no idea this would happen." She used her sleeve to wipe a tear from her cheek. "Right now, you need to be sharp and clear minded." She needed to remind herself to be the same as she spoke. "You have to help us find Lenore and deal with that creep that took her."

Willow's words seemed to make an impact, and immediately the stricken husband disappeared behind the sureness of an elite former KGB operative. The eyes belonged to a man ready to do whatever necessary to achieve his goal.

"Yes." He searched the lot, momentarily confused. He turned to John, "I need transportation."

"Come with me." John said. They walked to the agent and John spoke briefly to Kelly, then turned to Gregor.

"Take Kelly's car and head back to your house. As soon as they get Williams on the way to the hospital, Kelly will use this car. I doubt it, but Halvorson could make a ransom call. I'll get our people working on the phones. Don't worry. The best will be searching for Lenore." Anger flashed in the eyes of the normally controlled John Dixon. "This is CIA priority one. Halvorson's not going to win this one."

Willow had pulled her truck closer to the downed agent's car. John got in and nodded to Gregor and Kelly. The afternoon sun moved closer to the horizon.

* * * * *

Before the downed agent could be moved into the back of an ambulance, Gregor got into Kelly's vehicle and headed for home. He had no concern for speed limits, but made sure to stay aware of his surroundings. One crash today was enough.

* * * * *

"Where do we begin?" Willow asked, then held up a finger as she keyed the radio to answer a call. "It's for you."

"Courthouse." He said to Willow, then to the radio. "Director, we have a situation here." He related details of Lenore's kidnaping as well as the shooting of Leah Chase. Willow listened to the conversation, learning details of Leah's shooting. The agency would be in touch with the Fort Collins detectives regarding evidence gathered at the shooting and determine if it could be connected. The Director offered to send more agents.

"Yes sir. That's what I need. The locals and state police have put out an APB. They could be anywhere, but I'm banking on him keeping everything relatively close. I don't think he's going to harm her, but she needs to be found and Halvorson needs to be dealt with.

"We're heading to the courthouse right now to check on property transactions to see if he's got a place where he could be hiding. Remind me, when did Halvorson first get assigned to this area?" It was quiet for bit as the Director checked, then answered. John replied, "Okay, right. We only need to check recent transactions. That's good." The Director asked Dixon to convey regrets to Gregor. "Yes sir. I'll tell him. I appreciate all you can do."

He waited until Willow had parked directly in front of the courthouse, using the authority her truck garnered. She shut the engine off before they discussed contents of the call.

"This is Halvorson's first assignment in Colorado, and as far as we can tell, has no other connections. That should narrow our search window."

"That's if he *bought* property. He could also just be squatting on abandoned property. Many of the summer resident's homes are closed-up in early fall, like the Billings family. They don't want to deal with snow."

"Well, that's true, but let's start here."

The courthouse doors were being locked when they approached. John placed his ID badge up to the glass and the man opened the door, then locked it behind them. Willow was impressed to see how much weight CIA identification had. She had authority in her own profession and called upon it occasionally, but never received such immediate reaction.

There were precious few property transactions for the last few months. Dennis Halvorson's name didn't appear among them for Garfield County. With a promise from the county clerk to check with surrounding counties, John handed her a card with his contact number and scribbled the Parishnikov phone number on the back. The clerk, an acquaintance of Willow's, said she would also provide the Ranger with any information she deemed valuable.

"Give me a call either way," John said. "This is a matter of life and death."

"Absolutely, I'm on it." The clerk turned to the phone and started punching in numbers as John and Willow walked out the door.

"Dry hole. Now what?" Willow asked when they got outside.

"We know that he headed north out of city center. I'll ask for locals to check for eye witnesses, but unless someone saw the truck, he could also have hit I-70 and gone either way."

They stood in front of Willow's truck. He slipped his hands into his jean pockets and looked up at the late afternoon gray sky. "This case is damned personal."

"I know John. For both of us." She put her hand on his shoulder. "You've been in their lives far longer than me."

"Better take me back to my vehicle, Willow."

"Yep. I may have a few cages to rattle of my own," she said as they both got back inside the truck. "I think we should also alert the media and get it out there to see if anyone might have seen something."

John turned to the beautiful woman behind the wheel of the truck. "I'm very glad we met. It's good, knowing you care about Lenore. It means a lot."

"Lenore is a new friend and we have a lot of life ahead to share as friends. It's a connection I don't want to lose and I'm glad I met you, too." She glanced at him and winked. "She's right. You *are* a good guy."

* * * * *

Gregor slid to a stop as two Great White Pyrenees barked at the vehicle's abrupt and sudden intrusion. As soon as Gregor exited the car, the familiarity immediately produced wagging tails instead of threatening barks. Alex stepped onto the porch.

"Where is your vehicle Gregor? Where is Lenore?" the younger man asked. Marushka continued to watch the car, as if expecting Lenore to get out and join them. "What is not right with this?"

"Lenore has been taken. The agent Dennis Halvorson has taken Lenore," he said to his brother as he bounded up the steps and into the house. Alex followed.

"What will there be needing for me to do for this?" Alex would have much preferred to speak in his Russian language, but the promise he made to Lenore to use English stopped him.

The phone rang and Gregor stared at it, reflecting on the words John had said regarding a ransom call. He walked to the phone and picked up the receiver.

"This is Gregor Parishnikov."

"Gregor, this is JD, Leah wants to talk to you."

The last thing Gregor wanted to do was have a friendly chat, but he waited as JD transferred the phone to Leah.

"Gregor, what's going on. Something is wrong, isn't it?" asked Leah.

Gregor closed his eyes and couldn't speak for a moment. He knew she must be told, but he also knew it would be painful for her to hear.

"Yes, Leah, there is indeed something wrong. Dennis Halvorson has taken Lenore. We are beginning a search." He heard the phone drop and a few seconds of jostling before JD spoke.

"What did you say to her, Gregor? She just fainted. What's wrong?" Gregor could hear nurses answering a call button in Leah's room.

He relayed the information to JD and listened quietly as JD began telling Gregor of the shooting the previous night.

"This cannot be a coincidence. I must tell John."

"I called him a while ago, so he's aware of her getting shot. I think you must have been calling him about then, because he was sure intent in getting off the line. Said he had a situation." He stopped to tell the nurse that Leah had just received some bad news, then continued. "I know you're undoubtedly busy, but let me know if there's anything we can do from here. I know we'll be praying."

"Pray hard JD, for both of our wives."

It was then that Gregor realized he needed to let Lenore's sons know what had happened.

"One thing please, JD … our sons must be told. I do not know how to begin to tell Joel and Grant. I do not believe I should do this by telephone."

"I'll get it done and let them contact you."

Gregor's eyes began to tear and he couldn't stop. It was only this morning that he and Lenore were deciding how best to tell the boys of her pregnancy. He knew more pain at that moment than he had ever known during the solitary confinement and torture he had endured in the Soviet prison. He handed the phone to Alex and walked outside.

He could hear Alex speaking with JD for a moment. Gregor knew the call had ended when the phone rang again. Alex spoke to his brother from the doorway.

"There is a call from the doctor office. They wish to be speaking to you please."

Gregor heaved a sigh, as he trudged back into the house and accepted the phone from his brother, took a deep breath to calm himself and spoke into the phone.

"This is Gregor Parishnikov."

"Good afternoon Mr. Parishnikov." The doctor spoke with gentle authority. "I realize this is not a good time to be calling, but you need to know that Lenore is indeed pregnant."

Gregor again took a deep breath and cleared his throat. It took a few seconds before he could utter a word.

"I appreciate this wonderful news. I am sure my wife will be very excited to know this information." His voice broke trying to complete his sentence.

"Please, let us know if there is anything we can do."

"Yes, please, one thing. I am asking for all of you to be praying for the safe return of Lenore."

"Mr. Parishnikov, we've all been praying since you left and will continue. Be strong for her."

Gregor simply hung up the phone and turned to his brother who stood in the doorway. They locked eyes for a moment before Gregor could speak. Alex tilted his head, waiting.

"You are going to be an Uncle Alex for a third time."

Gregor walked past his brother and out the front door. He fell to his knees in the now dormant grass on his front yard. He spoke often to God, who had brought him back to his Lenore. In fact, he and Lenore prayed together daily, with grateful hearts for their lives together. He prayed now. He prayed fervently with a pure heart for miracles and guardian angels to protect his wife and keep her strong. He asked God to be his eyes and help him find his Lenore.

As he paused, he realized his brother Alex was on his knees next to him. His prayers were in Russian.

Gregor knew the words.

He knew God would absolutely know them as well.

CHAPTER 15

Lenore's eyes were open, her head pounded and her vision was blurred. The incessant drone of an engine magnified her headache, making it nearly unbearable. She kept blinking until she could clearly make out the source of bright light. A single bulb overhead seemed distorted and with a few more blinks, she could see that it had a fine mesh protective screen. *Why had someone done that?* she wondered.

She turned her head and surveyed the unfamiliar surroundings. She turned onto her side and could see a cardboard framed wedding photograph on the wall beside the bed. She blinked several more times before she could see clearly.

"No!" She sat upright and jumped off the bed stumbling to regain her balance. "No, no, no, no, no!" She stood in front of the photograph and tried to focus, shaking her head, not believing what she saw. The wedding photo had been cut from a magazine and put into a frame. Her face had been crudely glued over the face of the bride and Dennis Halvorson's face replaced the groom's image. She felt sick and looked around the room, her eyes locking onto the portable toilet. She ran, lifted the lid, and vomited.

She used the nearby camping sink to pump water into her hands. She splashed it onto her face and closed her eyes, hoping it was a dream. She dried her face with the sleeve of her sweater and then checked her wedding ring. Reassured, she kissed it; a silly gesture she did often.

The drone continued as she walked around the room. There were no windows and no knob on her side of the door. The walls were painted an absurd color of yellow over poorly finished lathe and plaster. A makeshift closet held a variety of plain, shapeless dresses hung on wooden knobs. Another shelf held sweaters, including the one she saw Dennis Halvorson purchasing.

Her eyes widened with the understanding of her situation. This was not a spur of the moment thing for Dennis. Her decision to make him a friend had turned into this.

Trying hard to hold back the panic seizing her gut, she scanned every corner of the room and ceiling for cameras or holes where someone could watch her. She could see a vent grid high up on the wall which she assumed provided warmth to the room. She stood on tiptoe and then stood on the bed and saw nothing that looked like a camera lens from any angle within the vent.

Stepping down from the bed, she continued her surveillance, noting plywood with pictures of outdoor scenes cut from calendars or magazines covering what could possibly have been a window. She tapped it with her knuckle. It absolutely covered a window. Rough cut wood surrounded it, fastened with screws to the wall. She tried to pry the edge of the wood with her fingertips. It had also been glued to the wall. She could also hear the generator running just beyond this wall; a recognized sound, having depended on one during a few power failures in past Colorado winters.

Lenore went to the door and put her ear to it. She could hear sounds of snoring over the pounding of her heart. She knew who slept on the other side of the door. She got down on her hands and knees and tried to see under the door. A felt strip, preventing her from seeing beyond the threshold.

She remembered the abduction and the needle being jammed into her thigh. She rubbed the spot, feeling a small discomfort. She wondered how long she had been out. She couldn't tell if it was night or day. With no light switch in the room, the single bulb enclosed in a mesh cover had to be controlled elsewhere.

She walked around the small room again, taking note of everything, hoping for anything that could be used as a tool or a weapon. She looked under the bed and noted its metal frame. There were bolts holding the bed together and a box spring fit into the frame, supporting the mattress. It would take some serious work to make a weapon out of the bed without tools. She had no doubt she would try.

The shelves were attached with blocks of wood glued together and screwed into the wall. She tried to pull a shelf down, but it wouldn't budge. She found no hairbrush or tooth brush; nothing to use as a tool or be sharpened into a weapon. She ran her fingers through her hair and her tongue across her teeth. She needed both brushes for their intended purpose right at that moment.

"Not hopeless, Lenore. Not yet," she whispered. She had to pee. A sad smile settled on her lips. Leah would have to whiz. She rubbed the heart on top of her new pinky ring. With Leah here, they could take on the world, she thought as she pulled down her jeans and sat on the necessary equipment. It reminded Lenore of her boys' miniature toilet used when they were potty training. It couldn't be much further off the floor. She checked the spot where Halvorson had emptied the vial into her leg. Only a tiny red speck identified the violation.

She flexed her bare feet on the worn floor covering and wondered where her shoes were. Her feet were cold. She hated the redundant pattern of green vines swirling around bright orange and yellow flowers on the worn beige flooring. She hoped she wouldn't be seeing it much longer.

Once again, she wondered how long she had been there and whether, or not her sons knew. Surely Gregor and John and a whole cavalry of people were searching for her. She thought of Halvorson's threat against Gregor and caressed her wedding ring again.

No, she would have to take care of the situation herself. She would not have anyone in danger.

Necessities completed, she washed her hands in the small camping sink and walked back to the door.

Lenore listened to sounds from the other side of the door. The snoring had ceased. The sound replacing it was moaning and her name being muttered over and over.

"Oh, no you don't! Not even in your dreams!" She pounded on the door and yelled. "You let me out of here and let me go home. Right now, Dennis!" She continued pounding. "I know you can hear me because I can hear you groaning, you pervert!" Again, she pounded with the sides of both fists and kicked with bare feet at the door without stopping until she became breathless.

The sound of footsteps stomping and a loud bang on the door startled Lenore and she backed away.

"You be quiet, Lenore. You just stop it!" Dennis yelled.

"No! You let me out of here right now!" She banged the door with the side of her fist.

An eerily quiet voice came from the other side of the door. "I can't do that yet, Lenore. You need to be deprogramed and cleansed. Then we can be together." He laughed quietly. "You sound so anxious."

Lenore smacked the door with the palm of her hand. "I want to go home to my husband."

"Absolutely not!"

"Why Dennis? Why can't we talk about this? Let me out and we'll talk … I thought we were friends."

Again, the quiet laugh.

"I belong with my husband, not you!" She ran her fingers through her hair.

"No. You belong with me. You'll see. You and I will be the perfect couple. I can be patient for now, but soon we will be the perfect lovers, too."

"I would rather die!"

"No, my darling, it will be your precious Gregor and that idiot John who will die if you won't be happy with me." He patted the door. "Our life together will be so wonderful."

Lenore's head reeled and she felt sick again. She knew nothing could be left in her stomach, but she gagged and retched and backed away from the door.

"Now be a good girl and be patient. I will bring you dinner if you will do as I say."

With a raspy voice she croaked, "I'm not hungry. I want to go home."

"This is home for now." His voice was harsh. "Get used to it."

Hearing his retreating footsteps, she slumped against the door, and slid down to the floor.

This looks hopeless. Tears welled up and she couldn't even muster the energy to get angry. Instead, she summoned the courage to stand up and walk to the foot of the bed, knelt, and began to pray with all her heart. She prayed for an answer; for help; for safety for her Gregor and for John. She prayed for her sons to be strong and grow into the men they needed to be if she couldn't get back to see them do it. She asked God to take her life before harm came to anyone else.

Then she cried.

CHAPTER 16

John said goodbye to Willow and agreed they would stay in touch with any information either could find. He sat down behind the wheel of his truck and as he turned the key to start it, the mobile phone immediately rang, startling him. He shook his head and picked up the receiver.

"Dixon here."

"Where do you need me?"

John Dixon had never been so glad to hear Frank Gillespie's voice. "Where are you now?"

"Just landed in Denver. Called HQ to let them know I'm officially back in service. Didn't know if you were back from the holiday. The Director filled me in and said to call you."

"Not sure where I need you yet. You got any clue as to whether Halvorson had property or a house or cabin in the area? He had to have a place in mind before he took her."

The line was quiet for a few seconds. Then John detected the sound of a cigarette being lit, inhaled deeply, and exhaled. He'd witnessed it many times. The sound of a busy air terminal made a distorted racket in the background.

"I recall him saying if he stayed in the area, he wanted regular digs for time-off." Another pause for inhaling and exhaling smoke. Frank had been on a non-smoking flight.

"Where, Frank? Do you have a clue?" John felt anything but patient.

"No. Not positive, but he said once he hoped Grizzley Creek didn't have any namesakes." Another pause. "Personally, I didn't like the guy, so I didn't exactly hang on his every word."

"Right. Anything else?"

"I want a piece of this clown when we find him. He started wearing shoes like mine, but he sure as hell didn't copy any of my ethics. He's dangerous." Another pause. "God help him if he hurts Lenore."

Frank mirrored John's thoughts. He wondered if he could simply turn his head the other way if Frank got to Halvorson first. He knew he couldn't. That ethics thing ran deep in John. That trait came from his grandfather, John Milton Dixon the original, as John always referred to him, not from the CIA.

"Okay, if you can sit tight, I need to make a couple of calls. Give me your number there. I'll get back to you as quickly as I can about where I need you."

Frank gave the number, then the line simply went dead. He never went in for the *10-4 shit*, as he referred to it.

First, John called the Parishnikov house. Alex answered and immediately handed the phone to his brother.

"John, what is happening in this situation? Do you know some news? I cannot stay here and do nothing."

"Might have some idea of where Halvorson could have taken Lenore."

"I am on my way."

"Stop! First, I need to know if Joel and Grant have been told? What about Leah and JD?"

"I have told Leah and JD. I have asked JD to contact our sons. I am certain they will want to be here."

"That will be taken care of. We'll have the boys flown into Aspen from Denver and have an agent pick them up to come to your home."

"Alex will be here for them. I must be doing something John. I will be where you are as soon as I can get there."

"Okay. I understand. I'll be at the agent house. By the way, Frank Gillespie is back and he'll handle getting the boys here. Don't worry."

"Very well. Thank you, John. You are all good friends to my family."

John hung up without a reply and reconnected with Frank.

"Here's what I need for you to do."

* * * * *

Leah answered the phone from her bed, surprised to hear Frank Gillespie's voice.

"Sorry to hear about your being shot. John wanted me to call and see if you or JD have contacted Joel and Grant yet. I'm supposed to make some arrangements, to fly them to Aspen."

"JD called when he picked up Joel and they're on the way to Denver to tell Grant in person. Joel is pretty upset, as you can imagine. I'm glad they're being told before it becomes national news."

"Right." He replied. Leah could hear Frank inhaling and exhaling a cigarette. "I'll meet them at Grant's workplace."

"Frank, you guys get Halvorson. You get him good. You take care of him however you need to, just bring Lenore back safe and sound." She stifled back a sob.

"Leah, we'll find her. You have no idea how bad we all want a piece of Halvorson. It ain't gonna be polite."

A sad smile settled on Leah lips hearing Frank's comment as he disconnected the call. She knew it would absolutely, positively *not* be polite.

* * * * *

When JD had given Joel the report on his mom's situation it took a minute for the young man to absorb the information. He threw things into a bag and followed JD to the car. Joel planned to go to Glenwood Springs, one way or another. JD called Leah from Joel's dorm before they left Fort Collins.

JD allowed Joel's silence for half the ride to Denver, then the kind man spoke.

"Joel, there's a lot of very good people looking for your mom. It'll be okay."

Joel sat quietly for a moment longer, staring out the windshield as they drove south toward Denver on I-25. He turned to JD.

"How can you believe that?"

"Well, believing anything else sure seems to be a waste of faith, don't you think?"

Joel shrugged. The 62-mile drive between Fort Collins and Denver seemed to be taking forever. He needed to be with his brother. He needed this to just *not* be happening. He had only recently learned the truth of what had really happened to his mom earlier this year in Kansas City. Now this? Glenwood Springs and his mom seemed a world away.

JD put a hand on Joel's shoulder. "Lots to think about, isn't it?"

"Unimaginable. I wish Leah could have come with us."

JD had no intentions of adding to Joel's stress by telling him of Leah being shot.

"Well, I guess she figures this is guy stuff here. Besides, she needs to stay by the phone at home for updates, don't you think?" he lied. He had to. "You know she sends her love."

That's when the dam broke and sobs racked the young man's body. "I don't know what me or Mom would ever do without you guys. Thanks for taking me to Grant."

JD kept a fatherly hand on Joel's shoulder a few miles further. His own emotions were a challenge to keep in check. He pushed the accelerator down. He had a feeling if he did get a ticket, considering the circumstances, a judge might be lenient. He really didn't care about a ticket at all. With Joel's directions, they were soon at Grant's office building, parking in the visitor space near the door.

"Look here, we're at your brother's office. Now take a deep breath and let's go get this thing done, okay?"

It seemed to calm Joel. JD handed him a box of tissues from the back seat and waited for a nose to be blown and eyes wiped.

As they walked to the glass and steel front of Grant's office building, Frank Gillespie opened the door for them. Tall and lean, he wore a dark gray overcoat and his normal unamused expression on a heavily creased face. He had great posture, but always appeared to be a little bent over. His eyes were in constant movement; a habit of too many years on surveillance and too many cat and mouse games in the world of covert operations. He was efficient and loved regulations.

"Hey Frank. I guess I know why you're here." JD shook his hand. Joel simply nodded.

"When I saw you pull in, I asked the receptionist to call Grant down here from his office. Figured it'd save time."

The elevator opened and numerous employees, along with Grant Appleby, stepped into the lobby. With his jacket slung carelessly over one shoulder, he rolled down his shirt sleeves. His briefcase was tucked under one arm. His eyes were wide as he strode quickly to his brother, dropped the jacket and briefcase, and pulled him into a hug before addressing the others. People walking past were too focused on their own agendas to pay much attention to the group near the front door.

"My secretary told me the radio reported a woman had been abducted in Glenwood Springs and that it possibly involved the CIA. She knew my mom lived there." He looked from JD to Frank. "I knew it had to be Mom and I started to call when my secretary said I had to get down here."

He shook hands with JD, then hugged him. "Thank you for bringing Joel here." He turned to Frank. "What do you know. Is there a ransom or what?"

"I'm here to accompany you to Aspen on a company jet, then we'll be picked up for the drive to the house. Hopefully they'll have found her by then, but we won't know any more until we get there." He turned back to JD. "Thanks for bringing Joel. Give my best to Leah. Glad the gunshot wasn't life threatening."

Joel and Grant both turned to JD who glared at Frank. "Don't worry about it, boys. She's doing fine, I promise. Talking and everything, as usual. We'll explain later. You just take care of one another. We'll stay in touch."

After JD hugged the boys, Frank ushered them from the building to his rental car. JD walked to his car and headed back to Fort Collins. By the time he returned to the hospital, the CIA chartered flight was already in the air and on its way to western Colorado.

CHAPTER 17

"Grizzly Creek. How familiar are you with Grizzly Creek?" John asked Willow over the phone.

"You're telling me he has her there?"

"Not for certain. He told an agent he hoped Grizzly Creek didn't have namesakes. He'd been talking about finding a place to go when he had time off."

"It's worth checking out … John, you do realize it's dark outside? We can't do much in the dark."

John looked out the window of the agent's house and could see a vehicle from the glow of the streetlight as it parked in front of the house. He watched Gregor exit the Pathfinder and sprint to the door.

"I know." He opened the door. "Greg's here. First light, okay?"

"I'll check the maps and be there well before first light."

"Thanks Willow. Get some rest if you can." As he hung up, he knew none of them would get any sleep this night.

"John. What is the news?" Gregor asked as he closed the door behind him. His jacket remained in his vehicle.

"The boys are with Frank, in the air and on their way to Aspen. Kelly will pick them up and head to your home. I'm going to encourage the boys to stay there with Alex. You agree?"

"I agree. I would prefer to be there with them when they arrive, but I need to find more to do here toward finding Lenore."

"I don't know that there's anything we can do in the dark, Greg." He pulled a chair back from the table. "I made coffee. Sit down and let's try to make some plans."

"What is the information you have?"

John took two large mugs from the cabinet, filled them, and put them on the table. He sat down across from Gregor.

"Frank said he once heard Halvorson talking about getting a place in the area to go when he had a day off. He mentioned a place or area called Grizzly Creek. Willow is going to check the maps and realtors to see if she can find a cabin in that area. It's worth a shot."

Gregor shook his head. "I am not familiar with this area." He drummed his fingers nervously on the table with one hand and ran his fingers through his hair with the other. Forced patience was not well tolerated.

Agent Pete Kelly came into the kitchen from the back of the house. "I smelled the coffee. Mind if I join you?"

Neither man spoke and Pete didn't wait for an invitation as he grabbed his own mug from the cabinet. He had confirmed with Williams at the hospital that Halvorson was responsible for injecting him, thus eliminating interference in the abduction.

"Pete, can you shed any light on this situation?" John asked. "Did you even remotely have an idea that Halvorson might pull something like this?"

Pete stood at the counter and took a sip before answering.

"I didn't, though we all considered him a little different. He'd make a remark occasionally, about having to surveil a Commie." He shot a glance toward Gregor. "I assure you Greg, none of the rest of us ever felt like that," he assured the Russian. His attention focused back to Dixon. "When we'd call him on the remark, he'd just laugh and say he was joking." He sat his coffee cup down and pushed up the sleeves of his gray Henley shirt then addressed Gregor. "Hell, we know you chose to be here and it sure wasn't anything just handed to you. You've earned a lot of respect from us and from this community. We'd give our lives for you and Lenore and Alex."

John looked on with pride as his agent spoke. Gregor nodded and looked down at the untouched cup of coffee on the table between his hands.

Pete took another sip of coffee, then continued. "We know from dealing with the public, locals feel the same. They're proud to know you or of you. Of course, Lenore and Alex are big hits, too. This community, this town … well, they feel almost protective of you guys. I hope knowing this didn't make us lax in our duties. No one saw this coming from within the Company." Pete picked up his coffee cup and took a drink, then addressed both men. "Halvorson's stepped over a very deadly line."

"Pete, we all feel the same," John agreed, "but we'll need to check the emotions. Finding Lenore; that's priority. What happens to Halvorson, should he survive, is up to the courts. It's going to be a damned steep price to pay."

The agent and Gregor exchanged glances. Neither intended Halvorson to survive for the privilege of a trial.

Pete offered the last of the coffee to John and Gregor. Neither accepted a refill. The pot was emptied, grounds discarded and both washed and readied for the next brew. He turned to the two men at the table.

"I knew he'd found a truck and had been working on it. I only saw it once; a great looking gray '48 Ford truck and he was damned proud of it. Sounds like the one spotted when Lenore was taken. Couldn't be two in this area. Had to be him."

"Helps having confirmation," John said.

Pete Kelly reached for his brown leather jacket and keys. "I'd better get on the road. Don't know how soon the jet will arrive in Aspen, but I imagine Gillespie is telling that pilot to pour the fuel to her. John, I'll confirm arrival."

"Thanks. Take care and remember you'll have some important cargo to bring back."

"Affirmative." He nodded to John and Gregor and walked out the door, leaving the two friends with mugs of coffee and many thoughts between them.

* * * * *

Frank offered Joel and Grant cups of coffee from the jet's galley. Both declined. Frank poured himself a cup more out of habit than desire. His hand automatically patted his pocket, where the pack of cigarettes would remain until he landed. He slipped out of his jacket, revealing the shoulder holster carrying his nickel plated .45 Colt Commander. He ignored Joel's "*WOW*" as he tossed the jacket onto the back of the seat in front of his own.

Grant waited until the agent was seated before asking obvious questions.

"What were you saying about Leah being shot? When did it happen? Joel and I both need to know."

Frank took a long drink of the less than hot brew. He shook his head and answered.

"Not much more than that. JD would have those details. I spoke to Leah and she sounded worried about your mom, but normal to me. The Director told me she was shot when she exited her car inside their garage. They were just getting home from the trip to Glenwood. Not a mortal wound, but it did put her in the hospital." He sipped his coffee. "No one knows who or why."

"Do you think it's connected to Mom's abduction?" Joel asked.

"I can't prove it yet, but I'd bet my life it's Halvorson; an agent recently replaced. It wouldn't be impossible for him to make the round-trip to get it done, in my opinion."

"Is he going to hurt Mom?" Joel asked. "What if he kills her?" His eyes were wide.

"Then we'll kill him back, Joel. *Harder!*" He sipped more coffee. "But I don't think that's his plan." He sipped again, made a face, rose, and walked back to the gally. He poured the offending beverage into the sink; glad the flight was only forty-five minutes.

"What about Gregor and Alex?" Grant asked as Frank turned to come back.

"Look guys, anything I say is purely conjecture, but I think he's done what he wanted to do. He's got what he wants." He plopped back into a seat across the aisle from the sons of Lenore and Gregor. He patted his shirt pocket for cigarettes he couldn't have, then grimaced and crossed his arms.

"But, what ..." Joel started to ask.

Frank held up a hand. "Guys, that's it. We'll be there soon and you can grill John and your step-dad." Long days were normal for CIA agents, but Frank became just a little irritable at not being able to have a cigarette. He turned toward the window on his side of the jet.

The two young men stared at one another. Joel raised his eyebrows and Grant shook his head. Both young men turned their focus to their own window. The blackness beyond the wings of the jet would occasionally be interrupted with speckles of light in the landscape below, defining homes or communities, or low clouds reflecting moonlight from above. As they neared Aspen, they became engulfed in clouds and landing lights made blinding reflections against the whiteness. When they were free of the cloud cover, they were only seconds from the runway.

The jet taxied and stopped far from the airport buildings. The boys watched a dark blue sedan pull up next to the jet as the door opened and stairs lowered into place. The trio exited the warmth of the jet and descended into late November breezes, which did nothing to slow them. Pete opened car doors as they approached.

"Hi Joel, Grant. I'm agent Pete Kelly." He shook both their hands. "I'm taking you to the house. You'll stay there with Alex." He turned to the agent lighting up a cigarette. "Frank," Pete nodded. Frank acknowledged his reply with a nod and a plume of smoke.

Joel and Grant got into the back seat of the sedan and settled the bag Joel had brought and Grant's briefcase between them. Frank took one last long drag from his cigarette, crushed it under the sole of his wingtip on the tarmac and got into the front passenger seat. They headed north from Aspen.

*****

Alex bounded out the door and met the sedan as it stopped. Marushka and Nikolai didn't bark. The familiarity of a company vehicle approaching slowly, along with the presence of Alex, gave them assurance.

Joel and Grant exited the vehicle and walked to Alex, who surrounded both of his nephews into an enormous hug. Marushka and Nicolai circled the trio, then sat side by side, alert.

"Gregor is in Glenwood with John. We are to be staying here together. It is what we are instructed to do," Alex stated.

"What do you know, Alex? What's happening right now?" Grant asked. Joel only stared and automatically petted Nikolai's enormous head as his hand was nuzzled by the creature so attune to the raw emotions of one of his new favorite humans.

"I am to call and tell them you have arrived. Perhaps they will have news." He turned to Pete and Frank. "Thank you for bringing my nephews here. I will be taking care of them. Please go and find Lenore. I will let Gregor know they are here, safe."

Grant and Joel shook hands with the two agents who were eager to get to work. Frank hadn't even taken time to smoke a cigarette.

"Stay safe. We'll be in touch." Pete nodded and got back into the car.

Frank uncharacteristically turned to the young sons of Lenore and hugged them, then put his hands on Joel's shoulders "You have the best there is looking for your mom. Hang tough." He walked to the passenger side and climbed in, then Kelly put the car in reverse and backed out of the drive.

The stories they had heard of the curmudgeon old agent vanished as the trio watched the tail lights recede.

$$* * * * *$$

"Greg, it's Alex." John handed the phone to his friend and turned back to the range. He filled a kettle with water and prepared tea for Gregor, knowing the Russian man preferred it to coffee. John had always kept tea handy for Gregor, though visits to this house had been rare in the days when John had been assigned to monitor the former Soviet operative.

Gregor spoke briefly, thanked Alex, and waited while the phone was handed to Joel.

"Gregor have you heard anything? Do you know where Mom is?"

Gregor closed his eyes. The feelings of guilt for it happening in the first place and wondering if they felt betrayed, overwhelmed him.

"Joel, we believe we do know where she is. We are waiting until daylight." He had to take a deep breath to control his emotions. "I swear to you Joel and to your brother, I will bring your mother back. The man who did this will pay dearly for what he has done. Please know we are doing everything we can to make this happen. You are safe there with Alex. That would be what your mother would want. Do you agree?"

"Y-yes. I agree. We just wish we could do something to help."

"My son, I believe the very best thing you can do for your mother's safety right now is to pray very hard. Will you do that?"

"I will Gregor. Um, Grant wants to talk to you."

Joel handed the phone to Grant, then picked up Spot, who had come into the room after hearing familiar voices. They headed for Lenore's art room.

"Hi Gregor. I had a couple of questions."

"Of course, Grant," Gregor replied.

"Do you think that guy is planning to hurt Mom? Be honest." Grant's voice was deeper than his younger brother's, magnifying his concern.

"Grant, we believe Halvorson thinks your mother should be with him instead of me, because I am a former KGB operative. I do not think he will hurt her." He did not want to mention the fact that if she did not comply with the deranged agent, the outcome could absolutely be different. He prayed his Lenore would be wise about such things and cooperate until she could be found and rescued.

"My next question is, how'd this happen since you guys are always under surveillance?"

Gregor only then realized they not only hadn't heard the story of how the abduction occurred, but why they were even at a doctor's office. He did not want to tell them. He knew Lenore would prefer he did not. The fact that Lenore herself did not yet realize she was pregnant, settled his decision.

Gregor told of leaving Lenore alone in the vehicle when he went in to an office to take care of something. The agent in charge had been rendered unconscious by Halvorson, making certain her abduction could not be challenged.

"Understand, Grant, this man will not succeed in this. I have let your mother down by not being there for her when this happened. I assure you I will never stop until she is safely back to all of us. I am so sorry this happened."

"We aren't blaming you, Gregor. If someone is determined enough and deranged enough to do something, they're going to do it. I'm glad you weren't there, because he might have killed you to get her. I know she couldn't have handled that." Grant took a steadying breath, "Do what you need to get Mom back. You and John are the ones who can do it." He nodded at Alex. "We'll stay here with Alex. He'll keep us safe so you don't have to worry about us." He cleared his throat, swallowing his emotions. "You know, we love you, Gregor."

✶ ✶ ✶ ✶ ✶

Willow had only dozed. Being energized by the task ahead, sleep would not come. She stepped into the shower and quickly washed. It helped to have a semblance of routine. She dried, walked into her bedroom, and opened an antique cabinet. She took out a small bundle of dried sage and stood naked, facing east as her grandmother had instructed. Clearing her mind of all except the ceremony, she lit the sage. Blowing out the flame, she nestled the smoldering sage into an earthenware bowl given to her by her grandmother, and placed it on the floor in front of her. She directed the smoke to first cleanse her hands then directed the smoke over her face and to her heart.

She directed it to her arms and legs, her back and front. She lifted each foot and allowed the smoke to bathe them in the centering smoke of sage. The cleansing would clear her mind and spirit, enabling her to receive information from the mountain.

Never an overtly religious person, Willow believed God to be the "Great Spirit" of her father's ancestors. Clinging to vestiges of Native American rites as instructed by her grandmother, her sage ceremony always seemed a natural and necessary thing to do, before embarking on any search and rescue mission.

Her paternal ancestors were natives to the area where she now worked. They were Utes. The Ute Nation was no longer located in the Colorado mountains that Willow called home. They had long ago been removed, and settled on a Utah reservation following the Meeker massacre and Colorow's War. Treaty negotiations and agreements allowed them to continue hunting and fishing in Colorado, and allowed the use of their sacred hot springs. Willow's father swore they were direct descendants of Colorow, the infamous early leader of the Ute Nation. Her Grandmother would always quietly shake her head and shrug her shoulders.

On this mission, Willow prayed deeply for help from the ancient ones, and from God, to help her locate Lenore alive and return her safely to where her heart was content with Gregor.

With prayers finished, Willow smudged the rest of the sage into the simple earthenware bowl to extinguish it and began working her hair into a single braid to fall down her back, securing it with a blue rubber band. Dressing for the task ahead, she layered clothes, preparing for any temperatures or weather conditions she might encounter. Sturdy boots, suitable for rugged terrain and lined for warmth, were pulled on over thermal socks and tied securely. Before putting on her leather coat and fleece-lined cap, she checked her 9mm Sig Sauer and slipped it into the holster strapped onto her belt. It had a full chamber and multiple rounds were in the box she would carry along. She hoped she did not have to take a life this day, but prepared herself to do so if necessary.

She would meet up with John, and head for a place she knew to be perfect for hearing what the mountain would have to say. Grizzley Creek was known to be full of gullies and heavily forested but Willow had a gift for listening to the mountains. Every area had its own unique sound and scent. Any variation could help her tune-in to

Lenore's location. She had led rescue operations in every season and weather condition. Because of her specific skills, numerous hikers, two lost children, one escaped prisoner and even a horse, who had been frightened by lightning, had been located by Willow within the last few summer months. She prayed she would not fail in the challenge of finding her friend Lenore.

Willow half listened to the radio as they gave the latest weather report. Snow was not in the forecast for the next forty-eight hours. She would see what the mountain had to say about snow, but weather changes would not impede her ability to find Lenore.

CHAPTER 18

Lenore hadn't slept. She had no idea if it was morning or night. The food she had been offered had been refused. Persistent urging from Halvorson had enraged Lenore, particularly when he had called her *Darling*. She had thrown the cup of soup at him, screaming for him to just let her go. He seemed genuinely shocked, standing in front of her, looking down at the beef and barley soup dripping from his shirt and pants onto the floor. Instead of reacting in anger, his eyes had teared and he told her to get some rest. He would try to make something a little more to her liking, later. He had quietly picked up the empty cup and returned a short time later to wipe the rejected soup from the floor.

The agitated prisoner again looked throughout the room for cameras, and could see no surveillance equipment. Anything she might use for a weapon had either been glued or fastened securely. Lenore's feet were cold and she wondered again about her shoes and searched unsuccessfully. She arched her back, and adjusted the fit of her bra, where underwires had become increasingly uncomfortable from having the darned thing on for, who knew how many hours.

Underwires! She excitedly pulled up her sweater, slipped her arms out of it, unfastened, and removed her bra. She felt the underwires which gave *extra support where it was needed.*

Lenore began to push the first flat wire, encased inside soft padding around the edge of the cup, to one end. She chewed and bit and pushed until the end tore through the fabric. She allowed a quiet little giggle. Her dentist and friend, Dr. Kate Major, would no doubt scold her for using her teeth in this manner, but if this worked, she would also give her an, "Atta girl!", and a free toothbrush. She went to work on the second one.

She managed to get the protective covers off the ends of the metal pieces by once again using her teeth, to expose the sharp ends. She tucked the small pieces of plastic into a pocket and admired the sturdy flat wires. Lenore had no doubt she could fashion them into some sort of weapon. She put her bra back on and settled her sweater back in place The lack of extra support would be nothing to worry about for the time being.

Lenore pulled the blankets and sheets back from the side of the bed. She used the wires to poke a hole in the side of the mattress, slid them inside and smoothed the sheets and blankets back into place.

She decided when food was next offered, she would eat. She knew she needed the calories and energy it would provide. She intended to fight for her life.

*****

Frank Gillespie and Pete Kelly arrived a half hour after Alex had phoned to let John and Gregor know Lenore's sons were safe.

"What's the plan?" Frank asked as soon as he walked in the door. He slid out of his coat, carelessly tossing it onto the sofa in the living room. He strode into the kitchen and began preparing coffee. Pete closed the door and hung his own coat on a nearby rack, leaving Frank's where it landed.

Gregor paced with a cup of tea in hand, as John brought Frank up to speed on where they were in the investigation.

"As soon as Will gets here, we'll head toward the Grizzly Creek area. Probably separate and see if we can locate a cabin."

"Who's this guy Will?" Frank growled. "How's he gonna help?"

"Will works for the search and rescue department as a law enforcement ranger for the U.S. Forest Service. She's the best at her job," John noted.

Franks eyebrows shot up and he looked hard at John before he spoke.

"Did you say *she?*"

"Yes. She knows the area, Frank, and has a real success record. We couldn't be in better company. She's also half Ute, which I'd say gives her an additional advantage."

Frank turned back to the task of making coffee and grumbled, "Hell, I'd hire a psychic, fire-juggling gypsy dwarf if it would help us get Lenore back."

Gregor closed his eyes, and John rolled his. Pete just shook his head, grabbed mugs from the cabinet and placed them on the counter near the coffee pot.

A knock at the door got their attention. Pete crossed to the living room and opened the door to Willow.

"How soon you guys ready to roll?" She asked, then strode into the room assessing the four men who watched as she took her hat off and unzipped her coat.

"Did you find a cabin on your maps?" John asked.

"A few possibilities. According to the clerk at the courthouse, a piece of property had been for sale recently and the description said it included a rustic cabin. I just feel it's more likely than one that's modern and more accessible." Willow tossed her hat onto a chair and slipped out of her coat, hanging it on the back of the chair. She opened a long white tube holding a rolled map. "He would want something secluded where he figures he would be well hidden. We can check it out and if it's right, decide how to approach."

They cleared the table and rolled out the map. Willow indicated the likely area, noting the lack of marked roads and no actual indication of a residence. "It doesn't get much more rustic if it doesn't even have indications on how to get there. I know how to pinpoint where it is."

The four men looked at Willow, waiting for more.

"Let's just say it's an old *Indian* trick and let it go at that." She started rolling up the map to fit back into the tube. "I also have someone at the station handy to check the older maps when I get it narrowed down. You guys need warm clothes, make sure your weapons are loaded, our radios are all on the same channel and keep cool heads." She looked each of them in the eye. "We'll find her. We'll get her."

There were no challenges to her Rocky Mountain rescue experience and law enforcement authority. Something about the serious, dark eyes mirrored their own resolve. Each person in the room busied themselves with preparations.

John returned to the kitchen after adding a borrowed pair of long underwear beneath his jeans and wore a pair of hiking boots he had retrieved from his truck. He recalled having purchased that pair of boots from Lenore on their first meeting at the shoe store in Fort Collins nearly a year ago. So much of life had changed in that one year. He asked Gregor if he needed a weapon.

"I will not be needing a weapon." The former Soviet operative answered with cold eyes. It didn't mean he already had one.

John looked at Franks feet, normally clad in Florsheim wingtip dress shoes and noticed the protective rubbers covering the agent's prized shoes. He did not comment.

Cold weather gear, ammunition and assorted weapons were gathered. John, Pete, and Frank had donned protective vests under their coats. Three agents and one very determined husband followed Willow from the house and separated into three vehicles. John and Willow got into her service truck, Frank and Pete got into Frank's prized 1965 Ford truck, which he had left at the agent's house prior to flying out on vacation. Gregor got into his Pathfinder with a radio provided for communication. Frequencies were set and they drove from the house, determined in their goal.

Sunrise was still over an hour away.

* * * * *

Lenore awoke with a start. She had fallen asleep at the foot of the bed and mentally chastised herself. Cold and exhausted, if there could be any chance of escape, she needed nourishment. It had to be many hours since breakfast. She had no reference of time in the small, windowless room. Having emptied her stomach when she vomited contributed to the hunger.

She had no idea if the water in the portable sink was safe to drink and was ready to take a chance. She stood at the sink when a knock at the door startled her.

"Darling, um, I mean Lenore, are you awake? You really need to eat and drink something."

She opted for cooperation.

"Yes, I'm awake and I'm very hungry and thirsty."

"Alright, you need to move away from the door."

"Yes, I'm on the other side of the room."

Lenore made sure to make enough noise that he could detect her position. The door opened slightly and Halvorson looked in.

"Good girl!"

His words made her cringe.

He brought a sandwich and chips in on a paper plate and a paper cup full of water. He left the door ajar behind him and watched as Lenore took the cup of water and drank the entire thing quickly. She bit into the sandwich, not taking any time to savor the turkey and cheese on wheat bread, and chewed quickly. She swallowed, took another bite, and pushed it to her cheek before speaking.

"More water please, Dennis." She held the paper cup out to her captor.

"Of course. I'll be right back." As he left the room Lenore could see a little of what lay beyond the door before he closed and relocked it. She also noted his having not completely closed the door while in the room. It might be a definite advantage for her. He seemed anxious to keep her comfortable; abnormally so. She shuddered.

She continued eating and listened for Dennis' return. When the door unlocked, she heard only one mechanism disengage, and she didn't hear a key. Again, he left the door slightly ajar. He must have felt pretty sure she didn't plan to run.

"Thank you, Dennis. The sandwich tastes good." She accepted the refilled paper cup and sipped.

He smiled. "I'm glad you like it, Lenore. Would you care for another?"

"Oh, no. This is plenty. I feel much better already." She managed a forced smile.

He absolutely beamed. "Good. Good! I want you to always be happy, you know."

"Of course, Dennis. You know this is going to take some adjusting for me, don't you?"

"Yes. I know. You've been a captive of the Commie for so long." He shook his head and added, "You will have to re-program, for sure. Just be certain I'll always have your best interest at heart. You must learn to trust me and rely on me for everything."

"Yes Dennis. I'll try." She choked back the urge to strike him or throw up at that point. She took a deep breath and smiled again.

"Would you like to take a bath now? I know you love bubble baths and I'll be happy to prepare one for you." His voice had become raspy.

This time, control vanished. She ran to the port-o-let and lifted the lid and pulled her hair away from her face just in time to start retching.

"Oh, my darling Lenore. Did the sandwich make you ill? What can I do?" He stood at her side and patted her back.

Don't touch me! She wanted to scream. *Let me go! I want to go home! I hate you!* reverberated in her brain. She knew it would not be a solution at this point. The heaving subsided and she pushed the button to pump water into the basin of the toilet and then pushed the flush lever.

"Just let me clean up here. I think maybe I ate too fast." She stepped away from Dennis before he could touch her again. She pumped water into her hand from the nearby sink and sucked it into her mouth, rinsed and spit. She took the paper napkin from lunch and wiped her face.

"Shall I get you something else?"

"No Dennis. Nothing right now. I want to lay down and rest. Can you leave me alone please?"

"Yes. I will let you rest." He picked up the plate of remaining sandwich and chips, and the wadded napkin. The cup of water was left on the floor beside the bed. "I'll let you rest for a while, then you really will need to try again to eat something. Perhaps simply some crackers?"

The concern in his voice unsettled Lenore. "Whatever. Please, just leave."

She waved him away, and Halverson quietly left the room. She heard one lock engage again.

Lenore lifted the bed cover and sheets and felt until the two underwires were detected. She slid them out and examined them. More than once, she had felt the flat blue steel break while wearing an underwire bra, producing a startling stab. These could be made into a weapon. She bent the pieces nearly in half with some effort. Using her sweater to protect the heels of her hands, she put the wires on the floor and pressed until the sides were closer together. She knew now it would simply be a matter of creating a handle. She crossed her eyes in exasperation.

"Necessity is the mother of invention," she whispered. *I wonder who said that?* she thought, then added, *besides me?* She vowed to look it up as soon as she got home.

Home.

So many homes in her lifetime. Childhood homes hadn't always been happy, but she could remember happy times. Homes with two husbands before Gregor had been so different. Craig, her first husband and father to their boys, was a good man; a good provider. They had just grown apart. They needed such different things out of life. He thrived in cities and business and getting ahead. Lenore just wanted smaller comfortable places to raise their boys.

With respect and due consideration, they both agreed to go separate ways. The boys were never used as leverage or fell victim to the stigma of being children of divorced parents. They were always amicable. Visitations were planned first and foremost about what best worked for the boys.

Lenore's second marriage to Nick had been vastly different. Initially, it had been good. They had great adventures with four-wheeling and camping. He seemed to really care about her and both of her sons. By the time Grant had moved to Chicago to go to art school, Nick had changed. He drank heavily and seemed to delight in provoking arguments, most of which involved Joel. The younger son of Lenore could do nothing right, it seemed. At the time, she had no clue Nick's numerous affairs had produced a pregnancy and he needed to get out of their marriage. When threats and his violent temper became more frequent and truly frightening, Lenore knew they had to go. She prepared to make a move for the safety of her son and her own sanity.

Then, she met Gregor. She tilted her head, and closed her eyes.

Nothing in her life would ever be the same. It had been a hard-fought love. They both knew what they wanted, but it took a year to come to them. Her life since then had been absolute bliss. She had a love she had only imagined could ever happen. They created a home. Her home. Her Gregor. Her family. A tear slid down her cheek. She wiped with the heel of her hand.

Lenore shook her head and took a controlled breath. If Gregor could withstand torture and isolation in a Soviet prison to get back to her, she could figure out a way to get back to him.

A handle. What the heck could she make a handle out of? Everything in the room was so firmly glued and screwed to the walls. She picked up the paper cup and sipped more water. She considered for a moment using the paper cup to form a handle, then realized he would wonder what happened to the cup. She frowned.

She pulled the sheet back to put her weapon material away and wished she had a rubber band or something to hold them together before she inserted them back into the mattress.

"Ha!" She said out loud and immediately covered her mouth.

Lenore ran to the other side of the bed furthest from the door and pulled back the cover and sheets. She used a piece of the sharp metal to slice down the side of the mattress, then sliced again an inch away from the first cut to remove a strip of material about a yard long. She saw batting material inside the exposed mattress and knew it could be used to make a handle. She would need time to put things together, so the pieces of metal were tucked inside the tear along with the material. She replaced the bedding and returned to the other side of the bed, smoothing the comforter back into place there as well.

With an almost giddy excitement, Lenore forced herself to settle onto the bed and at least pretend she had slept. She felt so tired and hungry. As much as she needed to stay alert, her eyes closed and she slept.

She would have no compunctions about doing whatever necessary to get away from Halvorson before someone tried to rescue her and got hurt, or worse.

CHAPTER 19

On a county road near Grizzly Creek, Willow stopped the caravan. She and John got out of the truck to meet with the others. The team assembled near the truck and listened, never questioning her direction.

"You guys wait here. I'll take John and drive up the road over there." Willow indicated a rarely used U.S. Forest Service Road. "If I can get a better sense of where the cabin might be, we'll head in and surround it from different directions." She looked each man in the eyes. "Agreed?"

They all nodded.

The group got back into their vehicles to wait for further directions and let engines idle to keep warm. Willow and John drove ahead and stopped at the entry to the service road. She got out of the truck and used a key from an attached ring on her belt to open a padlock, allowing the chain to be lowered. John drove the truck past the entry and then moved back to the passenger seat.

John glanced at Willow. "I hope we get to Lenore before she tries to escape."

"Why would she do that?" Willow asked, steering her truck on the rutted road.

"I know how her mind works. She'll try." He shook his head. "She has a tendency to think she's Superwoman."

"You think you're maybe too close to this situation, John? Lenore told me how close you were at one time." She glanced at the passenger sitting beside her in the truck. "You can't go making judgement calls based on the woman you knew in the past. She's changed."

"Can't help it, Willow. She can't change how she thinks entirely. I know that woman. I loved her." He sat quietly for a few seconds. "I'll always love her, but the way I love her has changed." The statement surprised him. He hesitated, then added, "Lenore is a very dear friend."

Willow pondered his words for a few moments, then asked, "So you've been able to change the way you feel about Lenore from a romantic love to that of friendship? Seriously? Are you delusional, John?"

John stared out the window, jostling in the truck as it maneuvered over the old rutted road. "I know it'll always be more than friendship down deep. Lenore and I pretty much shared a lifetime for nearly a year. I've seen her so broken I didn't think she would come back. I've seen her hurt and scared and I've shared precious moments of true happiness. I've loved her through it all."

He grabbed the dashboard as the truck jostled through another rough area. He turned his eyes to Willow. "My love for Lenore had to change. I'd never betray Greg. Besides, Lenore would never let me. She's the wife of my best friend." He let those words hang in the air for a moment. "I stepped aside and let her choose when I brought him back to her. There was no fighting for her. Then I stood there with Alex as she promised to love and honor Greg, wishing her words were for me, but as soon as those words were spoken, it changed." He caught Willow's glance. "I'd give my life for either of them."

"Okay, let's say I believe you. Don't you think you're still too close? Think about it, Halvorson's sharper than your average KGB agent trying to abduct her. He knows her history. He'll take precautions to prevent an escape."

"I'm close. Can't deny that, but it also gives me an edge. I know Lenore *and* Halvorson. I know what challenges they face daily as well as their pasts. I'd say it puts me at a decisive advantage. I *know* she's going to try." He managed to say it without sounding defensive. "I also know he will never be able to prevent her from trying."

"Well then, John, let's find Lenore before she tries to escape and gets hurt."

Willow slowed the truck and stopped. She looked out the window and the windshield, then turned off the engine. They got out of the truck and quietly closed the doors. There were no fresh tracks in the skiff of snow that had fallen a couple of days earlier. The snow would soon be belly-deep on the native elk in the area, ensuring any clues would remain buried until the spring thaw. Willow and John were confident in their task.

"Let's go see what the mountain has to say." She took the flaps down on her leather cap to protect her ears from the cold and began walking. John met her brisk stride after snugging a stocking cap down over his own ears. The stocking cap did not defeat the sound of the winds whispering through the pines far above them. A hint of light in the early morning sky told them sunrise would come soon.

A hundred yards down the road, Willow found a deer trail forking off the road and followed it to an outcropping of rocks.

"We'll climb up there," she whispered, daring to break the natural hush of the forest. She pointed to the top of the outcropping. "We should be far enough away from the truck to make sure any creeks and pops from the cooling engine or odors produced by the truck, don't obscure or confuse natural odors and sounds."

As they neared the top, she turned to John. "I hope you know this might take a while. Can't rush the mountain, you know?"

"I'm fine with that." He assured her as he sat down on a smooth boulder near the top; grateful for the extra layer of clothes he had donned.

Willow walked to the other side of the outcropping, removed her cap, and stood; her profile glowing as the sun broke over the mountains. Her people had conversed with these mountains for a millennium. If there might be something to learn, John believed she was tuned in and paying attention.

As John watched, Willow closed her eyes and slowly turned her head from left to right, then turn her entire body to the left, and remained perfectly still. John began hearing sounds of which he had previously been unaware and removed his own cap as the sunlight reached him. A flutter announced a trio of dry aspen leaves stubbornly clinging to an otherwise bare tree. He watched a chipmunk scurry from beneath one group of rocks, followed a path only it could discern, and disappear under another group of boulders. He wondered why it wasn't already hibernating. Perhaps they had disturbed it.

The rush of wind coming up the mountain lured dry leaves near the base of the rocks into a final dance. Soon they would compost and feed spring's new growth. As if scolded for the intrusion of too much sound, the wind quieted and the dance ended.

Willow listened for something not akin to the usual symphony of this Colorado mountaintop.

"There." John's thoughts were interrupted when Willow spoke quietly. She turned slightly as if tuning in a directional receiver. "That's not natural."

John strained to detect what Willow heard. She glanced at him and he shook his head, letting her know he didn't hear what she heard.

"Listen beyond what you are hearing," she whispered. "Listen for what you don't hear."

John closed his eyes. Nothing but the whisper of wind through evergreen trees and deadfall leaves tickling to the whim of the winds.

No. Something … else. He opened his eyes and looked at Willow.

With a slight nod, Willow indicated a direction. John turned his head toward the valley to the west and once again closed his eyes.

"That's an engine," he whispered.

She smiled.

"Not a vehicle engine. Generator."

Willow nodded. Again, she turned her head one way and the other, then focused and pointed.

"I know it's coming from that direction, but the sound is muffled. It could be closer or further than it sounds. The generator might be inside a building or something." She jammed the leather cap back onto her head. John replaced his stocking cap.

"You're thinking that generator is being used by whomever has Lenore?"

She turned to John. "According to the map, there should be no habitable residence anywhere near that area. I don't believe it's a coincidence." She turned, took a deep breath, and checked the morning sky, then back to John. "We need to find her today. We will have snow before the day is out."

"Weather reports aren't predicting snow for at least forty-eight hours."

Willow turned to John and flashed her beautiful smile. "I can taste it in the air. Don't let these clear, sunny skies fool you."

They got down from the rocks and walked quickly back to the truck. Willow took the map from the tube and they spread it out on the hood of the truck.

"We're here," she indicated. "The sound is coming from this direction." She drew a line with her finger, narrowing the area. "There can't be too many spots in this vicinity where a cabin could even stand. Pretty rocky and steep for the most part, so that narrows it down for us considerably."

"How do we narrow it down further?"

"Let me contact the station. I've got the guys ready to do some checking on the old maps to check for a cabin. Nothing shows on this one. Can't take old stuff off premises."

Willow pulled out her radio from her coat pocket, then spoke to the rangers, giving and receiving directions until she was satisfied. She knew about where the sound had to be generating. She rolled the map up and slipped it back into the protective tube, then tapped John on the shoulder with it.

"Let's go get the guys."

"Wait." John removed his coat and then unfastened his protective vest. "You need this."

"No John. Then you won't have one."

"Take off your coat and put this on." He wouldn't take *no* for an answer.

Willow slipped out of her coat and accepted John's help in putting on the vest. His hands lingered on her shoulders.

"I don't want to worry about another beautiful woman today, so don't argue." He gently tilted her chin up; his kiss was soft. "Now I can concentrate on my job."

They both put coats back on, got into the truck and headed out to meet the rest of the group.

* * * * *

A knock at the door awakened Lenore. She felt confused for a minute until her eyes fell on the photo pasted to the wall. She jumped out of the bed and checked to make sure the wires were out of sight before answering.

"What? What do you want?"

"Lenore, it's been two hours. You should eat something. Does anything sound good?"

"No … yes." She ran her fingers through her hair and then over her face, trying to get more alert. Food. She needed to eat. "Peanut butter and potato chip sandwich. That's what I want."

"Alright. I can make that for you. Do you want coffee?"

Oh, that sounded wonderful. It would taste great, but maybe she could scald him with it. She also realized it must be morning if he offered coffee.

"Yes. Coffee. Extra cream." She questioned her own request. She never had cream in her coffee. She just never liked it. "I need water, too." Peanut butter and potato chip sandwich? Why on earth did that sound good?

"Very well Lenore. I'll get what you want. You'll have to eat slower this time so you don't make yourself sick, alright?"

She rolled her eyes. "Sure Dennis."

She went to the portable camp toilet, slid her jeans down, and sat on the absurdly low seat. She produced scarcely a dribble. She pinched the skin on the back of her hand and, knew she was getting dehydrated and really needed to drink water. She washed her face and hands at the portable sink and dried on her sweater sleeve.

She needed to eat, drink, and make a weapon. She would need privacy, which Dennis had thus far accorded her. She hoped to catch another peek into the room beyond the locked door. She paced and ran her fingers through her hair. She needed her shoes! How could she run for her life if she didn't have shoes on her feet? She knew she'd try, with or without them.

CHAPTER 20

Once again, Willow unrolled the topographical map of the area. Four men stood beside her, intent on the words and indications on the map.

"The old maps show a hunting cabin about here." She tapped a spot. "It's been uninhabited for forty plus years. The roads in this area have been neglected, too. We could be challenged. Probably go in on foot from here." She made sure each of them could see what she indicated. "We don't want him hear our vehicles anyway."

The four men were united in their agreement, relinquishing their usual authority to the expert in search and recovery in the back country of Colorado.

Agent Pete Kelly spoke. "Just show us where you need each of us."

"Okay guys, it could get rough and we don't know what we'll be met with … traps, climbing, even an ambush." She stared at Frank. "I also need someone at the road to give accurate directions on how to get here." Then she looked over at Pete.

"Got it," he said.

"I may not be a huge fan of rough terrain, but I sure as hell want a piece of this clown." The older agent met Willow's eyes. There would be no challenging him.

"Don't underestimate Frank. He can handle it," John assured Willow, much to Frank's surprise. He knew Frank didn't put rubbers on over those wingtips to stay on the sidewalk.

"I'll call for backup and give directions," Pete confirmed. "I'll have my radio on." He would also request an ambulance, though he hoped it wouldn't be necessary.

Willow rolled up the map and inserted it back into the protective tube. She handed it to Pete, with instructions, "You hang onto this. If you need it to give direction, open it up. Just make sure it goes back to the Forest Service." She didn't need to complete the thought of *in case I don't make it out.* He nodded agreement.

They were two hours past sunrise and daylight was short in the mountains this time of year.

* * * * *

Lenore had finished her sandwich and surprised at how good her choice tasted. The coffee also tasted great with cream.

"No wonder Leah likes cream in her coffee," she whispered to herself. "I may try sugar in it when I get home."

Halverson knocked before he unlocked the door and brought in a pair of slippers. They were soft soled and more like a moccasin than a shoe, but she knew she could run in them. It was unsettling to realize he knew her shoe size. He apologized for letting her feet get so cold.

He brought two paper cups of water and once again reminded her to drink slowly. She didn't need the warning. She had to make sure this food and water stayed in her system. She needed the fuel.

"What else do you need, Lenore? Are you ready for a bath?"

She shuddered. "Not now Dennis. I'm tired. I need to rest for a couple of hours, alright?"

"Alright Darling, I mean Lenore." He smiled. "You rest."

As soon as the door closed and she heard the lock engage, she went to the far side of the bed and pulled the sturdy wires out from the mattress. The strip of material and a wad of the mattress batting were pulled free. She began wrapping the two bent wires first in the batting and then used the material to weave in and around the wires and batting until it felt secure enough to be used. She could see, when the door had been opened a bit, that it was daylight. She knew she had to make her escape, or die trying.

She rummaged through the stack of sweaters and chose two; one pullover and the other, a cardigan, was added over her own light sweater.

She went to the end of the bed, got down on her knees and prayed for help to escape this man who held her against her will. She asked for strength to run and angels to direct her because she had absolutely no idea which way to go.

Then she stood.

* * * * *

Nearly a mile from the county road, the four rescuers walked the less traveled trail, honing in on the hum of a generator. The sound was clear, directing them like a beacon.

* * * * *

"Dennis! Dennis, I need your help." She tried to sound frantic. "There's a spider in the toilet." She pounded on the door. Grinning she thought, *now here's an opportunity for him to be the knight in shining armor.*

* * * * *

When they heard the pounding, Willow grabbed Gregor by the sleeve to hold him still. He glanced at her hand, then looked into the eyes of the ranger. She shook her head. The Russian man closed his eyes for a moment, then nodded in compliance.

The pounding ceased and John pointed ahead. "Keep quiet, your eyes open and your weapons ready."

They would move in, assessing the situation as they went, hopefully surprising Halvorson enough to avoid endangering Lenore.

* * * * *

"Hurry Dennis. I need to go pee and there's a spider."

Lenore heard the lock being disengaged.

"OK, darling," he said with a chuckle. "Step back from the door and I'll come kill it for you."

Lenore stepped aside and gripped her makeshift weapon, hiding it in the folds of her sweater.

Halverson stepped through the doorway and, as he had done before, he left the door ajar. He started toward the portable toilet, then stopped and turned toward Lenore.

"What are you wearing?" he asked.

"Just trying on my new wardrobe. You don't mind, do you?" She smiled and batted her lashes. "Now, the spider? I really need to *go*! It's huge and right there behind the toilet." She gestured with her free hand.

He nodded and turned toward the toilet, getting down on one knee to check for the offending arachnid. Lenore took three quick steps, then stuck the weapon hard into his neck and raked it back toward his ear. When she shoved him down onto the portable toilet, she didn't wait to see what damage she might have inflicted. Instead, she ran to the door, slammed it shut, then engaged the deadbolt with fingers shaking.

The sound of an enraged, injured man pierced the quiet of the cabin and she could hear him slamming his body against the door.

Lenore turned another deadbolt on the back door and as she jerked open the door, the movement of a set of keys caught her attention. She grabbed them from a hook and ran out of the house. The cold slammed into her and she winced, stopping only long enough to assess her surroundings and locate the parked Ford pickup.

Lenore glanced back as she heard a crash coming from inside the cabin. She reached the truck, silently thanking her high school driver's education teacher for insisting they all know how to drive standard shift vehicles. She climbed in, stuck the key into the ignition and pushed in the clutch, then pulled the choke and engaged the starter. The 1948 Ford pickup rumbled to life. She looked toward the house and saw Halvorson walking with a deliberate gate toward her. She slid the gearshift into reverse and slowly let the clutch out as she accelerated.

* * * * *

They heard the truck's engine roar to life. Willow pointed to a stack of deadfall. Tracks on the other side had been made recently. John pointed to each rescuer and then to the area he wanted them to enter. They knew the truck was moving.

* * * * *

Lenore watched Halvorson raise his arm, pointing his Walther .380 toward her, just as the truck died. She had forgotten to disengage the choke. As she tried to start the now flooded engine, Halvorson reached the truck and jerked open the door. Blood covered the front of his shirt and the nightmarish look in his eyes matched the horror she felt.

Lenore plummeted him with blows from clenched fists and kicked with her feet, struggling to stay out of his grasp. Halvorson ignored her efforts. He pulled her from the truck and threw her to the ground, then picked her up like a rag doll, placing the gun's icy muzzle against her cheek. The custom fitted silencer wasn't needed.

"Why did you do that, Lenore?" His voice, a high-pitched wail. The air was fouled with the metallic odor of blood and Lenore looked sideways to see the crimson stain seeping down his shirt. His breath came in bursts of vapor into the cold air. He squeezed her to him and jammed the gun even harder into her cheek.

"Agent Dennis Halvorson, stand down!"

Halvorson glanced up and stared at John Dixon.

"Drop your weapon!" Dixon hoped that Halvorson's training would surface long enough to react with ingrained compliance.

Halvorson looked at Dixon with incredulity. Lenore's terror-filled eyes were locked onto Dixon's.

The deranged agent laughed. "Stand down? No, no, no. I *know* how this works. I drop the weapon and you take me into custody." Halvorson pushed the icy muzzle of the weapon deeper into Lenore's cheek. "You'll just give her back to that Commie."

Dixon steeled his jaw, then replied, "In the name of the Central Intelligence Agency of the United States of America, I *order* you, as an agent of this agency to stand down, Agent Halvorson."

"No Dixon. She's supposed to be with an American, don't you see?" He looked at the HK P7M8 John pointed at Halvorson's head. "You need to put *your* weapon down." He smirked in defiance. "*You* stand down, Agent John Dixon!"

John kept Halvorson's eyes locked on his, but could see Gregor moving silently toward Halvorson and Lenore from behind. Frank stood a few yards to John's left, with his trusty nickel-plated Colt Commander pointed at the deranged agent for a kill shot. Willow stood near Frank with her Sig Sauer focused on target as well. Neither could chance it. John needed to provide a distraction.

"You know you aren't going to win here, Halverson." John continued to lock eyes with the unstable agent.

"Oh, I may not win, but neither will you or that Commie. You may kill me, but before you do, I'll shoot her in the face, then who'll want her?" He laughed maniacally. "I still win. If the only way I can have her is in death, so be it!"

"I find it interesting you seem to hate a Commie more than you love Lenore," John said to the unstable man.

"No. No that's not right." Halvorson looked confused, but maintained his grip on Lenore. He pushed the weapon deeper into her cheek, making her yelp. "I love her more than anyone could. She just needs to come back inside and be de-programed."

Gregor closed in, just a few feet behind the two. John knew he had to act. He continued to aim his weapon at a spot between Halvorson's eyes and began squeezing the grip below the trigger as he slowly walked forward. He hoped the deranged agent would choose John for his target and not Lenore. As predicted, Halvorson took the weapon from Lenore's cheek and aimed it at John.

"Your choice, Dixon!"

"No!" Lenore screamed and began thrashing. Halvorson's grip on Lenore loosened, to secure his aim. Lenore dropped to the ground as Gregor Parishnikov dove toward Halvorson. Gunfire echoed in ricochet absurdity from four weapons. John Dixon was hurled backward from the force of Halvorson's bullet. Halvorson fell to the ground and the weapon, too late, was knocked from his hand when three bullets pierced his body. None were the preferred kill shots because of Lenore and Gregor's proximity to the line of fire. The abductor writhed in pain several feet away from Lenore. Smoke from the four fired weapons hung heavily in the air.

Gregor did not hesitate. He grabbed Halvorson head and locked eyes with him. "I do not believe you deserve to live and be tried for the choices you have made."

Halvorson struggled to speak, but his words were clear enough.

"You go to hell you fuckin' Commie."

In one swift move, Gregor snapped the neck of the agent. He watched Halvorson's golden eyes cloud over, as life force left his body; small whisps of steam continuing to curl from three wounds. He dropped the now limp man and ran to Lenore.

"Are you alright, Lenore?" He slid to his knees, holding his wife.

"Yes. Yes," she sobbed. "Go to John."

Gregor gently let go of Lenore and ran to where Willow knelt on the frozen ground beside John and began applying pressure to the wound.

"Get him?" John asked, looking up at Gregor.

"Yes. He is dead."

Lenore approached, knelt beside Willow, and touched John's cheek. "John, why did you do that?"

"Had to." He raised his eyebrows at Lenore and smiled. "The … baby."

Then the brave agent lost consciousness. Frank Gillespie stood nearby, yelling into the hand-held radio to agent Kelly stationed back on the main road.

"Agent down. I repeat, agent down. We have an injured female." He glanced toward Halvorson's still body. "One perpetrator deceased."

Willow assessed the wound. She looked up at Gillespie. "Tell them to hurry!"

He needed no prompting. "Get whatever in the hell is available and get it here *now!*"

Kelly's voice crackled back on the radio. "Heard the gunfire. Got one ambulance already on the way. I'll call for another."

"I don't understand, Willow." Lenore shook her head, tears flowing. "He drew fire to save me. Why?"

Willow instructed Gregor to continue putting pressure on the wound. With hands of experience in dealing with injured citizens in the back country of Colorado, she lifted John's hand to check his pulse and gently removed the stocking cap partially skewed on his head.

"That's how a hero operates, Lenore." She gently soothed John's hair, tucked the stocking cap under his head then turned and hugged the shaking brunette. "He had to."

The words John had spoken to Willow filled her thoughts. *I'd give my life for either of them.* It had not been an idle statement.

"It's the same reason he insisted I had to wear his protective vest." Her normal steady voice cracked. "He was in hero mode, and he gave me no other choice; no talking him out of it."

"Pretty well sums him up." Frank shook his head and added, "All the years I've known Dixon, the guy's always out to save everyone but himself."

Gregor continued to apply pressure to the wound as Frank jogged back to the trail, and began removing the pile of brush and limbs obscuring the entrance. He would direct the ambulance to the clearing. In less than a half hour the area filled with red and blue strobes of light coming from county and state of Colorado law and emergency vehicles.

The midday shadows had shrunk into the surrounding forest, bathing the clearing with a few precious hours of sunlight. Paramedics pulled equipment from an ambulance and jogged to the downed agents, glancing at the staring eyes of the deceased agent. As protocol dictated, one paramedic quickly checked for a pulse or signs of life, looked at his watch and noted the time. Their first-priority, as always, was to the living.

The professionals started working to assess and stabilize their patient. Gregor, Lenore, and Willow stood up from where they had knelt beside their friend. A second ambulance arrived and as paramedics exited the emergency vehicle, Frank pointed to Lenore. They began urging her to let them check her and take her to the hospital. Lenore resisted being led to the back of the waiting ambulance and away from Gregor, Willow, and her dear friend John.

"Lenore, John's going to be alright, now get your ass in that ambulance!" Frank pointed and frowned.

"He is right, Lenore. Please, let's get you checked by the paramedics." Willow hugged Lenore, then turned her toward Gregor.

The anxious husband pulled his wife into his arms, then helped her towards the ambulance, with Lenore limping due to the gash on her foot. A young deputy sheriff stepped in front of Gregor. "We have some questions that need answered before anyone leaves. There's a dead man over there." He gestured toward Halvorson's body. "We need to find out what happened to him, and who is responsible?"

"Yes," Gregor glared at the deputy with cold dark eyes. "I am most responsible for the dead man there." He handed her into the care of the paramedic, who helped her into the back of the ambulance. He started around the deputy to follow his wife. Again, the deputy stopped him, this time placing a hand on Gregor's chest. Gregor's eyes flashed with anger.

Frank walked to the deputy and put a strong grip on his shoulder. "I think you'd better back off. His wife is heading for the hospital."

The deputy frowned and continued to prevent Gregor's movement. "Yes, I understand that, but a man was killed here. He just admitted to it, so we need to investigate. No one can leave until we do."

Gregor looked at the hand on his chest and moved to grab it. Frank stopped him by raising a hand, flashing his CIA credentials, and spoke firmly to the deputy.

"You let us worry about that. We all had a hand in bringing that asshole down." He gestured to Halvorson's body with his thumb.

"This crime scene is *officially*, the CIA's responsibility." He cocked his head and looked squarely into the eyes of the deputy. "Now, you are hereby *officially* advised to back off," he paused for emphasis, "or else."

There was no challenging Frank's authority, and the deputy stepped away from Gregor. Frank nodded his head toward Lenore, without breaking eye contact with the deputy. Gregor didn't hesitate. He raced for the ambulance and jumped into the back. Pete Kelly closed the doors and pounded on them, yelling, "Go, go, go!"

The deputy immediately walked to his patrol vehicle to call the sheriff, currently enroute. With his question apparently answered quickly, he walked back to Frank.

"Sir, if there is any way we can assist, please let me know. The sheriff is on his way."

Frank responded with an inaudible grumble which the deputy didn't bother to ask him to repeat. The unamused, seasoned agent walked back to where the paramedics were working on John. He watched, standing beside Willow. Neither spoke. Pete continued to direct and secure the scene.

* * * * *

Lenore struggled, trying to get into a sitting position, but a strap secured her onto the gurney.

"Let me up. Let me get up." She reached for her husband's arm. "Gregor, help me get up."

"Ma'am, we need to keep you strapped down for transport." The paramedic advised as the ambulance lurched and slowly maneuvered down the rutted trail, toward the more traveled county road; the one which would take them to the highway.

Gregor spoke softly to Lenore. "He is right, Lenore. You will be safer this way."

"*No!*" She yelled and again grabbed Gregor's arm. "I have to sit up."

The paramedic nodded to Gregor and loosened the strap holding Lenore. She immediately sat up and struggled to remove the two sweaters she wore.

"Get these off of me." She started pulling the sweaters over her head. "Get 'em off. Get them off me now!"

Gregor and the paramedic began assisting her efforts. The outer one was streaked with Halvorson's blood, and John Dixon's as well.

Blood had soaked through to the sweater underneath. Both were removed, leaving only her own light blue sweater. She kicked off her one remaining slipper, having lost the mate in her struggle, and pulled her legs up close to her body. The paramedic secured the discarded items in a plastic bag and offered Gregor a towel which he first soaked with water from a bottle. Gregor wiped Lenore's face gently and then began to wipe John's blood from his own hands. The paramedic added the soiled towel to the bag of sweaters and continued his assessment of Lenore.

Lenore reached for her husband. "Hold me Gregor. Hold me tight and never let go."

"Yes. I will hold you. I will always hold you. You are safe now."

Her breathing slowed and she relaxed. She laid back and allowed the paramedic to replace the strap, though he kept it a little looser than before and raised the head of the gurney. He checked her respiration and pulse, then took a blanket from a compartment. He and Gregor snugged the warm cover around Lenore.

"You're doing fine Mrs. Parishnikov." He began to assess an injury to her foot. "You might need a few stitches on this cut," he advised, as he began to remove debris from the wound and clean it with alcohol wipes.

If it hurt, Lenore never flinched. She nodded and kept her eyes locked on Gregor's. The turn onto the county road made the ride smoother. The siren alerted traffic to clear their way.

"Gregor, what was John saying about a baby? Why did he say that, Gregor?"

Gregor held Lenore's hands to his lips and kissed them. "It is because you are pregnant, Lenore." He gently smoothed her tangled hair. "The doctor called. They ran the test and confirmed we are to be having a child." He stroked her face as tears filled his eyes.

Lenore stared at him, as if not believing what she heard. "I am? We are?" She shook her head, to clear her thoughts.

"Congratulations Mr. and Mrs. Parishnikov." The paramedic continued to monitor Lenore.

"Oh Gregor, what have I put this baby through? What if all this causes a miscarriage?"

"They'll check you out thoroughly when you get to the hospital," said the paramedic, "but it appears you've suffered little more than bruising, and a cut on your foot. They'll make sure, of course, but all your vitals appear to currently be within normal ranges."

"We will have a healthy child, because you are strong. Our child will thrive," Gregor assured her.

"Oh Gregor, what about John? We can't lose John."

The paramedic could offer little hope. "He's in good hands. He'll be in the other ambulance not long behind us." He opened a cabinet and retrieved a roll of gauze. "They'll stabilize him at the local hospital, then likely Life Flight him by 'copter to a Denver trauma hospital."

Gregor and Lenore knew there was nothing they could do but pray for God's mercy on their dear friend and skilled hands to do what they could.

CHAPTER 21

"You can't check out, John. Not allowed!" Willow hugged herself against the emotions.

Somewhere in a deep, quiet place the soft voice found purchase.

"I think I'm just getting something figured out, so you can't go before I can explain what I'm feeling."

Who's saying those words? Why can't I just go on to that bright place right over there and rest? Just for a while. I'm so tired.

The paramedics continued their work while Willow knelt beside the paramedics and spoke soft, soothing words. "Listen to me, John. You can't give up. You need to stay here with me."

There's John Milton Dixon the original. What's he doing here? Why is he shaking his head no?

"John, I need for you to stay, because," Willow urged, then with a catch in her voice, "I think I might be falling in love with you." She pulled the leather cap off her head and hugged it to her chest.

Love? Who's saying those words.

"You have so much left to do. You can't quit now. You just need to fight hard now. Fight, John!"

Grandfather don't walk away. I want to go with you. With one final turn and a wink to his grandson, John Milton Dixon, the original, tells his grandson to go back. He'll see him again one day, when it's time.

"That's it, John," the soft voice urged. "You can do this."

Oh, the confusion; the pain! Why do I have to do this? It's so quiet and peaceful there.

"John. Open your eyes," the soft voice urged again.

Yes, I need to open my eyes to see the face that belongs to the voice. I know that voice. I know … John's eyes fluttered a bit, opened and focused on the beautiful face.

"Willow." He wasn't even sure he had spoken it out loud. Emergency lights created a panoply of red, white, and blue on the face, but he knew it; knew her. The tears on her cheeks glistened, reflecting the carnival of lights.

"That's right John," she said, leaning toward him. "You can do this. It'll be okay. I won't let it be anything but okay."

He struggled, "I … is she?"

Another voice spoke. "Yes, you saved her. I promised her you'd be okay so she'd get in the damned ambulance, so don't make me a liar."

Frank. That's Frank. He turned his eyes and tried to focus on the craggy face of Frank Gillespie.

"Halvorson!"

"Save it Dixon," the older agent scolded. "Halvorson's dead. You'll have a complete debriefing when you might be lucid enough to remember it."

The paramedics blocked John's view of his most trusted agent as they lifted and secured him onto a gurney. An oxygen mask further prevented conversation. John's eyes searched for Willow. He felt her soothing touch on his hair and he turned his head to see her face; that beautiful face, beside him.

"Be strong and fight, John. We'll meet you at the hospital as soon as we can." He felt her kiss on his forehead, then the face of the paramedic moved into his view, adjusting the oxygen mask and tightening straps holding him onto the gurney. He struggled for every breath.

"It'll be rough for a minute, sir." The paramedic warned as they began moving toward the ambulance, and he didn't exaggerate. Every bump from the rugged terrain was excruciating.

"Mr. Dixon." The paramedic yelled over the noise of more vehicles and the clutter of voices and radios. "We'll take you from here to the local hospital by ambulance. They'll get you stabilized and then you'll most likely be transferred to a Denver trauma hospital by a Life Flight 'copter if they believe you need more than they can provide locally. I gave you something for the pain. Should be kicking in."

It was the last thing he heard as a peaceful warmth settled in.

* * * * *

Willow stood beside Frank, watching the ambulance maneuver toward the county road. A coroner's vehicle replaced the ambulance; no emergency lights needed. The evening shadows were oozing back out of the forest and into the clearing, as the sound of the siren grew faint. They were just beginning to feel the cold. The sky was heavy with clouds.

By the time a competent investigative team of CIA personnel arrived on scene and were briefed by Frank, they had little to do to but secure the area until daylight.

Snowflakes were whirling around, creating a confetti effect. Willow, Frank, and Pete walked out of the clearing, and onto the forest service road. The snow had settled on any surfaces not protected by trees.

"You okay to drive?" Frank asked.

"My ego says I should be, but my common sense knows better." Willow glanced down at her hands, still covered in John's blood. "I'm still too emotional, I guess. How about you?"

"We'll take my truck," the seasoned agent offered, always in control of himself and the situation. "Can you get someone to pick up your vehicle?"

"Yep. I'll ask the guys at the station to come get it. If you'll give me a sec to clean up at my place on the way, and grab some stuff for Lenore, we can go to the hospital together."

"Kelly, you take Greg's vehicle. Meet us at the hospital." He turned to the agent. "That work for you?"

"Affirmative."

The trio continued their trek toward the county road and the vehicles, silent; each mentally dealing with their experience. Pete headed toward the Pathfinder.

Frank and Willow continued walking toward Frank's truck. Only the sound of their footsteps on the sparse sandy terrain of the county road intruded on the silence. Even the small amount of snow provided insulation from the normal forest noises. It surprised Frank when Willow turned and gave the agent a hug. It surprised her when he hugged her back.

"Hope you don't mind, Frank. I don't know about you, but I really needed a hug."

"For Christ's sake don't tell anyone, but I did too." He rested his hand on Willow's shoulder as they walked.

"Looks like you lost one of your rubbers," Willow observed. "Your wingtip's pretty torn up. You've got a lot of dirt on it." She didn't want to point out that it probably included a combination of dirt *and* blood.

"Hell." He reached down and jerked the other rubber off. "I'm thinking about giving up these damned wingtips anyway. That fu … excuse me, that *maniac* Halvorson ruined their uniqueness."

Frank started to just toss the rubber off into the brush, stopped, frowned at it, then stuck it in his coat pocket instead.

The two weary rescuers continued to the truck, closed the doors to the outside, grateful to sit down at last. The reliable '65 Ford pickup started and Frank performed a U-turn to head back toward Glenwood Springs.

* * * * *

Alex jumped for the phone when it rang. Grant stood in the doorway and Joel came running from his mom's art room, Spot still in his arms. Alex spoke and listened for what seemed like eternity to the two younger men.

"Yes, I will tell them. We will be driving to be there." Alex hung up the phone and turned to his nephews. "The Agent Pete Kelly says Lenore is in the hospital but she does not appear to be injured. They are wanting to be sure."

"Is Gregor alright?" Joel asked as he put Spot on the floor and slipped into his shoes.

"I have been told he is with your mother and they are both alright." He grabbed three jackets from their pegs and tossed two to his nephews. "The agent Halvorson has had his neck broken by Gregor, but not before shooting John."

"Did he kill John?" Grant asked. Joel's eyes were wide, waiting for the answer.

"Kelly does not think John is going to be dead. He is to be in the air to Denver for special doctors."

The three men walked out the kitchen door into the attached garage, only then realizing their choice of vehicles were a wrecked Saab, an agent's vehicle for which they had no keys, or a beautiful red classic Ford Mustang.

Alex shrugged, went back into the house to retrieve keys for the Mustang, came back out the door and said, "Get in."

Joel climbed into the small backseat and Grant took the front passenger seat as Alex slid in behind the wheel.

The garage door opened and the rare classic 1969 Ford Mustang Boss 429 rolled out with three men inside. The garage door lowered, Alex turned on the headlights and drove away from the house.

"Will Gregor mind that you're driving this?" Grant asked from the passenger seat. Joel sat behind his brother, intent on watching Alex's driving skills.

Alex laughed a hearty Parishnikov laugh and shook his head. "My brother will not mind. This is merely a vehicle. A nice vehicle, but it will be more important to him that we are being able to go to where they are."

He turned onto the highway that would take them to Glenwood Springs. The lights of Glenwood Springs reflected on low hanging clouds. Alex pointed out the clouds and said snow would soon be falling in the valley.

CHAPTER 22

"They got Mom! She's okay."

Leah grabbed JD's arm and relayed the news. "She's okay." Then back to the phone. "Joel, what about everyone else?"

"Well, I know Gregor's okay. He's here at the hospital with Mom and they're in the emergency room just to check her out. Gregor will come get us when we can see her. Alex brought Grant and me here to meet them after we got a call from Pete Kelly." He hesitated before continuing. "I don't know if I should upset you, but I think John's hurt bad. He got shot. They had him here for a little while and now they're flying him to Denver."

Leah closed her eyes.

"That guy Halvorson; he's dead," Joel assured her.

"Did John shoot him?" Leah asked. JD raised his brows, hearing only half of the conversation.

"I don't know. Maybe. After he shot John, Willow and Frank shot him, then Gregor broke his neck. I'm glad."

Leah looked at JD with raised brows. "Well, I agree. He deserved it. I'm glad, too Joel!"

"Frank said you got shot. No one will tell us anything more."

"Well Joel, I did get shot, but I'm fine. Please don't tell your mom until things settle down a bit. Okay?"

"Okay. How bad is it, Leah?"

"A bullet ricocheted off Baby and into my hip. They've fixed me up just fine. The doctor says the scar on my hip will probably look like a butterfly." She laughed. "I think I can live with that."

Joel laughed. "I guess if you gotta have a scar, you may as well have an interesting one. I think they're pretty sure the same creep that shot you is the one who took Mom. So, I'm doubly glad he's dead."

"Me, too!" She winked at JD. "You give your mom and that stepdad of yours a big hug from us. We'll get together as soon as you get home. I'll probably be out of here tomorrow."

"Okay. I'll tell Mom and Gregor I called. Love you."

"Love you! Love to your brother and Alex, too."

"Wait! One more thing."

"What, Joel?"

"Alex brought us to Glenwood Springs in the Mustang! Pretty cool, huh?"

"Joel, I think that's about the coolest thing that's happened in a long time," she chuckled. "Was it fun?"

"Yep. We had a great ride. Alex drives good for being from Russia."

"I imagine Gregor and Lenore have been good teachers for him, don't you?"

"Oh, no doubt. Mom taught me to drive in the mountains when I turned 15 so I could pass my driver's test."

"I seem to recall that time in your lives." She nodded to JD.

"Not exactly like getting to drive a Mustang, but it was fun. Maybe someday Gregor will let me drive it."

"I'm sure he will."

"I'd better go. Tell JD thanks again for taking me to Denver. See you soon."

Leah gave the phone to JD to hang up. "They're fine, but John's on his way to Denver. He's been shot. It must be awfully bad if they're flying him to Denver." Tears spilled onto her cheeks. JD hugged her close and tried to reassure her.

"Might just be because he's CIA, you know, extra precautions. Let's hope that's it."

She sniffed and wiggled her fingers toward a box of tissues, and JD brought it to her. With three pulled from the box, she blew into one and tucked the other two under her pillow.

"That's got to be it. It can't be anything else. It just can't." She shook her head. "Not now."

"Let's think positive. No need to borrow worries." He put the box of tissues back onto the tray table. "I noticed you failed to mention that the shot went through your side before it ricocheted off Baby into your hip."

"Oh, he didn't need to hear details. Besides, the Dr. called it a through and through or something and it didn't hit a single thing vital, except my skin and a few muscles and a wee bit of pride. No one's even going to see *that* scar," she assured him. "I'm thinking I may just have to surround the scar on my hip with a tattoo, to emphasize the butterfly shape."

"Only you would consider this a fashion accessory." He shook his head, kissed her on her cheek and sat down on the edge of the bed.

They both were quiet, hands entwined, staring out the window as night lights of the city illuminated the front range of Colorado. Soon Leah began to relate Joel's great adventure in the Mustang. The life of their dear friend John stayed close in thought.

✴ ✴ ✴ ✴ ✴

Lenore and Gregor decided to not tell their sons of the pregnancy for the time being, feeling the present excitement would be enough to deal with. Gregor went to the waiting room and ushered Joel, Grant, and Alex back to Lenore's room, where she sat up in the bed with her foot elevated.

"I thought you weren't injured, according to Pete." Grant gestured to his mom's bandaged foot. "You're in a regular room, not just the emergency room."

"Yeah, and what about your face?" Joel asked.

"Boys, I'm fine. I got a cut on my foot trying to run. Couple of stitches fixed me right up. They're just being cautious." She stopped and turned to Gregor. "Wait, what's wrong with my face?"

She started to get up from the bed but Gregor gently put his hand on her shoulder and pulled the bed table across her lap. She opened the top so she could see into a mirror.

"Wow," she wiped her cheek to see if it might simply be soiled, and flinched. As neatly as an ink stamp, she had a circular bruise on her cheek where Halvorson had repeatedly jammed the barrel of his weapon into her cheek.

"Does it hurt?" asked Joel.

"No. I didn't even know it." She turned again to Gregor and pointed to her cheek. "You didn't say anything about this."

"To be honest, all I could see was your beautiful face." He smiled which totally disarmed her.

"We are very glad for this is being your only injuries, because I am looking forward to being the third Uncle Alex," he announced with a broad smile.

Gregor and Lenore's eyes grew large. Joel and Grant looked from Alex, to one another and back at their mom.

"Mom, are we missing something here?" Grant asked.

"Well. I guess we need to tell you something." Lenore frowned at the still smiling Alex. "We were hoping for a more appropriate time, *Alex!*"

"Have I put the cat out of the bag?" He asked, raising his eyebrows.

She sighed, then said, "Something like that."

Gregor took Lenore's hand. "We had not the opportunity to tell this before."

Grant and Joel nodded, waiting for more.

"When Halvorson took your mother, we were at the doctor's office to confirm what we believed we already knew."

"Yes," Lenore continued, "but then the power went out and one of the nurses said she believed it was just a sign of early menopause and lots of *older* women have hysterical pregnancy scares." She scowled. "I was upset and when Gregor went back inside to talk to them, I forgot to lock my car door"

"They called later to confirm, but your mother had no idea until after her rescue."

"Wait. You're telling us you're going to have a baby?" asked Grant.

"You mean, you're pregnant? Like, for real?" Joel added.

"For real. Sorry to spring it on you like this."

"I am sorry for turning over the beans as well." Alex said in his attempt to apologize, his smile gone.

"Mom, well, aren't you too old?"

"Apparently not, Joel." She smiled at her youngest son.

He chuckled. "Yeah, I guess not."

"I want you both to understand, you and Grant are our first children." Gregor assured the two young men as he held Lenore's hand. "Now we are having another child. Will you be as ready to become big brothers as your uncle Alex is to become an uncle for the third time?" he asked.

"Well, of course." Grant replied.

"Holey buckets! I'm going to be a "big" brother. Wow!" Joel announced.

"We're glad you *turned over* the beans, Alex! Now we all know!" Lenore smiled at her brother-in-law, and was delighted to see his return.

When the excitement of the announcement finally abated, questions of what had taken place on the mountain became their focus of conversation. The biggest concern became John's condition.

"We will travel to Denver as soon as we can get Lenore released. Alex, this includes you."

"But what of Marushka and Nicolai?" Alex asked his brother.

"We'll have our friends watch the house."

A more trustworthy couple could never be found. They had watched and cared for Gregor's home for nearly a year, long after the money he had reserved for them had run out. John Dixon had made sure there were enough funds to maintain his friend's Colorado home, though there were times he had wondered if it might be all for naught.

Gregor generously rewarded the young couple, after his release from the Soviet prison and his return to the United States. John had flatly refused to be repaid for his contribution. Gregor and Lenore knew the debt could never honestly be compensated by money.

"Mrs. Parishnikov, there are two people out here who would like to visit. You have quite a crowd already." A no-nonsense nurse noted with a firm line on her lips. "We usually limit visitors to two. Think you can handle it?"

"Absolutely!" She swung her legs over the side of the bed to sit. "I'm ready to escape anyway."

A few second later, Frank and Willow entered the room.

"We'd have been here sooner, but I had Frank take me home to change clothes. I brought a sweater and pair of jeans for you if you need them. The jeans may be a little long, but they'll work." She shook her head. "I have no idea of your shoe size, so couldn't help there."

"Bless you, Willow. I sure couldn't put those dirty clothes back on." She reached out for her newest friend and pulled her into a hug. "You're so thoughtful."

Frank cleared his throat to get attention of the group.

"I spoke to the Director. He'll have a jet in Aspen as soon as we can get there. All of us will head to Denver."

Gregor kissed Lenore on the forehead. "I will go secure your papers for release. I will inform them of the urgency." He sprinted from the room.

Frank ambled out the door and followed Gregor, certain a CIA badge would have a little more weight than the plea of a husband. It had certainly helped in getting himself and Willow into an already crowded patient's room.

"These must be your sons, Lenore." Willow nodded to the two young men standing at Lenore's bedside. "Let's see, this is Joel and you must be Grant. Am I correct?"

"Yes, I'm Grant Appleby." He offered his hand and Willow gave it a firm shake.

"I'm Joel Appleby. Nice to meet you, Willow." He also shook her hand. "Thanks for helping rescue Mom. You must have awesome skills."

"Thank you, Joel. I admit my skills were sort of inherited. I have a wonderful Ute Grandmother, who taught me to listen to the mountain," she noted.

"That's pretty cool."

"It is, isn't it?" The beautiful lady chuckled and the young musician posed another question.

"I'd like to learn from you. I have a pretty good ear."

"We'll see what we can do about that," she assured him.

Lenore enjoyed watching her son and Willow talk of listening to the sounds of the mountains and trees. She took Grant's hand and held onto it. He squeezed her hand and said quietly, "Glad you're okay Mom."

Gregor and Frank came back into the room followed by the nurse with a wheelchair.

"Mrs. Parishnikov, the CIA has deemed you ready for discharge," she stated with a straight face.

"Okay, everybody out except Willow, so I can get a shower and put on clean clothes," Lenore said, as she slipped off the bed, balancing on one good foot. As the visitors vacated, the nurse stood at her side, resolute in her duty. Lenore allowed the assistance and appreciated it. When she had showered and dressed, the nurse pointed at the seat of a wheelchair.

"Don't you have a crutch or something?" Lenore asked the unamused nurse.

"Hospital rules. You must ride." She finally smiled at Lenore. "I need to give you some instructions on our way out."

Willow opened the door and the trio began their trek down the hallway, past rooms with doors both closed and open. They drew little attention in the late hour.

In the lobby where the others gathered, Frank wanted to make sure everyone was on the same page. "Agent Kelly is here," he pointed with his thumb. "He brought the Pathfinder."

Pete Kelly nodded.

"Frank, I need to stop at the house to get shoes. I can run inside," Lenore hesitated, then added, "Well, no, I think I can tell Willow where the shoes are that I want."

"Not a problem at all, Lenore. We're going to drop off the Mustang and meet up with an agent to drive the other company car. We'll all be more comfortable for the drive, and the Mustang will be safely in the garage. No sense leaving the Pathfinder at the airport either." He smiled at her. "We can put it in the garage as well. Are you okay with that?"

"Sure!" Lenore replied. Frank smiling? It felt kind of disturbing to her, like discovering your high school math teacher drank beer or liked the Beach Boys. It didn't seem to fit.

"Frank, have you received any information regarding our friend John?" Gregor asked.

"When I talked to the Director, he said John had arrived at the hospital in Denver and they had him in surgery. That's all he knew."

Swirling flakes of snow greeted the entourage as they exited the hospital. Lenore got out of the wheelchair with thanks and determination. She let her two grown sons help her to the waiting Pathfinder. Pete Kelly opened the rear door for her.

"Will you be comfortable back here Mrs. Parishnikov, or would you prefer the front?"

Lenore started to ask him to call her Lenore, but a chill reminded her that it wasn't a really good idea. "I'm sure this will be fine."

Frank got into the front passenger seat beside Pete. Willow and Gregor sat on either side of Lenore. She felt very safe; crowded, but safe. Alex, Grant, and Joel ran across the parking lot to get the Mustang. They swept off the coating of snow from the windshield with gloved hands. As soon as they pulled up behind the Pathfinder, the two vehicles headed for the Parishnikov home, leaving Franks prized pickup in the hospital parking lot.

Pulling into the drive, lights from the vehicles illuminated the wrecked Saab. Lenore turned to Gregor.

"What happened to the Saab? How on earth did it get wrecked?"

Gregor began explaining about how the accident occurred, when he tried to follow Lenore and Halvorson. He had been running on adrenaline for so long, he had just begun to be aware of bruises and aches from the wreck.

"Good Lord, Gregor, it looks like you could have been killed," Lenore said.

With a hug, he assured her he was injury free, then got out of the car to go into the house.

It took very little time for Willow to retrieve shoes and a jacket, as well as undergarments for Lenore. She started out the door, then realized Lenore only needed one shoe. She turned back and ran again to Lenore's closet. She dropped the unnecessary mate and grabbed a pair of socks.

Gregor phoned the young couple of whom he knew he could rely on to watch things, and briefly explained the situation. Several hundred dollars were left on the counter to cover any possible expenses.

With the Mustang and the Pathfinder parked in the garage, Lenore, Gregor, Willow, and Frank climbed into Pete's car. Alex, Grant, and Joel got into the second car with the assigned agent. They would all fly out of Aspen and be in Denver shortly after sunrise. Frank and Willow were informed of Lenore's pregnancy and they were all appreciative of good news, amidst their concern for John.

CHAPTER 23

The waiting room was full of friends, families, and strangers, each person with an emotional investment of some sort in their location. Some read magazines or watched afternoon soap operas drone on. Others prayed or stared into nothingness with minds full of unanswered questions.

The group waiting for a word on John Milton Dixon III conversed quietly or paced, changing positions to accommodate newcomers to the room in need of seating or a just a restless need to move.

Gregor noticed Joel had become quiet and walked across the room to stand beside his young stepson.

"Joel, are you troubled?"

Joel shook his head no, then jammed his hands into his jacket pockets as he addressed his step-father.

"Gregor, I'm thinking of changing my major from music to criminal studies. I want to become a part of the CIA. Maybe FBI." He looked into his stepfather's eyes. "Will you help me figure it out, you know, how to do it? You could help me know what to study." He glanced across the room at Lenore. "How do you think Mom will handle it?"

Gregor smiled and put his hand on Joel's shoulder. "Perhaps we should take a walk and discuss." He gestured toward the door. Lenore, deep in conversation with Willow, gave an acknowledging nod. He walked with Joel to the exit.

The Colorado sunshine kept the chilly November air tolerable. They zippered their jackets and found a bench to sit on, facing the sun and sheltered from the breeze. They sat quietly for a minute before Gregor broke the silence.

"I understand what has fueled your decision, Joel. I will not tell you that you cannot pursue a different career choice." He said, patiently. "I want you to understand, there are many things to consider."

"You think I'm just wanting vengeance?" Joel asked, tucking hands into his jacket pockets.

"No. Vengeance has been served," he paused then added, "Be assured, the taking of another's life, even as deserved as this case, is a part of the career you consider." He looked directly into Joel's eyes. "It can cloud your view of the beauty and happiness in your entire world."

They sat, watching cars jockey for space in a crowded parking lot.

Joel broke the silence. "Gregor, there is so much bad out there. I feel like I need to help get rid of it, or do *something*."

"This world will always have bad people making very bad decisions and creating very dangerous and deadly situations. It is impossible to change this fact." He turned to Joel. "You have a much more powerful weapon. You have music."

The young man shook his head. "How can that be powerful? How can that change *anything*?"

Gregor put his hand on Joel's shoulder. "I want you to imagine for a moment, a world without lullabies to sooth crying infants, or love songs to inspire romance between young, or even old couples," he chuckled. "Think of a world without resounding rhythms to inspire dance, or stir an army? It would be a most miserable world." He watched the impact of his words on this not so young man. He took his hand from his step-son's shoulder.

Joel considered the point of view, then turned to Gregor, "Twice my mom was taken. *Twice*! I hate that! I want to *know* my mom is safe and it will *never* happen again." He waved a hand. "How is music going to make any impact on that?"

"It cannot. You also cannot become something you are not meant to be. I do not want you to think that by becoming a part of the CIA or FBI or any other criminal justice group, that it could prevent some deranged mind from doing the unthinkable."

Gregor had Joel's attention and continued. "John and I, and several other well-trained people, were unable to prevent what happened to Lenore." He frowned and shook his head slowly. "It is a most helpless feeling."

"But I'm just going to be a music teacher, Gregor."

"Joel, you have asked me what I think, and I will always be honest with you. Use the weapon God has chosen for you. You are a gifted musician. You may someday write an inspirational piece that will change the direction of someone's life or as a teacher, show a troubled soul how to create and love music as you do." He put his hand back on Joel's shoulder. "As far as how your mother will feel? Although I know that your wonderful mother will always support whatever choice or whatever path you decide upon, I am quite certain it will break her heart a little if you abandon your gift of music."

Gregor moved his hand from the young man's shoulder and they once again sat quietly.

"I can see why my mom fell in love with you. You're a wise and kind man, Gregor. Thank you for helping me with this." He was sincere. "I guess I need to start working on a lullaby for my new baby brother or sister."

"I believe you should." Gregor laughed deeply, and as the two men stood, Joel gave his stepfather a generous hug.

They walked back into the hospital and into the waiting room, just as a nurse and the surgeon came to bring the "family" up to date on John. She ushered everyone into a small conference room. The nurse introduced the trauma surgeon.

Doctor Garrett removed his surgical cap, revealing a messy head of thick brown hair and leaned against a counter. He looked as tired as he should be. His green scrubs were wrinkled and wet with sweat from hours in the operating room. He wore a pair of Chuck Taylor high top basketball sneakers which had seen better days. He wasn't concerned with style or trying to impress anyone. He needed comfort when he worked to save lives in the operating room. He waited until everyone was settled and quiet.

"John made it through surgery. He's being kept in intensive care right now. It could be several days before I will consider him stable. The bullet entered the right side of his chest and shattered a rib before penetrating the lower lobe of his lung, collapsing it. It created a hemothorax, or blood in the pleural cavity, as well as air, or a pneumothorax. The insertion of a chest tube in the Glenwood Springs emergency department stabilized him enough to survive a life flight here to the Denver trauma surgery team. We won't know if there has been damage to his heart for several days."

The doctor adjusted his stance, then continued. "The x-rays showed a bone fragment from the rib lodged inside the lung. We surgically removed it and closed the wound. The lung reinflated and appeared to be functioning, but he is intubated for now. At this time, we opted to leave the bullet that's lodged in the soft tissue behind his lung. Surgery to remove it would cause more damage."

He held the attention of everyone in the room. "Providing he makes it through the next twenty-four to forty-eight hours, he'll have a long recovery. His body will eventually absorb the excess blood in the pleural cavity. He appears to be a strong, healthy guy. If he wasn't, he wouldn't have survived this long. We'll keep him in a drug-induced coma until vital signs stabilize."

Doctor Garrett asked if there were questions, but none came. They were busy absorbing what they had heard. Questions could be addressed any time, he assured them. He and his nurse exited the room, leaving the family still quiet, digesting so much information.

The young nurse Grant had been talking to suggested they go home and come back in the morning. None of them moved, and she smiled. "I figured you'd stay. I'll bring some pillows and blankets for you later, after visiting hours. Just please be considerate of others here waiting."

"Of course, we will. Thank you for understanding." Frank smiled back at the nurse.

Everyone looked at Frank and back at one another, surprised with the uncharacteristic response. He didn't seem to notice their reaction.

Lenore held back a bit to allow others to leave the room before she maneuvered with the crutches Frank had commandeered for her upon their arrival at the Denver hospital. She moved slowly out the door and back to a chair. Gregor stayed beside her, made sure she was comfortable, then helped her elevate her injured foot on another chair where they sat down. Willow struck up a conversation with Joel about listening to the mountain. Frank headed outside to, no doubt, have a cigarette. Alex immersed in reading a newspaper. Grant continued talking to the young nurse, and both were absorbed in the conversation. Lenore noticed.

"You're smiling," Gregor noted.

She turned to her husband. "Yes. It just feels good to know John has this support." She nodded at Grant and the nurse. "Looks like those two have found common ground, doesn't it?"

Gregor agreed. "Yes. A mom will notice such things. I am still learning."

"You're doing just great. The boys love you and trust you." She kissed the hand holding hers.

"You have made them into very good and caring men."

"That reminds me, I know Joel told Leah I was rescued last night, but I need to confirm the pregnancy with her. I promised. I need to talk to Leah, then I can update her on John, too." She started to get up and Gregor gently eased her back into the chair.

"I think that will be a very good idea. I need to discuss some things with you before that, however."

Lenore tilted her head and asked, "Like what?"

"Leah is fine. This is the first thing you should understand."

Lenore started to speak but Gregor hushed her with a shake of his head.

"Though it has not been proven yet, it appears this Halvorson drove to Fort Collins on Sunday and waited at the Chase home until they arrived." He put his arm around his wife's shoulder and pulled her closer.

Lenore pushed away and looked in his eyes. "Keep talking."

"It is assumed Halvorson shot our friend Leah. Again, Lenore, I am telling you and you must understand, that *she is alright*."

"Oh, Gregor. No!" She shook her head and kept looking at him. "Not Leah. Not my Leah. What have I done? I've hurt two of my best friends just by having conversations with Halvorson?" She started to get up again. "Oh God. Oh God. I'm going to throw up."

Gregor reached for a nearby waste basket and Lenore made full use of it. Everyone in the room stared and Lenore's sons, Alex and Willow ran to her side. The nurse who had been speaking with Grant ran down the hall and returned with a wet face cloth and a dry towel.

"Mrs. Parishnikov, would you like to go to a private room and lie down?" Her sweet face was bathed with concern, and her beautiful doe-like eyes looked from Lenore to Gregor.

"No, I'll be alright." Lenore accepted the cloth. She wiped her face and patted it dry with the towel. "What I need is a telephone. Can you get an outside line for me?"

"Yes, I'll bring you a courtesy phone." The nurse took the waste basket from the area and walked to a nurse's station down the hall from the waiting room.

At that moment Frank came back into the room. He didn't apologize for parting the group surrounding Lenore.

"What's going on? What's wrong? Greg, what happened?" He knelt beside Lenore as she accepted a box of tissues from Willow.

"I have just told her what has happened to Leah. She will be calling to hear for herself that Leah is alright."

"Hell yes, I talked to her myself," he grumbled. "Don't go getting upset now. It's not good for that kid you're carrying." He reached out and hugged Lenore.

The shock of Frank's action made Lenore stop crying and stare at him.

"Frank, are *you* alright?"

"Sure. I'm great. Just gotta keep *you* alright." He stood with a grimace at the effort.

The phone was brought to Lenore and plugged in nearby. Frank took it from Lenore.

"I've got the number here."

Frank opened a small notebook and punched in the numbers. He made sure he had Leah on the line before passing to phone to Lenore.

Everyone except Gregor moved away to allow Lenore the privacy needed for her conversation.

"Leah, what have I done? How could I have been so stupid as to allow this to happen to you and to John? I'm so sorry. So sorry."

"Now Lenore, I'm fine. You did nothing wrong. You can't blame yourself for the insanity of that man."

"But Leah, it's awful. What happened? How bad are you hurt?"

"Not so bad. I'll have a little scar on my hip in the shape of a butterfly. He missed what he intended to do." She chuckled. "He was thankfully an *incompetent* insane idiot. Sounds like he won't be anyone's problem ever again!"

"No, he won't." Lenore's tears started down her cheeks. "I am so sorry this happened."

"Hey, have you got your best friend ring on? I do."

"Yes." Lenore rubbed the heart on top of it.

"We're best friends forever and nothing like an insane idiot or a little bullet will ever change it. Now, tell me what you found out at the doctor's office."

Lenore squeezed Gregor's hand. "We are pregnant, for sure."

"Oh, my goodness! So much shopping to do," Leah declared.

That brought a chuckle from Lenore.

The rest of the conversation centered around how long Leah would be at the hospital in Fort Collins and how soon they could be together. The vigil at the Denver hospital would continue.

Cheered from her conversation with Leah, she turned to Gregor, concern in her eyes.

"I don't know if it's just me, but it seems like something is different with Frank."

"I believe he has been acting with much authority, as he should. Is that what you mean?"

"No." She pressed her lips together and thought about it. "He seems, well, nice. Like someone soft and compassionate took over his body."

Gregor laughed quietly. "I have not known him as well as you, but I can see he is a kind person and very concerned about you and our family."

"Yes. That's it exactly! He's just not normally so, well, demonstrative. I wonder what's up?"

He hugged Lenore. "I have no doubt you will get to the bottom of this mystery."

Lenore and Gregor looked at Frank conversing with Willow. Both smiling.

"Weird," Lenore muttered.

CHAPTER 24

"Weston? Weston, where are you? We need to get going." Lenore stood near the front door on the porch, and called out.

The sound of barking puppies and a little boy's giggles preceded the appearance of dark curls on a short little bundle of love, being trailed by four rambunctious white Great Pyrenees puppies.

"Here I am Mama. I'm playing puppies."

"Well, now the puppies need to stay outside and you need to come in to get your face and hands cleaned up. Your hair is a mess, too, Weston."

"The puppies like to lick my hair. It feels *so* funny." He giggled his little boy giggle again.

She ushered the young boy into the house, leaving four precious faces standing on the other side of the screen, looking in, as she closed the front door.

"Well, it sure makes your hair look funny." She noticed. "Looks like a change of clothes is in order, too."

Mother and child ascended the stairs to the bedroom of Weston Dimitri Parishnikov. The nearly four-year-old stood patiently as his mother did an evaluation and decided a quick bath would be best. With a fresh bath and puppy hair damage washed from his curls, she put him in clean clothes, and combed his hair into place. She well knew, the normal activity of this little boy would doubtless rearrange any order she attempted. Satisfied, she gave him a hug.

"Now, let's see if you can stay clean and shiny until we get to the car, okay? No more puppies!"

"Okay, Mama." He took the steps one at a time to descend to the first floor. "I think Marushka wanted them to have breakfast anyway."

Lenore matched her son's steps. They walked to the kitchen door leading to the garage.

"You get into the car while I set the alarm."

Weston sat patiently in his car seat with his favorite stuffed animal in his arms, when Lenore came round the car to buckle him in.

"You look very handsome today, Weston." She kissed him on the forehead and ran her fingers through his curly hair. He rewarded her with a heart melting smile, before she closed the door.

She sat in the driver's seat and pushed a button to open the garage door. With her own seatbelt fastened, she checked mirrors and made sure no puppies were heading into the garage as she pulled out. She checked the fuel gauge and did a final check of the house. Their neighbors would be watching things and feeding the dogs while they were away.

"We have a long drive ahead, Weston. You have your *Stuffy Bear*, your books, and your water. If you need to go potty, you tell me, okay?"

"Okay Mama."

Lenore checked the rearview mirror to see the little boy who was growing up so fast. She adored his always cooperative attitude. Weston looked at one of his books as they drove toward Glenwood Springs.

After driving through town, she negotiated turns and entered Interstate 70 heading east toward the front range of Colorado. The familiar drive let them settle into the journey.

They no longer waited for surveillance agents to accompany them. After Weston was born and John Dixon had recovered from his nearly fatal gunshot wound, John and Gregor requested, and were successful in having all surveillance removed. It took several months of bureaucratic discussion, but logic prevailed over regulations. It had never been an issue after that.

An hour into the drive, Lenore noticed her passenger no longer joined in their usual sing-alongs and had succumbed to the cadence of the road. He slept peacefully; his Stuffy Bear clutched in his arms. As much as she hated to disturb him, an hour later, she needed to make a stop. Lenore knew if she needed to stop, Weston probably did as well.

With necessary things taken care of, they once again headed east. Weston stayed awake now, and Lenore was grateful.

"Mama, will Daddy have to change his name today?" He had a tiny frown as she glanced into the rearview mirror at him. "And Uncle Alex, too?"

"No sweetheart. No name changes for Daddy or Uncle Alex."

"Okay." His smile returned. "I didn't want to have a different name than my daddy."

She wondered why he had been concerned about it?

"What made you think that, Weston?"

He looked out the window, giving it far more serious thought than she thought a toddler should. He looked back into the mirrored image at his mama.

"I *pondercated* about it all day." Lenore nodded as she heard her son use the word Leah had created; a word they all used in their everyday vocabulary. "He has to stand there and talk and then become a different person, doesn't he?"

She sighed. "Well, do you remember we talked about Daddy and Uncle Alex becoming official citizens of the United States of America today?" She glanced in the mirror to see him nodding his agreement. "They are taking an oath of allegiance, kind of like a very important promise, to this country where we live. It's a very important thing, but he won't be different in any other way, I promise you. Daddy and Uncle Alex will always be just the same as they are right now."

A peacefulness settled back on his sweet features. "I'm glad."

"Me, too!"

They both laughed.

"Will my brothers be there and everyone?"

"Yep. After Daddy and Uncle Alex are sworn in, we all go to Uncle John and Auntie Willow's house."

"It will be like a birthday party," the thought obviously delighting him. "Will there be cake and presents?"

"Probably," she assured him. "I am sure your Auntie Willow will make sure you have some cake. I think your Auntie Leah will provide some gifts, don't you?"

"She's a good present giver, isn't she Mama?"

"The best."

Weston Dimitri Parishnikov settled back and hugged his stuffy bear. Weston's middle name, Dimitri, had been bestowed to honor Gregor's grandfather; a kind man who, with his wife, raised Gregor, and his brother Alex after their mother died. Gregor always credited his grandparents for teaching them honesty, the value of hard work and a love of God. The Soviet government tried very hard to erase those values, learned from the nurturing early years of Gregor and Alex. They failed. The very special grandfather Dimitri, was well worth honoring with the naming of her son.

Lenore always explained when asked about the name *Weston* by answering, "*just because*." She named him to be an individual, and character came naturally from both sides of his family.

*****

Lenore loved her hectic, fun life. Weston was an active, curious, funny little boy whom his parents adored. In just under four years, Lenore and Gregor knew that the happiness of every moment had been earned through struggles, and a God given love for one another. It would never be taken lightly. This child thrived in their love.

Lenore found the responsibility of shoe store ownership a good challenge. She knew what she was doing and had a competent staff. The light in her beautiful eyes and her natural beauty, seemed aglow with happiness. Her long dark hair had very little white weaving its way in. She vowed to never color it or cut it shorter. She figured she had earned any white hair and the length made it convenient to braid or simply pull into a tail.

Gregor was a good and kind husband. Their passion for one another had not cooled by familiarity. He still made her laugh and they were always ready for the next adventure together, as a family. He exceeded in the roll of being a patient and loving father to Weston. The child looked like his father, which always made Gregor stand a little straighter when someone pointed it out.

Gregor worked from home for the company he had been with prior to his year in the Soviet prison. Lenore joined him when she could, when face to face meetings were necessary for him to be in Denver. Occasionally it would just be him and Weston to make the journey. Weston would spend the day with Leah or one of his brothers. Father and son would often find adventures in the city before heading back to Lenore and home.

Gregor never missed an opportunity to take all three sons to the mountains he loved. He taught them ways to live off the land if needed, and traverse the varied terrain. It had been an excellent bonding opportunity. Lenore always considered it a special time for the men and enjoyed using her quiet time alone to paint or bake if not at work.

Joel and Grant loved Weston and visited as often as possible, always anxious to teach him, or be entertained in life as the youngest sibling saw it. Weston adored his *bigger* brothers, as he referred to them. The connection was deep; the love genuine.

Lenore loved the very special bond between them all, and knew they were blessed.

* * * * *

The clouds parted as they drove closer to the front range, with the Colorado sun shining from the cloudless sky. They were nearing Georgetown. With tourist season in full swing, traffic always became heavier. Lenore slipped her sunglasses from atop her head to sit properly on her nose and glanced back at her son, who squinted in the brightness.

"Weston, can you put your sunglasses on please?"

Glancing, she could see him reaching down next to his seat into his little stash of goods. After a bit she glanced again when he said, "Mama. Lookie!" He put his sunglasses on and waved at his mama's reflection in the mirror.

"Thank you, Weston."

Lenore's attention came back to the road in time to see a mass of brake lights just ahead. She braked hard and the seatbelt pinned her back against the seat. She heard screeching tires, and the thunder of a jake brake not far behind her.

"Hug Stuffy Bear, Weston!" she yelled. "Hug him close, and close your eyes."

* * * * *

The auditorium was filled with nervous and excited people, anxious to take their oath of allegiance and others simply wanting to witness their friends or loved ones becoming official citizens of the United States of America; their chosen home. The official ceremony celebrated the culmination of a lengthy period; the passing of exams, interviews, determination of eligibility and proper paperwork, to take the Oath of Allegiance. The process dated back to the 18th century. Gregor and Alexander Parishnikov were not nervous. They were filled with pride at becoming naturalized citizens. They handed-in their green cards, to be replaced with Certificates of Naturalization following the ceremony. They accepted the small American flags and took their place in the group.

Gregor had chosen to wait until his brother became eligible to pass the citizenship test so they could take the oath of allegiance together. They sat side-by-side. As the time neared, Gregor kept looking toward the back of the room for Lenore and Weston. They had missed a rendezvous in front of the building an hour earlier.

The loved ones and extended family of the Parishnikov brothers sat near the front, just behind the inductees. They were saving two seats for Lenore and Weston.

The television station crew where Alex worked as a meteorologist, decided to film a human-interest story on one of their own becoming a citizen. A stir and the hum of voices became louder and Gregor heard the words *wreck* and *pile-up* on I-70 just *west of Denver*. He turned to Alex, knowing he could access information from the film crew.

"Do you understand what they are saying? Could this be the reason my wife and son are not here?"

Alex walked to the back of the room, where a cameraman and reporter stood, and spoke quietly with them. Gregor watched as Alex listened and kept glancing toward his brother. The normal smiling Alex was missing. The face of a man full of concern walked back to sit beside his brother, in the second row of prospective Americans.

He spoke quietly to his brother. "There has been a multi-vehicle accident near the Georgetown exit. There are casualties. Let's pray our loved ones are not among them." He put his hand on his older brother's shoulder. "We must trust in this."

Gregor nodded silently. He closed his eyes, praying for God to keep his family safe.

Several people walked to chairs on stage in the front of the auditorium and sat, facing the crowd. A United States Citizenship and Immigration Service official walked to the center of the stage, stood behind a dark wooden podium, and asked everyone to please stand for the National Anthem. The rows of candidates stood, along with everyone in the auditorium. Gregor's heart was beating hard, both in excitement and in a growing fear for his wife and child.

A young Air Force cadet from Colorado Springs performed The National Anthem. His rich baritone voice filled every heart in the auditorium with patriotic pride. There were many candidates and guests dabbing at moist eyes by the end.

The USCIS official again approached the podium, and asked everyone to please be seated. He began to introduce a guest speaker but a commotion at the back of the room interrupted him.

One very loud little boy yelled at the top of his lungs, "Daaaaaaadeeeeeeeeeeeee! We made it!" He waved a small American flag on a stick as high as his little arm could reach.

An attempt to shush him by an obviously flustered and embarrassed mother seemed ineffectual, as the young child jumped up and down to see through the crowd, searching for his daddy.

"I'm so sorry." She said to the official. She finally got her son's attention. "Weston, you're interrupting that gentleman."

The excited little boy stopped and stared at the man standing in front of the room, his eyes large. "Ah-oh."

"Young man, please come here," the official said to Weston.

Lenore started to accompany her son, but the official held his hand up.

"No ma'am. I need to speak to this young man by himself."

"Okay Mama?" he looked at Lenore for approval.

"Yes, Weston. It's okay." She closed her eyes as her young son marched down the aisle, waving his flag at everyone. He stopped long enough to also throw kisses to his daddy and uncle, brothers, and friends, who all grinned and threw kisses back to him. A very short young man stood near the stage in front of a very tall podium.

"Hello." He looked up at the official.

"Hello." The official spoke to him in a firm voice, which captured the happy little boy's attention. "What is your name young man?"

"Weston Dimitri Parishnikov. That's my daddy right there and my Uncle Alex." He pointed and waved. Both men waved back. "That pretty lady back there is my mama. Hi Mama." He waved and Lenore waved back.

"Weston Dimitri Parishnikov, do you know you have interrupted something very important by your actions?"

He raised his eyebrows. "I'm sorry. We were late 'cause of an accident, and I wanted my daddy to know we were here, so he wouldn't be sad." He looked down and twirled the flag in his little fingers, then looked back up and tilted his head. "Are you the preacher?"

The official cleared his throat and attempted to remain stern. "No, Weston. I'm the official of this ceremony. Now, I believe everyone knows you made it just fine, don't you?"

"Yes, sir." He turned and waved proudly to everyone sitting in the auditorium, then turned back to the gentleman standing in the front of him.

Lenore put her head in her hands, wondering if she would be deemed an unfit mother for letting her small son disrupt such an important ceremony.

"I tell you what, Weston, if you will go *quietly* back to be with your mother, we will get back to the business of this ceremony and then you can visit with everyone afterward. Deal?" He finally smiled at the young child standing before him.

"Deal." Weston reached his hand up to the official, who stepped around the podium to shake the little hand offered on the deal. The delighted young man waved again to his daddy and uncle with his flag, as he skipped back down the aisle to Lenore. The two of them moved quickly to sit beside JD and Leah.

It took a few minutes before the room settled and the chuckles subsided. The television camera had captured the entire disruption. Lenore and Gregor would have a copy with which to embarrass their son at some important ceremony of his own one day.

Following two speakers and another song, the naturalization candidates stood to take their oath. A large screen had been set up in the front of the room with words for those who needed them. Gregor and Alex knew them by heart.

The TV crew was allowed to film from the front of the room as the candidates took oaths.

"I hereby declare, on oath, that I absolutely and entirely renounce and abjure all allegiance and fidelity to any foreign prince, potentate, state or sovereignty, of whom or which I have heretofore been a subject or citizen; that I will support and defend the Constitution and laws of the United States of America against all enemies, foreign and domestic; that I will bear true faith and allegiance to the same; that I will bear arms on behalf of the United States when required by the law; that I will perform noncombatant service in the Armed Forces of the United States when required by the law; that I will perform work of national importance under civilian direction when required by the law; and that I take this

obligation freely, without any mental reservation or purpose of evasion; so help me God."

Spontaneous applause and cheers erupted after the official from the USCIS confirmed and congratulated the new citizens of the United States of America.

Each new naturalized citizen proudly accepted their Certificate of Naturalization, a welcome packet, a large American flag, a Citizen's Almanac, a copy of the Declaration of Independence and copy of the US Constitution, in the form of a pocket size pamphlet.

Gregor Parishnikov and Alexander Parishnikov were American citizens. It had been a journey of difficult ordeals overcome in attaining this achievement. The two men walked to the back, to be embraced by Lenore and Weston, and their extended family.

The reporter and cameraman turned off the equipment and congratulated their colleague and his brother. They assured Lenore that young Weston would be a celebrity by the time the 10 o'clock news ended. She didn't know whether to be excited or embarrassed. Gregor assured her it was not offensive.

"What is this about the accident? You were not injured?"

"Well, no. Close, but no."

"Mama said she drove like it would make Uncle Frank proud." Weston beamed as he informed his daddy.

Gregor and Alex waited for clarification.

"Tell you what, let's get to the party and I can tell it once and be done."

EPILOGUE

The afternoon sun sunk closer to the mountains with the promise of a beautiful Colorado mid-summer evening at the home of John and Willow Dixon. The group kept busy grilling or swimming or simply sitting and talking with one another. Cool drinks and great company were in abundant supply and laughter punctuated the air frequently. Weston played in the pool with a new dinosaur float, a gift from his Auntie Leah. His brothers were having fun tossing balls to their little brother, or innocuous teasing with a game of "keep away". It all resulted in pure enjoyment for Weston.

Lenore relayed the tale of their narrow escape in the pile-up on I-70 earlier that day. She explained that upon hearing sounds of the truck braking behind her, she slammed her foot on the accelerator and swerved to the right, driving on the shoulder and beyond, kicking up clouds of debris and dust to skirt around the stopped traffic. Her vehicle had come to a stop near the front of the originating wreck.

Once the forward momentum ceased, Weston cheered from the back seat.

"That was fun, Mama," he said with delighted applause from little boy hands. It provided the calming affect her fast-beating heart needed.

They remained parked there for over an hour finding songs and stories to entertain one another. During that time, she told Weston her driving would have impressed Uncle Frank. Lenore and Weston eventually continued their journey after a wrecker moved vehicles, and traffic was allowed to go around the obstruction. She mentioned concern of Gregor being worried about their lateness, so Weston decided he should announce their arrival upon entering the auditorium.

* * * * *

Lenore's driving skills had impressed Frank Gillespie when he first attempted to follow her around Horsetooth Lake, and the back route to Highway 34 west of Loveland. It instilled a respect for her. Their mutual respect ran deep.

After Lenore's kidnapping and rescue, some of Frank's reactions to events had confused her. The normally curmudgeon personality had shown a softer side. Following John's release from the hospital, and back to limited duty, Frank then offered an explanation. He took a very rare vacation to attend a reunion, and reconnected with his high school sweetheart, Marsha. He planned to come back to Colorado and turn in retirement papers when the crisis had occurred.

Frank and Marsha had both remained single after high school. Life sent them on different paths. That first love had been stronger than either realized, and the power of their first reunion had softened even Frank Gillespie.

Frank and his wife, Marsha, enjoyed life in Florida most of the year. Their gulf shore home, expansive and with great sunset views, was beautiful. Visitors were always encouraged to come enjoy the sun. They traveled extensively and kept a summer home in Colorado. Frank had never spent much money on more than necessities in his service to the CIA, so his retirement fund proved to be substantial. They enjoyed all its benefits.

Marsha was a delightful woman who never missed an opportunity to express her love for Frank, nor set him straight if needed. They were a great match. She had spent her working years as an agent for the IRS. Lenore wondered at first how such a sweet lady could be an IRS agent. She realized the shadowy reputation of IRS agents hid the human factor. Lenore loved Marsha and enjoyed seeing her friend Frank so content.

Lenore grinned as she checked out Frank's latest footwear. He gave up his wingtips following the death of Dennis Halvorson. He didn't want the reminder of Halvorson having mimicked his footwear.

Frank asked Lenore to sell him shoes shortly after Dixon had been deemed stabilized, and they met at her old store in Fort Collins. He left the store that day with three different styles of dress shoes. Two pairs of boat shoes needed to be special ordered to custom fit a narrow size 13. He had quite a variety of footwear these days, though something about seeing Frank in sandals would always be a surprise.

A shelter in Denver received fourteen pairs of nearly pristine wing-tip shoes.

＊＊＊＊＊

Leah and JD Chase were still Lenore's closest family. Though not blood, the bond couldn't have been closer. JD would always be the gentle, easy-going husband of Leah, who was never easy going. Her exuberance could challenge a rugby team. They were always the best half of one another.

Leah had lost her enthusiasm for turning her gunshot scar into a butterfly tattoo. It seemed better than just the scar, but it still provided a reminder of a very frightening event. Over the past few years, new joys and the wonderful normalcy of everyday life became a blessing for all. Leah never missed an opportunity to shop for her new favorite little boy, and Weston adored her. Lenore and Leah's visits together were never long enough.

Leah and JD's daughter, Shelly, had begun a career with the City of Fort Collins and the wage and benefits provided well for her sons; Dustin and Danny. The boys were busy in school and sports and helping Grandpa JD at the shoe store after school.

JD had been instrumental in convincing the board of directors, to invest in a new shoe store in Glenwood Springs. Weston had just turned a year old when the store had its grand opening. Lenore learned all her management skills from the best, and had no problem running a shoe store in the busy tourist town of Glenwood Springs. She felt fortunate to be able to hire trustworthy and enthusiastic people to work in the upscale shoe store, and never worried about leaving the store for a few days.

＊＊＊＊＊

Joel and Grant Appleby were thriving.

Grant married Emily, the young nurse from the hospital just months after meeting. They would be making Lenore and Gregor grandparents in early November. They both enjoyed their respective careers, and were generous with their time and energy for family. Lenore loved Emily.

Joel graduated from Colorado State University with a degree in music education and a minor in criminal justice. The unusual combination raised a few eyebrows, but he felt he needed the knowledge and would find a way to put it to use. He had been accepted to graduate school and would further his music master's degree, and explore opportunities in the law enforcement field.

Joel's high school sweetheart had gone a different direction after graduation, but the new love of his life, Lynn, proved a perfect match. They were both music majors and athletic. The love of anything associated with running or hiking kept them busy, and they never missed an opportunity to visit. Lenore felt blessed to have such a sweet girl in her life and know that she and Joel were happy. Plans were being made for an autumn wedding at the Parishnikov home near Glenwood Springs.

* * * * *

Alex Parishnikov had become a celebrity. Gregor's younger brother was employed by a Denver television station, in the position of head meteorologist. Alex's skills made him a very valuable employee, forecasting the ever-changing Colorado weather with accuracy. His technical knowledge impressed the station management and his hunger for learning never ceased. The drive to succeed, eventually landed him an on-air position. The handsome man of Russian decent had a cheery personality and his calm, assuring manner during any impending weather situation, made him a hit with the Colorado viewing audience.

There were no special girls in his life, but Alex dated as much as his career and education allowed. He visited Gregor and Lenore often and was a very good Uncle Alex to Weston. They could talk for hours, or watch clouds and discuss the weather, or simply go outside at night and look at the stars, so vibrantly clear at the Parishnikov property. He had given Weston a very impressive telescope for viewing the immense skies over his Colorado home. He kept ski dates with Joel and Grant in the winter and camping or bike riding with them in the warmer months.

On most summer evenings, he was lacing up his spikes for a local baseball team, and he enjoyed watching the Colorado Rockies play at every home game. Lenore knew the "All-American" game Alex had heard about before coming to the United States fueled his passion for the game. He played third base or outfield and became good at both. He was an All-American now as well. He bought Weston his own glove, baseball bat and cleated shoes. Intent on grooming the youngest of the family to become a baseball player, he took him to games when he could.

Lenore always admired how far her husband and Alex had come since being released from the Soviet prisons, and being allowed to come to the United States. Their freedom would never be taken for granted, and she often wondered why so many in the United States, didn't appreciate the God-given, blood-earned blessing. Both men would treasure today's gift of citizenship for the rest of their lives. They would defend their new country, to any, and all. The American flag would always be on display in their homes.

* * * * *

John Milton Dixon III would ever remain Gregor's closest friend. The years and circumstances had strengthened what they once just tolerated as an assignment by both. Their friendship became its own treasure.

John was a man passionately in love with his beautiful wife, Willow; a love fully returned. Following the shooting and recovery, he soon stepped down from duties with the CIA. He felt fit, but the incident had taken something out of him, and he knew the Company would be better served with someone else. He rarely missed it.

Most summer days were spent in the Glenwood Springs area, where Willow continued her work as a Colorado Law Enforcement Ranger, and director for search and rescue. They had a ranch not far from the Parishnikov home, so the two men took opportunities to ski, fish, and hike often. Lenore and Willow enjoyed becoming close friends and Weston never missed an opportunity to show *his* Willow some special rock or plant he had discovered. He absorbed everything she told him about being a part of nature, and how to listen to the wind, and the song of the trees. She always taught him to be especially kind to the earth.

The Dixons retained a home in Denver where they welcomed company and encouraged visits. John knew Willow's heart would always be in the mountains of Colorado around Glenwood Springs.

He would never deny her any connection to her life there. Willow's grandmother accepted John and he never missed an opportunity to listen to her stories. If a search and rescue came up anytime throughout the year, John never hesitated about Willow's response. Knowing her gift of finding people, he encouraged her. He would fly her anywhere she was needed.

John and Willow recently announced they would be having a child early the coming year. They didn't yet know if it would be a John Milton Dixon IV, and opted to wait until the birth to find out. They simply knew, this child would be loved by so many.

＊＊＊＊＊

Lenore looked at the gathering of people so dear to her heart and wished she could paint a picture to show all the love and happiness she felt, or have Joel compose a piece of music to capture the joy and utter contentment she felt, so she could play it over and over for the rest of her life to remember this time.

The little girl from a Kansas refinery town, who once ran with dirty bare feet from one patch of shade to another on the hot sidewalks of summer, no longer ran. Lenore knew contentment and felt very blessed.

She was at peace.